RETURN TO EDEN

COLIN TAYLOR

RETURN TO EDEN

Copyright © 2022 Colin Taylor

All rights reserved. The author asserts the moral right under the Copyright, Designs and Patents Act 1988 to be identified as the author of this work. No part of this publication may be reproduced, stored in a retrieval system, or transmitted, in any form or by any means without the prior written consent of the author, nor be otherwise circulated in any form or binding or cover other than that in which it is published and without a similar condition being imposed on the subsequent purchaser.

ISBN: 9798367090581

Part one: Banishment

Chapter 1

The lights! Where were the lights? Geordie had said he would see the lights, but Geordie was dead and there were no lights. Finn stood at the edge of the ice wall that surrounded the pit, staring out, with crushing disappointment, into the clouded darkness.

He had always known as a fact that the pit was completely surrounded by this bleak whiteness of snow and ice, as though some giant had taken a massive scoop out of the ice hill so that the mine buildings and the winding gear could be fitted into it.

Yet now, as Finn stood exhausted from his climb up the ice wall, he felt the true isolation of the community he lived with as if for the first time. In the pit their fixation with digging out the coal that kept them all alive, allowed few thoughts on the chance that there were no others.

Geordie had said Finn would see the lights, the lights of the others that lived around them, in the wilderness of ice and snow that covered everything. Geordie had seemed so sure. Only there were no lights and he knew in his heart that it meant there were no others. They were alone. They truly were alone. The guards had told the truth. There was no one. If that were so, then why did the Director not take steps to crush the rumours? Everyone knew that there were other survivors who somehow clung onto life in this grim frozen landscape. It was common knowledge. Now he knew that knowledge was wrong.

Finn sank to his knees, his round face twisted with anger and frustration. Lifting his clenched fists above his head, he smashed then down onto the ice again and again, shouting his rage into the heedless wind. How could he travel to Eden without the help of others on the way? He had planned with Geordie for so long. Geordie was gone, yet Finn now knew he could escape. The spiked shoes and hand picks he'd made had allowed him to climb the sheer ice wall. He could climb it when he was ready and escape. Now he must return to the pit before he was missed.

The disappointment had drained his energy and a shiver passed through him. The heat he had generated while climbing was beginning to fade. The icy wind cut into him, piercing his inadequate clothing, cutting through to the tender skin that had only ever known the warm underground corridors of the mine. A creeping, numbing cold was beginning to spread into his bones. He must move before he froze.

Carefully he got up and keeping to the shadows so as not to be seen, he moved around the uneven pit rim. Despite his caution, this proved to be his undoing. Finn did not see the white clothed guard creeping up behind him and he did not feel the blow that crashed onto the back of his head that sent him falling, unconscious, to the ice.

***

He became aware that a bright light was shining into his eyes. Rolling over onto his side to avoid it, he realised he was bruised and aching all over. His exploring hand felt the swollen lump, covered in dry blood that darkened the short brown hair on the back of his head.

Sitting up, he looked around the bare room. He knew he must be somewhere in the pit and not far from the main living area, because he could hear and feel the humming vibrations of the generators that powered all their lives. Although he could not be sure how long he had been unconscious, his instincts told him it must now be sometime near the morning shift change.

He could imagine the exhausted workers coming back from the coalface, their places being taken by the fresh shift, ready for their eight hours of coal cutting. It was the never-ending backbreaking labour of digging out the coal that all their lives depended on. There would be families coming to life in their side gallery homes. People would be going about their allotted tasks; always aware of the Directors words "Those who work, eat." The cooks would be preparing the morning meal for the outgoing shift and the shower cavern would be cleaned after the workers had removed their black covering of coal dust. From the gap under the door he could smell the all-pervading earthiness of the mushroom growing galleries mixed with the sharp stench of the composters dealing with the everyday waste of the whole community.

They were all going about their business, living their everyday lives in the suffocating confines of the pit. Everyone essential, everyone needed. And now he felt the shock of knowing that soon he would no longer be a part of it. He knew what happened to those who did not obey orders.

The sudden turning of a key in the lock shook him from his thoughts. Two black clothed guards beckoned him out. He followed them. There was no need for force or restraint. Where could he possibly escape to, down here in the pit?

Not recognising the tunnels they walked through; he realised this must be the guard's quarters. They stopped in front of a door and a guard knocked, opened the door and entered.

In the plainly furnished room there was a desk and the Director herself was sitting at it, shuffling through some papers. Finn stood in front of the desk, the silent guards standing behind him.

The last time Finn had been this close to the Director was when he had been presented with his tek badge in front of the whole of his shift. He had qualified as a first-class engineering technician at fifteen years old, the youngest ever. He could remember how proud he had been and how superior he had felt to all the other labourers. He was educated. He was exceptional. That day was two years ago and close up, the Director looked old now, her hair solid grey, her face lined and sagging.

She looked up and stared at him: considering, calculating. His big green eyes met her steely grey gaze unblinkingly.

"You fool," there was no emotion in her husky, coal dusted voice, just a cool appraisal of the situation. "Why did you do it? Oh don't tell me," a slight irritation crept into her tone. "Why is it always the intelligent ones who want to know? Why can't you keep your curiosity in check, get on with your job, and enjoy the rewards. And you were the best. The best I've ever seen in my lifetime. It took time and resources educating you and you've thrown it away. You could have been chief engineer one day. In charge of the whole of the mine's technology. You would've been told the truth when you reached management level."

She paused, leaning back on her armless chair. Exasperation showed on her wrinkled face.

"You think we don't know about the beliefs of the workers. You think we don't know about their dreams."

She paused again and Finn shouted, "Then why don't you tell them the truth? What's wrong with them knowing there's no one out there?"

His pale face reddened with his only partly

suppressed anger.

Behind him there was a faint movement from the guards. They would restrain him if necessary.

"Why don't we tell them? Why? Because of the fear, despair and panic it would provoke. They need this dream, their illusion, because there are no others, we're alone: no one to trade with, no one to talk to. Nobody else, except maybe a few snow pirates and we've seen precious few of them recently. There may be no one in this whole damn white world of ice, except us. Maybe we're the last. Do you want them to know that? Do you want them to give up, finish it? Do you? We could be humanity's last chance," She looked away for a moment in despair. "We could be the one last gasp before extinction. You really want me to tell them that?" she paused, smiling sarcastically at him. "No you don't, do you? You're not that stupid. You may be strange and different, but you're not stupid. You're intelligent. You know what I have to do."

Finn moved as if to say something.

"And don't tell me you won't reveal anything. You might say that now, you might even mean it. We both know you wouldn't be able to stick to it. You might last a week. In the end you'd have to let it out. You know I can't have that." She paused again for a moment and looked at him. "No, you're out. We need to keep the workforce on their toes. We haven't had a banishing for some time. You'll do."

She gestured to the guards. Finn waited silently. He had known it would come to this.

"Get him out of here," she shouted wearily as the guards hustled him out.

"One pack at seven, banishment at eight, after the night shift comes in. They can all witness it then"

Banishment. The word went around the pit quickly as rumours always do. Who was it? Who was missing? It didn't take long to find out it was Finn. There were shouts of disbelief, mixed with pleasure from some that were pleased this arrogant tek was getting his comeuppance.

Chief amongst the emotions that surfaced was excitement. Everyone liked banishment. They would all be there, except the emergency crews, almost the whole community: well over two hundred people. It would be soon. The crowd of silent watchers gathered in the long gallery. Packed in, they left a narrow path along the middle that led to the outside doors. They waited expectantly for Finn to appear.

They had walked him to the small side space in the dwelling tunnels, which was no longer his home. Following the tradition, he had gathered his clothes and all he could cram into the 'one pack' he was allowed. He hadn't taken it with him on the climb. It was there bulging and ready: ready for his escape with Geordie to Eden. Geordie. How Finn wished Geordie was with him now, to face the banishment. A long sigh escaped his lips. How long, he wondered, did he have to wait? The Director's words rang in his ears.

"Humanity's last gasp."

No! There was Eden. He knew Eden was there. Geordie had said so. He was sure it was true and he would prove it by going there. He couldn't wait to get out now. Even without Geordie, he was going to Eden.

He had already planned to escape anyway. Only not like this, not banishment. Not with everyone knowing. He had wanted to slip away unseen. He knew what the banishment would be like, because he too had joined in with the screaming and shouting in the past, feeling the exhilaration and relief of the group. Knowing it was not them being banished, savouring the delicious feeling of solidarity against the outcast.

Finn walked down the corridor leading to the doors

of the long gallery, thinking of the walkways that took you up the ice wall and out of the pit. Even from here he could feel the gathering excitement, the smell of righteous indignation. Finn was one of them and he had failed. He would pay the price. The guards opened the doors and he looked out into the gallery. The crowd listened patiently while the charge and punishment were read out. Then it started.

The first shout rang out. Beginning quietly, with that one cry, the chant of "Banished! Banished! Banished!" quickly rose to a raucous crescendo. The sound rang in his ears, assaulting his brain, enveloping his body.

He hadn't expected to be so totally overwhelmed by their anger and hate. Intellectually he knew that this was foolish, but the raw emotion thrown at him was devastating. His body reeled before its onslaught. Tears welled in his eyes. He knew these people. Now they didn't see him as one of them. The guards formed a physical barrier between him and the crowd. Even though he hung his head, Finn could feel the intensity of their jibes and insults, the roar of disapproval and the gathering chorus of "Out! Out! Out!"

So this is what it felt like. He had seen others go:

begging, crying, screaming and having to be dragged. Some, a very few, were strong. Walking with quiet dignity as the taunts washed around them like angry waves battering against an unmoving rock. Even the final cry of "Out! Out! Out!" with arms outstretched and pointing fingers jabbing the air in self-satisfied relief it wasn't them, didn't break down some people's composure.

He had thought to walk proudly along the rows to spite them. Yet now he only wanted to reach the walkway doors and get out. To be out and away from this awful battering. As they turned on him and vented their anger and frustrations, he broke into a shambling run.

Then he was through the doors and free of it. Without speaking, the guards escorted him along the walkways leading to the top of the ice wall and pushing him out of the gate, locked it behind him. He was banished from the cocooned security of the pit. He felt the stinging wind in his face. His survival now rested entirely on himself.

He was out.

Chapter 2

For a frozen moment, Finn stood outside the pit gates, the sounds of the banishment still ringing in his ears. The unexpected anger and hate had left him numb and confused, yet he knew what he had to do.

He lurched forward across the hard-packed snow; his short, powerful body shrouded in all the clothes he possessed. Walking generated heat and in this frozen world you had constantly to fight for heat. The book said so. Without the book, his survival would be impossible. He had found the Survival Manual tucked away in the pit library, and it said, unless you have shelter, keep moving or you'll freeze.

Still shocked from the emotional bruising of the banishment, and careless of his direction, he walked away from the claustrophobic pit, into the faint light of pre-dawn, into the freezing wind of his cold new world.

Geordie had told him Eden lay in the South West.

Eden: where you were free. For no one worked in wonderful, far-off Eden. No one cut coal, tended mushrooms, cooked, cleaned or did any of the countless things the pit needed. You were sure to find your heart's desire in Eden. Though everyone knew the legend, only Geordie knew where it was. Finn longed to be in Eden.

Not until the sun came up would he have any idea in which direction Eden lay. Then he knew how to find it. The Manual explained how to find the compass points. The sun always came up in the East. So to find Eden he had simply to walk in the opposite direction to the sunrise in the morning and follow the sun in the afternoon. When the sun shone. It was really that simple. He remembered the rhyme Geordie had taught him about Eden:

'You'll know it when you see it.

It shines in the setting sun,

But you won't see Eden till you know it's there.

It's not for everyone.'

But Geordie was dead and the rhyme made no sense. Oh Geordie! Why did you have to go when I needed you most? Tears sprang from his eyes, the sharp wind freezing them on his round pale cheeks before he could brush them away. A low moan escaped from his lips and he flinched as if a blow had struck him in the chest.

He gasped and pulled a freezing stream of air into his mouth. His teeth ached with its ferocity. He stopped, staring into the distance until the pain eased and the feeling passed, then taking the cardboard snow goggles from his pocket, he adjusted them so that he could see through the eye slits.

The landscape was becoming brighter as the sun rose and snow blindness was the last thing he wanted. Finn walked. The hard physical exertion blunted his emotions. It did not stop him thinking.

The snow squeaked and crunched as it compacted beneath his feet. He had not thought that travelling through the snow and ice would be so noisy. Wherever he looked through the slits in his cardboard goggles, all was white.

Questions arose within his mind. How could he melt snow for water? He had no pans, no fuel to heat anything. He and Geordie had planned to seek help from the others along the way. Now he knew there were no others. All he had was the dried fish and mush bread in his 'one pack', enough maybe, for the next two days. Then what would he do?

Dark thoughts of starvation and hypothermia crept into his mind, and his pace faltered. The urge to stop and sleep here in the snow was strong. Yet that was what they would all think, in the pit. That he would die without a trace. Somehow, he must prove them wrong. He had exchanged the certain for the uncertain. He had lived with certainty all his life, from child to young man. He had seen what that certainty would hold. He had known the path his life would have taken. He would have lived and died in the pit, mending the machines, eating the food, been safe and secure. There were no other choices within its boundaries. It would have been for him as it had been for all, since the cold came.

He wanted more to his life. He and Geordie had planned it. Now he was living the uncertainties of this ice world. He might live, he might die. He would make his own choices. He was free of the pit and its cramped life.

Let them keep their certainties. He would trust himself, and go where he wished. Not that he had much choice. Banishment wasn't really a choice. Finn laughed out loud at the irony of his predicament. Plumes of warm breath clouded from his mouth to freeze on his already frosted clothes as he stared at the sunrise.

Once, working outside on the surface buildings, he had seen the sun: an insipid yellow disc that gleamed palely in the blue sky.

He hadn't seen a sunrise before. Now it came as a surprise when the sky lightened, and gradually a brilliant circle of dazzling light crawled above the horizon.

He stood in awe of the red rimmed, gold disc that appeared. Finn had not known such beauty before. It stunned his senses and he gasped at the faint cushioning of clouds that turned first pink and then ran through all the shades until it shone golden and complete above the gilded snowscape.

As the sun rose higher, Finn corrected his direction and a slight optimism crept into his mind, soon to be replaced by exhausted frustration as the hard ice surface gave way to soft drifts of snow. To stop his feet sinking, he put on the improvised, tennis racket snowshoes he'd made.

Finn was strong and fit, his muscles honed by long

hours of cutting coal and stoking the furnaces that provided heat for the steam generators. Yet despite that, lifting the improvised snowshoes used a different set of muscles to those he had developed in the pit. It was draining and his legs ached. He trudged on into the wilderness.

It was about midday that Finn looked up and realised he must stop. Clouds were gathering and the sun had gone. He could no longer be sure if he was going in the correct direction.

The wind, light at first, was now blowing harder, cutting into him, slowing him down. What was the weather going to do? The snow was building to more than a few flakes. Was this going to be a heavy fall? Would he have to make a shelter? He had the knife and the knowledge. The Survival Manual explained how to do it.

The falling snow was rapidly restricting his field of vision. He had to build a shelter soon! Behind him the snow was level. Ahead it changed. The land sloped down into hills and jagged lumps. A shelter would be more protected there.

Finn removed his snowshoes. They had performed well on the soft flat snow. He knew they would not last long when climbing over such uneven terrain: especially in the gloom of a snow storm. Even one at midday! He urged his aching body forward down to the uneven ground.

Unslinging his rucksack, Finn took out the heavy saw knife he had made in the pit workshop and started to cut into the flat ice. It dropped away sharply to his left, which was good. He did not want his shelter to be covered in snowdrifts that might suffocate him. He needed a trench two metres long by half a metre wide, deep enough to cut a shelf into one side to lie on. In fact, apart from the shelf, very much like an empty grave, although Finn knew nothing of graves. The pit recycled its dead, it didn't bury them.

Cold air would fall off the ledge into the trench and any warm air would rise. A cold sink the book called it. Put a roof over the trench and you would be safe for the night. He cut deeper, hauling out long flat blocks for the roof. Suddenly he stopped and stared down through the ice.

There was something dark beneath him. The distorting ice made it hard to see what it was. He cut down, exposing a flat stone surface. A wooden trapdoor with a ring handle was set into the stone.

Why was there a trapdoor here, in the middle of this desolate landscape and what were the chances of him finding it?

For a moment he had an impression that he had been guided to find it. He dismissed that foolish notion from his mind. It was just amazing luck that he should dig in exactly the right place.

It took all his strength to move it. The ice had frozen hard and he had to cut around the edges with the knife to release it. It opened to reveal a staircase disappearing down into darkness. Where did it lead? He had no idea. Yet, any shelter was better than spending the night outside, he entered, pulled the trapdoor closed and descended into the shadows.

The wooden stairs zigzagged around an empty middle space. A tower! He had seen pictures of them years ago when Matty was teaching him to read. He had to feel his way now and it was difficult to know how far down he was. After a while the blackness became less intense and by looking over the rail at the edge of the staircase, he could see light at the bottom.

Emerging from the gloom he stood on the last step, waiting for his eyes to adjust to the half-light that somehow managed to penetrate here, far below the ice sheet.

The beating of his heart slowed. It was quiet now he didn't hear the continual moan of the wind at the surface. He had not known such silence before. Here, there were no workaday noises, no friendly normality, and no sounds of people. Always in the pit there had been the noise of people living their lives, always the hum of the generators that drove the machinery and the far-off rumble of workers on their shift at the coalface, hacking away at the black veins of coal that were the lifeblood of the pit. It continued all day and all night, although who could tell day from night in the pit? There were few private clocks or watches. The only clocks they needed were the electric clocks that ruled their work shifts. Their technology was about survival.

He blinked in the dim light. A board hanging on the wall next to the door announced in faded letters, 'St Peter's Parish Church: Notices'. A church? What did St mean? Who was this Peter? What was Parish? Questions he could not answer.

As his eyes grew accustomed to the strange bluish light, he realised he was looking into a large building. It was a hall about fifteen metres long, just like the gathering place in the pit. Whitewashed stone walls led up to massive timbers supporting the roof. It was shaped like two boxes stuck together end to end: the furthest box slightly smaller than the first. He wondered at the purpose of this place.

At the end of the small box was an immense window, or rather several adjacent windows, joined together in a graceful arch. Another small circular window was set a short distance above the apex. This was where light penetrated. Fascinated, Finn walked towards it, marvelling at the way the coloured glass was arranged into pictures.

The noise of his footsteps, no longer muffled by snow, went flying around the building. His every movement sent ripples of sound through the fabric of the icebound structure. The frozen stone walls reacted to every nuance as he walked.

Instinctively, he looked up and stopped. There, in the shadows, hanging high on a massive beam across where the two spaces met was a large wooden cross. That alone would not have stopped him in his tracks. What really amazed him was the effigy of a semi naked man, with long hair and beard, held on the cross with huge nails through hands and feet. Thorny plants had been woven into a circle and stuck onto his head. Blood ran from the puncture wounds. Yet despite the man's obvious suffering, the sculptor had put an expression of extreme peace and tranquillity on his face.

Finn stood for some time wondering why this image was here. He had seen people suffering before, caught by machinery, and crushed beneath rock. Never though, had he ever seen such tranquillity depicted through such pain. Eventually he dragged his eyes away and walked on.

The light that penetrated through the thickness of ice that separated the building from the snow crust, was split and amplified until its beams shone at all angles through the huge coloured glass windows. Pools of colour lay on the frosted floor and as he trod through them the floor sparkled.

He moved through a rainbow of colour that he had neither experienced in the dark pit nor on the blinding white snowscape. It dredged up strange feelings inside him. If he had been able to vocalise them, he would have said that the feeling was sacred: a connection to God, the source of all things. He could feel it, yet did not realise its significance.

He stopped before what he had taken to be a shadow

on the floor. It was actually a large hole. He stood on the edge and looked across, his engineers mind wondering if it was safe. The hole had to be at least two metres wide and maybe two or three metres deep.

At the bottom of the hole, something shone. As he moved the light did too: he was unable to focus on it. Why was there a hole here? Someone had deliberately dug through the floor. He could see tool marks on its sides. Who had done this and why? What was this place?

He looked around, studying the strong walls and pillars. They were quite able to withstand the pressure of the ice surrounding them. Yet the windows were glass. How could fragile glass keep the ice and snow out? How had they survived the pressure? He looked through the hole again. Something shimmered there like water, yet like no water he had ever seen.

He must examine it more closely. There should be a way down. He looked around him, searching the shadows. There! A door set back behind a stone column. He walked towards it, the sparkling frost crunching under his feet as he did so.

The door was made from some ancient ridged wood, with a metal ring handle like the trapdoor in the tower. He pulled. It didn't move. Locked? No, it was a latch. He pulled again, twisting the metal ring, gave it another heave. He heard the clunk as it came up. The door moved slowly on rusted hinges and there before him was a broad spiral staircase leading down into darkness.

He hesitated. He was not sure he wanted to go down, although was this darkness any different from that of the pit or the earlier staircase? The shining thing was down there and he wanted to see what it was. Carefully he crept down the steps.

Near the bottom of the staircase he could see again. He no longer had to feel his way. The stairs opened out into a shadowy room with a low ceiling. Massive pillars and arches held the weight of the whole building. The debris had been removed from beneath the hole and piled nearby. A huge circular stone bowl, standing on a low pedestal, had been set beneath the hole.

As his eyes became accustomed to the dim light, he walked to the bowl. Was this the source of the light? The bowl was half full of mirror-like ice. Was this where the shining light came from? He lifted his head and looked up.

With a gasp he staggered back, clutching at his face. A searing, bright, violet light had flashed through his eyes into his mind. Something was in his brain. Pain, fear, anger, and then something else beneath the anger. A calm and unruffled depth of feeling, overlaid, but not destroyed by his agony. Finn's sturdy legs collapsed. He sat with a jolt. What had happened to him in that instant of looking up? He suddenly felt overwhelmingly tired. His body fell sideways, and in a moment, he was in a trance-like sleep that was full of dreams and visions.

Chapter 3

With a sudden, sharp, intake of breath, Finn emerged from his fitful sleep. The light! What had it done to him? He felt echoes of the pain and fear it had brought. His mind chased the half-remembered images, the strange, yet familiar pictures that tantalised his still sleepy senses. His emotions were raw and tender from those unexpected, half-forgotten visions. Yet despite the pain and the anguish of these bewildering and unwelcome feelings, he knew that in some way, all was well. He could not say how he knew, just that he did.

The creeping cold of the floor had entered his young body. His muscles had stiffened, and his joints hurt. He moved slowly, in the unavoidable agony of returning circulation. How long had he been lying there in the dark he wondered, beside the stone bowl. Was it still daylight outside? Did the violet light still shine, ready for other unsuspecting travellers?

Finn stood. He looked at the frozen surface carefully, not wanting to repeat his earlier experience, but the ice no longer reflected the light.

He turned and started climbing the stairs. What was this all about? He reflected on the chain of coincidences that had drawn him here: banishment, walking in the right direction, cutting the shelter in exactly the right place, looking up at the light. Was this pure chance? What was he was doing in this place?

You were led here.

He stopped, astonished. How did he know that? The answer had flashed through his mind. Led here? Who had led him here? Why? How had it done this? Words came again.

The light.

It was the windows. It had to be something to do with the windows. Where else could the light have come from? It had to come from somewhere high.

He ran up the remainder of the steps and went to the hole in the floor, calculating the line that the light must have taken to shine down onto the bowl. Finn stared at the huge windows with a mixture of curiosity and apprehension. He wanted to know what was happening. Yet he was also trying to ignore whatever it was the light had unleashed within him.

He stared. There was something shiny on the wall, just below and to the right of the topmost round window. What was it? There was another further along and then another. Shiny metal pegs, like spikes or nails, had been hammered into the gaps between the stones of the wall. There were two rows. One placed roughly a metre and a half above the other.

His gaze followed them as the rows went away from the windows to the right, over to the corner, across the other wall and down to the floor. Someone had fixed them there so you could climb up to the light. It had to be that.

Gasping with excitement, he removed his pack and, in a moment, was trying his foot on the first pin. It held the weight of his stocky body, quite easily. Spread-eagled and holding on to the upper row with his long fingers, he moved crab-like to his left. Moving, one foot at a time, along the bottom set, eager to find the source of the light.

After dealing with the corners, he paused to rest and clinging to the pins, turned his head to look. There was something in front of the circular window. Turning back to the climb he moved carefully along.

Crashing down onto the hard stone floor would be disastrous.

As he neared the top, his view of the window was obscured by a large stone that jutted out from the wall. Negotiating that, Finn found he was able to turn his head and look closely at the window.

The glass curved out like the magnifying glass he used in the pit when mending small machinery. What took his breath away was what hung in front of the window: a beautiful, faceted, purple crystal with a pointed end.

Fascinated, he stared at it. Its violet centre moved beneath his gaze like flames in a fire. His consciousness drawn within it; Finn felt himself falling into its endless violet heart. He dragged his eyes away and was surprised to find himself still clinging to the metal pins. The sensation of falling had been so strong, he was sure he'd let go and was plunging to the stone floor.

He realised now that the rounded window focused the light from outside, which shone onto the crystal and was then reflected down somehow through the hole in the floor onto the ice in the stone bowl. Again he wondered who had done this and why? They had gone to a lot of trouble to set it in place so high above the floor. How was the crystal held here?

Holding on with one hand, Finn swung closer and reached out with the other hand to grab the crystal. His fingers closed upon it and he pulled the crystal towards him. Yet when he opened his fist to look at it, it was gone! The crystal was still hanging in front of the window.

He tried again and again. Each time he tried, it eluded him and hung there, mocking his efforts. Somehow it slipped through his fingers. It wasn't where it should be. He could still see it's fiery, violet middle that focused the purple light. Yet no matter how hard he tried; he was unable to take hold of it.

After a while, he stopped trying. He didn't understand. He could see it, yet somehow it wasn't there. Was it not in this world? Keeping perfectly still he stared at the crystal for a long time, until his limbs ached. It was there. Of that, he was sure. Yet equally he was sure it was not there, because he was totally unable to touch it. Round and round went the thoughts. Either it was there in this world or it wasn't. How could it be anywhere else? There was nowhere else.

Frustration mounting, Finn suddenly turned and roared his anger at the crystal. The crystal shuddered and swung away from the onslaught and then swinging back towards him, hurled the sound back. Finn rocked, hanging on in startled surprise that an inanimate object could do such a thing.

As the echoes died away, he stared at the crystal and once more felt the pull of the violet flame. He looked away. Maybe he was doing this the wrong way round. Carefully, without looking at the centre of the crystal, he reached out his hand. The crystal stayed where it was. His fingers gingerly pushed forward. They reached the crystal and moved through it.

Finn jerked them away in surprise. Pleasant, tingling, warmth spread along his wrist. With a smile, Finn moved his feet one peg closer and reached out again. His fingers went right through the crystal and banged against the wall beyond. His feet slipped and, off balance, scrabbling for support, his left hand closed on something hard and cold. Was it the crystal? No! Regaining his balance he opened his hand to find he had plucked a large iron key from its resting place in a nook beyond the crystal.

The key was thick rusty iron, not steel. He knew

steel. He worked with metals in the pit. This was iron, heavy and old. It had to fit a door somewhere in the building. He had to find that door. He knew he had to.

Was this the key to the whole mystery? He laughed at his own feeble joke, the sound echoing around the building again.

Placing the key in a pocket, he made his way down, relieved to be on the floor. Where was the door that the key would unlock? It was certainly not obvious.

Searching, he noticed that opposite the door that led beneath the floor were more pillars and there in the gathering darkness was another wooden door, similar to the first one. The key fitted. Finn dragged the door open and looked inside. He stared in disbelief. Something must be looking after him, because this was the answer to all his needs. Inside, towering above him, were shelves of stores. There were tents, food, clothes and so many other things that he didn't recognise. He knew, yes, he knew, that there was everything here that was going to be essential to his journey. Finn stared, amazed at his good fortune. If he had known what prayer was, he would have said this was the answer to all of his prayers. He was saved.

Chapter 4

Finn laughed: a mixture of relief and exhilaration. His deep voice echoed around the building, reminding him that he was still alone in his strange new world. Everyone in the pit had expected him to die in the white wilderness, even though they knew there were others out there. Finn wouldn't know where the others were and besides, why would they help Finn anyway? He would die a cold, lonely death and "serve him right", most of them would say. Yet to his amazement, not only was he alive, he had all he needed to stay alive. He was staring at it and as he walked into the hidden storeroom, touching the marvellous hoard in awe and wonder, he couldn't stop himself from grinning at his good fortune. Guided or not, he was here and those fools in the pit could keep their damn safety. He was free of it all.

While training as a tek, Finn had frequently used materials from the massive engineering storeroom.

Marvelling at the huge resource of materials on the shelves, he would wonder where it had all come from. Was this what a "normal" mine would keep or had it all been collected deliberately after the snow came? Finn would wander amongst the shelves, often forgetting what he was supposed to be collecting, picking up strange items and trying to work out what they might have been used for. He could almost see the 'before' people using the objects.

Suddenly he was back in the pit, walking into the store room, with Geordie pointing out the tools he needed to repair the electric truck in the lower galleries. Hindle, the chief engineer trusted him to do it.

Finn was important. He wore his tek badge with pride. The others, what did they know? He was the one. Quick and clever, he knew where a problem would be. Wiring, chips, circuits, switches or motors, it didn't matter what it was, he could find the problem and fix it.

It was a gift, a sense of knowing where it would be and then following his instinct. Once he'd read a manual or seen a circuit diagram, he didn't need them anymore. All he needed was to follow his intuition. No problem. Geordie had honed this gift. He had sharpened it over the years until Finn was the best tek ever.

Finn stared around at the loaded shelves in the church. This storeroom had the same feeling of plenty as that storeroom in the pit. Who had put all this here? Who had collected it? More importantly, were they coming back soon, before he had time to take what he needed?

He dismissed the thought from his mind. He had cut through over two metres of ice to reach the trapdoor in the tower. There was no other way in and beside there was a thick layer of dust on everything. No one had used this room for a very long time.

In the dim light from the room's high windows, he began to look for food. The mush he'd eaten before entering the building seemed like a lifetime ago. Coughing from the dust he disturbed, Finn picked a cylinder from a cardboard box and read the print on the label. Steak and kidney pie. He had no idea what steak and kidney were. Pie, he understood.

Self-heating, the instructions said. Self-heating? How did it do that? He held the top of the cylinder and twisted the bottom as the directions said. There was a grinding sound and immediately Finn felt heat coming through the metal. Amazing! He waited for something like the five minutes the directions stated before removing the ring pull top, wondering at the same time how the top came off so easily. A delicious smell made him realise how hungry he was. Grabbing a fork from a box on the shelf, he tried the contents. It tasted strange to a palate used to a diet of mush and farmed fish.

Mush. He thought of the mushroom growing galleries in the pit. They were warm, humid and dark, with just the glow lamps to guide the pickers through the rows of growing tables. Cropping the huge flat mushrooms was a duty Finn had shared with the other children.

Tracie was nearly always the quickest to fill her bucket to win the prize. They all made sure that none of the caps were smaller than the thirty centimetres wide required by the kitchen. Anything smaller was considered a waste and the picker was punished with extra toilet cleaning duty. With most mushrooms growing to more than forty, some even fifty centimetres, there was little chance of that.

He smiled at the thought of Tracie flashing her

dazzling white teeth in the dark. Smiling at him: for him. He stole his first kiss from her, hiding in a side gallery. Remembering the softness of her lips, he sighed at such innocent childhood memories.

Finishing the steak and kidney pie, he tried another cylinder: Irish stew. However the heat was generated, it worked wonderfully. Irish stew tasted good. Searching through the boxes, Finn found all sorts of unfamiliar foods sealed into different shaped metal and plastic containers. Most tasted okay when he tried them.

The best thing he found was the brown stuff called chocolate. That was the most wonderful food he had ever tasted. Sucking on a huge chunk he started making a pile of all the things he wanted to put in his backpack.

The pile accumulated so quickly that he knew he couldn't get even half of it in his pack. That was when he found the sledge. What luck! He'd seen pictures of sledges in books in the pit library. This one was big. The sort you could stand on at the back and glide down slopes and with room enough to pack everything on it. Would he be strong enough to pull it? Maybe. He'd face that tomorrow.

There were candles and matches. A lit candle gave a comforting half-light, casting flickering shadows across the shelves of the store room. No electricity here. It was such a contrast to the bright lights at a click of a switch in the pit. They always had light, even when one of the turbines was off line for maintenance, repairs or breakdown. There was always the second one.

Hindle taught the apprentices to work on them. He could remember how they had found the lectures boring. They had all wanted to be working on the turbine itself. Surprisingly, Hindle let them do the maintenance, under his supervision, whilst the second turbine emitted its high-pitched whine next to them.

The candle flickered and as he snuggled down into the sleeping bag, after relieving himself in a dark corner of the main building, his mind wandered and he thought of the wonderful luck he'd had on this amazing day.

Luck? There's no such thing as luck.

Isn't there? Finn thought about it. No, of course not.

It's all meant to be, isn't it?

"Yes," replied Finn.

We brought you here.

"You did?"

Yes, of course we did. How else could you complete your journey if we didn't help?

Help? Yes, he needed help.

It's all meant to be.

Meant to be, meant to be, meant to be. The phrase echoed through his mind.

"Yes, it's meant to be," he replied loudly.

Finn sat up suddenly. The candle still burned brightly. He looked around in the shadowy half dark of the candlelight, expecting to see who had spoken to him. Had he been dreaming? Was there really something watching him, guiding him? The thought was disconcerting. Yet he felt strangely comforted. The idea that he was not completely alone eased his solitude.

Finn woke several times in the night, feeling slightly nauseous. The strange food was not digesting too well. Yet, by the time light came through the window he was ready to eat more of it.

After regretting trying something called chilli con carne, Finn had the tricky task of manoeuvring the sledge up the tower stairs to the surface. Sweaty and red faced with the effort, he stared at the new layer of snow covering his footsteps from yesterday. He could hardly believe that only one day had passed since his banishment.

Deciding what to take with him was difficult. He wanted as much food as possible, yet he needed to be able to pull the sledge.

Sorting through the pile of supplies he'd made last night, he made his choices, some carefully and some by instinct. Tent, sleeping bag, matches, a small stove, fuel and as much food as he could possibly fit in. He chose all the light, paper and plastic packages first. Only then did he add the heavy self-warming tins, resolving to eat them first, to reduce the weight he had to pull.

It was midday by the time he'd carried it all up to the surface and packing it took even longer. Choosing clothes was easier. The survival book said lots of thinner layers were better than one thick one.

Thermal underwear, three pairs of padded trousers, the outer one waterproof, tops, lightweight windproof jackets, and something called a cagoule to cover it all. He chose a white one. Walking boots, just his size, with a deep tread to grip the ice and snow. Crampons, metal frames to strap to the boots, with spikes to stop him slipping on ice.

Finn found the pile of skis when looking for boots and socks. Choosing some at random, not understanding their differences, he put them on the pile.

There were proper snowshoes too, replacing his improvised tennis rackets. He found something called a ski mask. Made from a very smooth, white material it had eye and mouth holes and completely covered his face. It felt very warm. He finished it all with a ski hat, and then threw in one or two spares.

There were maps: a whole pile of them on a back shelf. He unfolded some. Not that these maps would be of much use to him. They were from the before times. He wouldn't recognise the landscape now it was covered in snow. Studying them, trying to make sense of them, he was amazed to discover massive towns and cities marked in. He calculated, considering the occupants of all the houses. Thousands of people must have lived here on this land, maybe tens of thousands, even hundreds of thousands.

Perhaps Geordie was right, the land had once teamed with life, and now they were down to just a few hundred people. No wonder then, that the Director of the pit looked so old. The future of the whole human race weighed heavily on her shoulders.

He stared at the map, thinking of the people in the pit. In a moment of insight, he had a feeling of being linked to them, of being one with all the humans he had ever known.

Like plants with underground spreading roots and at intervals a plant grows up from those roots. Each plant looks separate, yet is joined all the time. Why would he think of this? Was some awesome truth being revealed to him? Was it the light again? What had he seen yesterday to cause him such mental pain. Hurriedly, he pushed the uncomfortable thought away and busied himself with the packing.

Time was passing. His shadow from the setting sun was lengthening. The brief day was passing quickly. Should he stay for a second night? He didn't want to blunder around on the snow in the dark and it had been a tiring day. Leaving the packed sledge, there was no one to steal it, Finn returned once more to the storeroom and slept.

Chapter 5

Finn began his learning curve next morning straight after breakfast. Without any practice, he started. It didn't occur to him that he might injure himself and die a lingering death on the snow with no one to care and no one to see. There was no time to think of what might happen. He just had to do it.

Pulling the heavily loaded sledge was not easy. It took all of his strength to move it into the wind. Head down, he leant into the traces, staring down at the snow, sometimes standing almost horizontally over it, the straps biting into his shoulders.

Once the sledge moved, it gathered momentum and was hard to stop. He had to slow down gradually or it would bump into him. Fortunately the snow and ice here sloped downhill. He had very good balance and the crampons strapped to his boots gripped the ice. Yet he slipped frequently and fell often. Even the ski poles he'd picked out didn't always stop his falls. His body hurt. He had bruises and bumps all over him.

The wind had cleared the dry snow, exposing solid ice that glinted in the bright sun hanging in the eastern sky behind him. In spite of his bruises, after a while, he began to understand.

Slowly, exhaustingly, he learnt. The sun was high and bright now, the sledge still incredibly heavy and awkward and Finn was sweating hard from dragging it. Despite the gently undulating surface he was travelling on, he made slow progress. This was more difficult than he had thought it would be. It was better when he was going downhill. He soon learnt that as soon as he got to the top of a steep enough incline he could stand at the back and push off, the sledge would keep moving with just a shove every now and again. The problem was steering. If he wasn't careful and hit a bump he could end up in the snow with a broken sledge.

Maybe he was lucky, because it didn't happen, and anyway the hills were little more than bumps really, so most of the time he was pulling.

Time passed.

He slipped and a searing pain flashed through his body as his head smacked onto the solid ice. Black clouds, shot through with red, filled his consciousness. He lay inert. As he tried to move, the pain struck again. Finn cried out in his agony. Struggling to his feet, he stood on the ice and screamed at the sun.

"Help me! Why don't you help me? You're looking after me, aren't you? Then help me now why don't you?"

Finn whacked his ski poles down onto the ice and stood for a moment, breathing fast. Suddenly he laughed. What would Geordie say about this behaviour? Tell him to get on with it and stop being stupid. Finn reached down to the sledge and pulled out some of the chocolate. Shoving a big piece into his mouth he started off once more.

His world shrank to what he could see directly in front of him as he leaned into the harness. The white and blue of snow and ice at his feet, together with the sky when he looked up to check his direction, were the limits of his physical horizon.

Eden was a distant dream. He had no idea how long it would take him to get there. Geordie was gone; all he had were his memories of the pit. There was nothing else in Finn's world.

He persevered and, despite his aches, after a few more hours the effort required to pull the sledge became automatic and his mind relaxed. Images of his existence in the pit came to him as though he was reviewing his life. The memories were a comfort and yet he felt fear growing within him. What had he to fear from his recollections? He didn't understand why he felt fearful. Was there something wrong with his memories? Had the purple light changed him that much? It didn't matter how hard he tried to deny it, he knew there was more within him than there had been. Something was working away beneath the surface of his mind. Having no means of knowing what it was, he escaped into good memories, allowing his mind to wander. Not having to think about putting one foot in front of the other, all he needed to do was detach his mind, be somewhere else and let his body work automatically. It was better that way.

His earliest memory was of the cat. A tortoiseshell called Tiddy. It was beautiful, sleek and well fed, although he didn't feed it. There were always plenty of rats and mice in the pit. It would sleep next to him and he would snuggle up to its warm body.

Something strange crept into his mind. He did not

remember it until now, although it must have been there all along. Tiddy was sitting on the mushrug that covered the bare rock their dwelling space was cut from. Finn saw that Tiddy was gazing at something. When he looked, he realised Tiddy was staring at nothing. There was nothing there to look at. Yet the nothing she was watching moved and Tiddy's eyes moved with it.

Finn stared, concentrating on the spot she was looking at, trying to see what she saw. Like when he saw something out of the corner of his eye, a spider running across the floor. His eye would catch the movement of the spider and he would look directly at the movement and see the spider.

This time, when he looked, there was nothing there. Tiddy could see it, whatever it was. He could not. Only he knew there was something there, because he'd glimpsed it out of the corner of his eye.

Finn momentarily stopped and then walked on as the sledge slid up to him. Why had he not remembered this before? Was it just an inconsequential memory, or was there something important about it? There was more than he knew to this world, he realised that now.

It was time to eat. Finn picked out one of the self-heating meals and twisted it. Brushing the icicles from his mouth and nose, accumulated from his breath, he ate quickly, shoving the food into his mouth, unwilling to spend more time than he had to, standing there in the freshening wind. He was getting used to strange tastes and didn't even bother to read what it was he was eating. It was fuel. He needed fuel for his body whether he liked it or not. Afterwards he gulped down some water from the bottle that had been warming beneath his clothes in the pocket of his inner jacket. It was better than drinking half frozen melted snow. He hadn't realised how thirsty he would become, breathing the freezing, dry air blowing across the ice.

He had no means of knowing how far he'd come or any real idea how long he'd been walking since he'd left the church behind. In the pit, buzzers, bells and orders made sure they were all in the right place at the right time. How else could so many people survive unless their lives were ordered?

He suddenly realised that in some strange way, he missed the order of the pit. The closed in, safe feeling that the pit gave. The ubiquitous humming of the turbines as they turned. The sound of scraping shovels as the coal was heaped into the furnaces. The hiss of the boilers as the water turned to steam and powered the turbines. He missed the taste and smell of the coal dust that permeated everything, and everywhere.

Finn laughed out loud, steam clouding from his mouth. How could he possibly miss anything in the pit? Yet he did. He had spent so long living the dream of Eden that he had forgotten that the pit had been his home for all his life. The pit held a strange mixture of emotions for him. He had hated the authoritarian life. Even so, the pit had taken his life and formed it. Geordie would have been unable to eradicate all of that, even if he had wished to. No, he had to accept these contrary feelings and live with them. He was free, physically, yet where did his heart lie? Was there still some part of him that dwelt in the pit? He walked on. Concentrating on putting one foot in front of the other and letting his mind wander again.

Children wandered where they would. There was nothing dangerous in the living quarters. Finn was more adventurous than most. He remembered the peculiar smell of the weavers' gallery. Where the mush stalks were laid for drying before the outside fibres were separated and used to make cloth on the looms.

He would wander down there and watch the

workers making cloth on the wooden frames, using the-metre-long dried stalks of the giant parasol mushrooms. Esmerelda always talked to him as she worked. Finny she called him.

"Finny! You come to see me," she smiled at him, her teeth shiny yellow in her ancient lined face. He had no idea how old she was. Apart from smile and frown lines people didn't really show their age in the pit. Oh, their hair went grey or fell out, but without the sun's rays to damage it, their skin aged slowly. Her age wasn't important though, it was her attitude to him that mattered, her kind words and smiles. She always had time for him, no matter how much work there was piled beside her. She ruffled his hair, which he loved, as he sat beside her, playing with the discarded fibres from the skin of the mushroom stalks.

Finn watched, mesmerised, as her deft fingers magically worked the machine that produced the coarse rough cloth all the workers wore, except for the Director, the managers and guards of course, who wore fine woollen cloth made from the fleece of the sheep kept for that very purpose.

Finn knew nothing of this, he liked 'Relda and 'Relda liked Finn. He would listen to her laughing and chattering with the other women as she worked. Not understanding meant little to Finn. Being there with 'Relda was what he liked, and she would often ask him to run little errands for her.

"Finny, go get me a new bundle of stalk fibre, love," or "How about getting me a nice drink of water from the bucket, my little Finny."

Finn adored Esmerelda and she gave him all the affection that the shy little boy needed, like the grandmother he had never known. He was devastated when she died.

Finn was there as usual. He was getting her a drink from the bucket: it was thirsty work with all that fibre in the air. They were all laughing at something. Finn turned with the cup of water in his hand in time to see her fall from her seat and lie still. The doctor came, although there was nothing he could do, and they took her away, and Finn stood there watching.

That was the last time he entered the weavers' gallery. It was a memory he tried not to acknowledge, yet the tears slipped from his eyes to freeze on his cheeks, straight from his once frozen heart.

Finn paused in his labour. He didn't know which drained him more, the physical intensity of dragging the sledge over the ice and snow or the memories that crowded into his mind. He stopped to catch his breath.

The cold was intense. It gnawed at him, leaching the heat from his body, leaving him unable to stand still for more than five minutes at a time, because of the numbing effect on his extremities. Yet he could go no further today. He sat on the ice, the wind so cold he could feel the sweat freezing onto his clothes, yet not wanting to move. He sat beside the sledge, sheltering from the wind.

Pulling the sledge was much like stoking the furnaces in the pit. You could only do so much and then you had to have a break. The difference was that in the pit you could walk out of the furnace room and cool off. Here on the ice, stopping meant cold. The almost instant loss of all the heat he generated pulling the sledge. When he could no longer stand the cold, he would start pulling again.

Finn hungered for heat. Heat! He could almost feel the dryness of the air and the heat from the furnaces in the stoking room that singed the hairs from your skin. He ached to feel the sweat running down his body as he shovelled coal through the open furnace door.

Everyone took turns at feeding the furnaces, even a

tek had to do his shift. He could see them all working, their bodies toned and muscular from the hard work of shovelling in the intense, skin blistering, heat. They wore just enough to cover their modesty and the sweat poured from them. He could feel the heat spreading throughout his body, driving the cold from his limbs. He luxuriated in the life-giving heat, breathing in the scorching dry breath of the furnace, sliding his shovel under the pile of hard glittering coal, pulling it out fully loaded, turning and flinging it through the open doors of the furnace.

He came back from his reverie to find, to his astonishment, that he did indeed feel the warmth of the furnace throughout his body. The cold had gone. How had this happened? Did his thoughts somehow affect the reality of his physical body?

He looked down and was surprised that the ice beneath him was no longer frozen solid; there was a slight puddle beneath his waterproof trousers. Had his visualisation of the roaring furnace affected his physical surroundings?

As he stood up beside the sledge, he could feel the heat from his thoughts percolating through his body. What had he done? Was this another effect of the purple light? Maybe he would try it again the next time he felt really frozen. He continued on his way with new strength.

The sun glared at him from the cloudless sky, dazzlingly low across the flat snowscape. It shone full in his face and despite the dark snow goggles he was wearing; Finn had to half close his eyes against its brightness. It was time to stop for the night, before the sun dipped below the horizon.

He unpacked the tent. It ballooned in the wind and he had to fight to put it up, using the last reserves of his strength. Although he had practiced it by the church, it was still an unfamiliar task and it took time to get it right.

Flinging what he needed into the opening, he climbed through and zipped it up. Zips had been an unknown to him. They didn't have them in the pit and it had taken him a while to work out how to use them.

He had spent a while playing with them, pulling them up and down, and wondering at their construction. This tent was from the before times, when they had so many wonders that were now only myths and legends in the pit.

The first priority was to light the stove. He needed

heat. With still-cold, fumbling fingers he struck the match and sat before the roaring stove. Gradually, the heat built up in the tent, percolating through his layers of clothing and he began to relax. The survival book said to make sure you dried your clothes properly or they would freeze on you and cause frostbite.

He knew what frostbite was. He didn't want any part of him frozen. His cheeks stung as the heat began to spread and his circulation came back. The icicles from around his face began to melt and he wiped them away. He must be more careful tomorrow and cover his face better. He rubbed his red cheeks, the stubble from his three-day beard was rough on his hands.

The new boots had rubbed his feet and brought up blisters. Finn knew better than to burst them. He'd had far too many on his hands from cutting coal and stoking to do that. He cleaned them and rubbed in some cream from the storeroom called antiseptic.

He made soup with dried ingredients from the storeroom, unzipping the groundsheet and digging up snow to melt in the pan. He drank it scalding hot, relishing the heat that coursed through him. Chocolate completed the meal. He relieved himself by unzipping the groundsheet in one corner, digging a hole and then replacing the snow after.

This was his third day since leaving the pit. Without its communal washrooms and plentiful hot water, he was beginning to smell. Although he had soap, he didn't want to waste fuel to heat water and he couldn't bear cold. He'd have to stink.

With the stove turned off, he fell asleep in the sleeping bag and dreamed of hot showers: boiling water rushing over him, cleaning the black coal dust from his tired body. He luxuriated in it.

Suddenly he was gasping in freezing water. There was greenery all around him and blue sky above him. A strange woman was shouting and he slid underwater, to emerge inside his sleeping bag, within the dark tent, gasping for air. Air! The vents in the tent were closed. The tent had a covering of frozen snow clinging to it: sealing him in. He could suffocate.

The open vents let in some welcome, cold air. The dream had saved him. Finn wondered what he had been dreaming of. Was it Eden? Was the shouting woman someone who lived there? Was this the work of the crystal again? He drifted off into a deep sleep.

Chapter 6

He woke early and the day, which was to be like so many others, began. A rhythm to his life was taking form, different yet similar to the pit. Making camp at the end of a long day. Eating. Sleeping. His exhaustion meant he usually slept well, although sometimes he dreamt about the pit and of other places that he did not yet know.

Mornings, his body had stiffened during the night, muscles tight and protesting from the previous day's effort. His bruises hurt and his shoulders were red raw from the straps, despite the padding he'd put under his clothes.

It was difficult to face the day. To stay would be to admit defeat. Instead, he packed everything and pulled the sledge, making his small stops throughout the day to eat and drink, though never for long, and then made camp again in the evening.

In those early days of his journey, the sun always

seemed to shine and the terrain was flat. Mostly he travelled over ice swept clear by the wind. Sometimes there were patches of snow and he would change his boots and crampons and replace them with the skis.

Skiing was more difficult than walking. By pure chance he'd chosen the correct cross-country skis that he needed. If he'd taken downhill skis, it would be even harder to learn how to use them and cover distance. At first, he didn't understand why the heels of the boots weren't fixed to the skis. For a moment he almost thought they were broken. It was when he started moving that he realised how much easier it was to move because of it. It made him ache in different places, becoming another part of his rhythm.

He became accustomed to pushing into the prevailing westerly wind. Its force changed daily, sometimes hourly. Seldom less than a slight hum, some days it would scream in his face like a demon. Unexpected gusts almost pushed him over, it grabbed at loose folds of cloth and buzzed through the webbing of the sledge.

Yet on those rare days, when it was absent, and a freezing mist descended, he missed its presence. At night he would fall asleep to its music, sometimes waking, disorientated, to a strange eerie quiet, until he realised the wind had dropped.

It was at the end of the first week the storm stopped him in his tracks. The wind roused him in the night, whining around the tent like an animal.

It was worse in the morning, the tent wall bulging: the material cracking furiously. Every now and again a sudden gust rocked the whole structure and Finn wondered if the pegs he'd hammered into the ice would hold or whether the wind would blow the tent away and him with it.

He crawled out only when the wind lulled, checking the sledge wasn't buried and fetching more food. When he did so, the wind almost blew him away, lifting him off his feet. It cut into his body, flung snow in his face and he was glad to get back inside, deafened, dazed and confused.

While the wind raged, he dozed, curled up in his sleeping bag.

His thoughts inevitably turned to food. He tried to eat less, but the boredom of sitting in his tent in the darkness made him want to do something, anything. His impatience mounting, he fiddled with things, searched through his pack, lit the oil lamp when it became dark and he wanted to eat.

He watched the flickering light reflecting from his cup of water onto the side of the tent. The flickering produced colours on the pale material that moved as the tent moved. Colours? The light on its own should not produce colours. What was causing the light to shine that way? Was it something to do with the water? He stared at the tent side, watching the moving colours in fascination as the tent side flapped with the wind. The colours made patterns and suddenly, memories flashed into his mind.

He would walk to his quarters after school. Going through the interconnected galleries, climbing ladders to get there more quickly than waiting for the mini train or the lift. He held his nose as he passed the stinking compost vats with their rotting vegetables. The animal and human manures adding their sharp stench to the aromas that assaulted his nostrils.

It was one day, coming back that way as usual, that was not usual. There was no one tending the vats, only the young ones and oldies looking after them. He knew at once what it was. Only an accident in the deep levels could provide a reason for all the men and women to be gone. He read it in the oldies' eyes.

Father! It was his shift. He ran, through the empty eating hall and the kitchen, down towards the shafts. Suddenly he stopped. A tall thin man, Simon, his father's friend, walked slowly along the gallery. His bald head, covered in dark coal dust, was bowed down onto his scrawny chest as if it were too heavy for him. At the sound of Finn's running feet, Simon looked up. Finn stopped. Fear's frozen hand grasped his heart. Father! Where was Father?

Simon's eyes told the story. Father was not coming back, not today or any other day. Accidents in the deep levels seldom happened without their quota of dead and injured. Digging out the coal was a dangerous job. It had to be done. Their lives depended on it and sometimes it demanded a sacrifice.

But not his father. No. Someone else's. Not his.

He had seen the empty gazes of other children whose parents had died in the deep pit. Finn made no movement as Simon picked him up with his long skinny arms and carried him back to the dwelling place Finn had shared with his father. It was now his alone. That night Finn's cries mingled with those of the other children whose fathers or mothers had also not returned that day.

Finn gasped. He lay in the sleeping bag, panting with shock. Where had this memory come from? Of course he'd known he'd had a father; it was just that he had no memories of him. For as long as he could remember, Geordie had looked after him. Now he knew. He remembered.

His father had died. It had been a turning point in his life. It was after his father's death that Geordie became his constant companion. He taught him and told him about the outside. It was then that he learnt of Eden. A magical place where you didn't have to dig out coal and there was more to life than growing food to live. From this time on, he knew there was somewhere else and he and Geordie made plans to go.

The wind howled outside the tent. Inside, Finn sat silent and still, mourning the father he didn't remember.

Chapter 7

He approached the conical shape across the flat featureless terrain. It stood above the ice for a few metres and cast a dark shadow from the fast-setting sun. This was the only landmark for miles around. He needed to stop. Of course he could always put the tent up. It was just that it was late and he was tired.

What was it?

Maybe a building from before times. As he got closer, he could see branches sticking out of the snow. It was a tree! A dead tree, a conifer, its brown withered needles still intact, covered in snow.

He stood there wondering what to do. Around the base of the cone was a gap where the wind had loosened the snow. It should be possible for him to crawl under the branches. If it was windproof, he could sleep there for the night and not bother with the tent.

Taking off his harness and pack he wriggled

through the gap and climbed down the branches into the centre of the tree. It was clean and dry. The snow had not penetrated here and at the base of the tree there was a space where people had camped here before him. Grey ash and pieces of burnt blackened branch lay in the middle of a circle of flat stones. Evidence of others?

Tonight he would have no need to use fuel for his stove. He would have a fire, a real fire, blazing and bright. The smoke would filter up and out through the snow-covered branches. No one would see it. Not that there was anyone to see it, because there were no others. Just like the Director said. This fireplace was old and covered in dust.

He brought down what he needed and made himself comfortable. He used some dried mush to light the fire. The branches he gathered, crackled merrily and filled the space with the beautiful scent of pine. Finn closed his eyes and sat back, enjoying its warmth.

Immediately he was back, with other children, in the mushroom growing galleries of the pit. They were supposed to be scaring the mice away. Instead they played their favourite game of Finn chasing.

He ran from them, between the clumps of giant

parasol mushrooms that towered above, some over two metres high. Running only half in fear. They couldn't get him, though they'd beat him if they did. He was too clever by half!

The giant metre wide mushroom caps spread like huge umbrellas. Not that anyone in the pit had ever experienced rain or needed an umbrella. Their excited cries were heard by nobody. He ran further and further into the dimly lit caverns. Leaving the others far behind. It was then that they did it. Knowing they couldn't get him, they shouted altogether.

"Finn!"

Instantly, he was shrouded in choking clouds of spores, as a billowing, dark brown fog fell from the mushrooms' pink gills, blotting out the dim lights, enveloping him. The spores filled his ears, eyes and nose. He breathed them in, choking and coughing, unable to get his breath. His eyes blinded and streaming, Finn blundered through the parasols.

It was a worker who saved him. He heard Finn's coughing and wheezing. He dragged him out, took him to the washroom, rinsed the spores from his face and mouth. Why didn't the worker report him. Did he feel sympathy for Finn. If he did, he was the only one. And where was Geordie then?

Finn awoke next to the smoky fire, doubled over, coughing from the depth of his being. The smoke hadn't filtered out through the tree branches. As he smothered the fire, he wondered again, why these images were coming into his mind? Why did he only now remember them? What was wrong with his memory? Why did the purple crystal creep into his mind.

Would he find answers in Eden?

***

After the second week, the landscape changed. Hills poked through the icescape, each with its covering of snow and on precipitous slopes the ground showed through. The ice and snow were uneven. Travelling was hard. He had to find routes around huge drifts of snow. It slowed him and wore him out. He was glad to stop each night. The sledge was lighter, though, as he ate his way through his supplies. Would he have enough food to get to Eden? He could only wait and see.

Coming around a sharp hill, Finn was confronted by a cylindrical tower. Built from grey stone, it stood tall with small windows set into its walls.

Finn approached. This was a fragment of the wonderful world shown in the pit library books. He wondered what had happened to it all. What had happened to cover it in snow and ice?

This structure had been built to stand out proud of the land. It was only the second building Finn had come across since leaving the pit and the church building had been completely covered. His curiosity led him on and he entered through a broken window at ground level.

Inside the room, huge paintings covered the walls. Finn was fascinated, although he could see few details. It was dark inside with just those few small windows. Who would ever have the time to paint a picture that size? Life in the pit was about survival, not pictures. No one would have time to paint something that big, even if they had the materials. Life must have been so different in the before times.

Finn walked down a staircase and stopped at an open door. It was a bedroom and lying on the bed were the bodies of a man and a woman. It was not the sight of the dead people that stopped him. He had often seen dead bodies in the pit. Sometimes he had helped dig them out from under rock falls. Other times he had helped carry them to the composters, for the disposal ceremony, where after the relatives' goodbyes, they would be recycled and used to fertilise the crops. Death in the pit was normal. It happened frequently. The birth rate was high; children grew rapidly and soon replaced the dead workers. Those who mourned their passing soon forgot them. There was work to be done.

This was different. The bodies were dressed in beautiful clothes. They were not young. In pit terms, they were ancients. On a bedside cupboard there was a bottle that Finn guessed had contained alcohol. Beside the empty bottle was a plastic container lying on its side with a few spilt pills. Food bar wrappers were scattered around the bed. A half open box of them was on the floor.

All this, Finn took in at a glance. What stopped him was how they were lying on the bed. Their arms were locked about each other and they were holding on in the most obvious gesture of affection Finn had ever seen. This was love. Dying together after living together for a very long time

It was unlike anything he had ever known in the pit. People did not show their feelings in the pit. The authorities did not encourage emotions. Without them people were more likely to do as they were told. Pit life was all about doing as you were told.

Finn could not remember people touching him or showing much liking for him when he was young, except for Esmerelda. Other children avoided him or were nasty to him. They were jealous.

To see people showing this much love for each other was a shock, upsetting. He felt like an intruder in a sacred place. The church had been different. He had felt almost welcome there, led there.

Grabbing the food bar box, Finn quickly retraced his steps and making his exit where he had entered, he hurried away from the unsettling experience. Yet it clung to him, despite his uneasiness and it brought other images in its wake.

Ralphie was a barrel of a man. Short, thick set, well-muscled, with robust legs and long powerful arms, he walked with a splay footed gait: rolling from side to side as he went. As a child, Finn had often thought he would overbalance and go crashing to the ground. He never did. Children loved him. He could pick them up with ease and throw them up and catch them in the way children loved, grinning indulgently at their cries of delight. There was an air of permanence about him. Ralphie was solid, a believable, enduring presence: until the rock fall crushed him.

Finn remembered the recycling. That must have been before his father's death. Before he started studying as a tek and moved apart from everyone else. Before he realised how much he liked being apart from the others: uninvolved.

As the days passed, and his supplies dwindled, he came to know all the moods of the weather, as a sailor would the sea. He'd seen books that showed the sea.

He knew the weather's anger and its meditations and, on some days, its irritations, when it drove sharp, dry, ice crystals, fiercely into his face.

There were happy days of sharp, bright sun with just the slightest breeze. The air so clear he felt he could see all the way to his journeys end and his imagination would run riot as he visualised what Eden must be like.

There were days of storm when he felt he had to keep going, however slowly he progressed. Occasionally the wind brought clouds of soft fluffy snow that muffled everything. Then the wind swirled them around him until he would lose all sense of direction and be forced to sit in his tent until it stopped and he could push it aside in soft heaps and continue on his way.

Some days were exhilarating. If the wind changed direction and blew from behind him, he felt as if he was being pushed to Eden. Others were depressing: days of low cloud when his movements became a weary plod.

He experienced them all and still he could not prevent himself from sinking into a mind-numbing apathy as he trudged towards Eden.

The landscape changed slowly and sometimes not at all. Occasionally, he would find himself travelling on a wide, even expanse of snow that he eventually recognised as being a road. It continued for mile upon mile with only an occasional bump. He knew the before people must had driven vehicles on roads like this. It took him a long time to realise that the bumps were the frozen remains of vehicles.

The roads made his travelling simpler, except for bridges. It was easier to go under if he could. If the bridge was blocked, he would be forced to drag the sledge up, over, and down the other side.

Finn began to fret at any delay. His supplies would

not sustain him for much longer. He tried to restrict himself to make it last. He lost any fat that might once have clung to his body, becoming skin, bone and muscle. What would he do when everything was eaten? He though vainly of all he had left in the storeroom. There was no way he could have taken more.

The pit faded to a dim memory. He remembered it. You couldn't delete memories. Not like the computers he'd used in the control room to regulate the steam, run the turbines and control the electricity supply. His memories were like a series of black and white photographs. He could look at them. They just didn't seem real any more.

Just like his tek skills. He didn't need them on the snow. They were still there, but strength and endurance were what he needed now. He had no one to help him, no one to give him orders. Unlike the pit. There they had controlled him, yet also they had relied on him. They could not do without technicians such as Finn. They were as essential as food and water.

Who else could run the turbines and the other machines that made the heat and light that grew their food and kept them alive? Without him and others like him, there would be no survival and they knew it. It was not an easy relationship. The common workers resented the teks, even when the teks took their turns at cutting coal and stoking the furnaces.

He lost count of the days. It felt like forever. He was sentenced to pull the sledge for the rest of his life. He shared out his remaining food for each day and watched helplessly as the days passed by, each with its ration of food and fuel and its quota of miles. How many more were there to go?

The next day's sun had barely pushed its disc above the horizon and Finn was walking fast across the smooth snow. The previous night the wind had blown cold and noisy, keeping him awake and shivering, not letting him forget his hunger. If he didn't find a new source of supply soon, he would starve. Walking made him hungry and he ate more, yet he wouldn't find more food unless he travelled.

He must keep moving.

The snowscape changed. Huge chunks of ice faced him. He stopped. There, clearly before him, was a choice of two routes. The one to the left went downhill. On the right the ice towered above the path. What should he do?

He chose the harder path and after navigating the

ice, he found himself on a windswept plateau, the frozen land scoured clear of snow. Then he saw it, a valley winding its way south between the windswept ridges. To his surprise the valley was not full of snow. As the plateau gave way to shelter, he felt better, as if the valley was some creature looking after him. He had chosen the right path.

The gradient was gentle. Frosted trees covered the steep sides of the valley and the sun, shining at an oblique angle from the east, created rainbows as it shone through the ice-coated branches onto the path. He stared for a while, mesmerized, then walked on through the rainbow colours as he had across the coloured floor of the church.

The wooden hut was on the other side of the valley, set on a flat area six or seven metres below the ridge, within the protection of a group of dead trees

Shelter. What luck!

Excitement rose within him. After scraping the snowdrift from the door with a fallen branch, he entered. There was a bed, a cupboard, shelves with boxes and bags and, most wonderfully, a pot-bellied stove in one corner. He looked in wonder at the iron stove with its metal chimney poking through the back wall. Excellent! Fortune was smiling on him.

Turning, he saw the axe on wooden pegs above the door. An axe! His laughter broke the silence. Better and better. Using branches cut from the trees outside, he soon had a blast of heat roaring from the stove. He sat close, letting it percolate through his body.

Warmed through, he explored the bags and boxes. Flour, dried fruit and old vegetables, frozen. They would supplement his rations. After eating, he lay on the bed in his sleeping bag and sleep claimed him.

He woke to a cold dawn. The blazing stove fire had died down overnight. After resurrecting the embers and breakfast he considered his situation. What should he do? Stay or go? He was exhausted and the warmth was beguiling. The dead trees would provide fuel for the stove. Food was the problem. Could he reach Eden with what remained of his supplies? The Survival Book said keep warm, but if he stayed, he would run out of food, fast.

He must go. If he climbed back up on the plateau, he could try and see which way the valley might take him and then leave.

On the windswept crest, where the snow was scoured away, the frozen ground was clear.

Finn looked back across the valley as it meandered away. He could not follow it. A few trees on the other side showed a black tracery of branches against the pale morning sky as the sun climbed higher. He must go, and soon.

Finn sighed and looked south. Are you there Eden? Are you waiting for me? Would he ever get there? Despair grasped him in its hands and he stared along the ridge wondering how far he would get before the food ran out.

What were those small white blobs dotted across the landscape? Snow drifts? Bushes? Curious, he walked towards one. Getting closer, he could see they were bundles of curly white wool. Wool? Wool only grew on sheep. In the before times, sheep had grazed on grass that grew on fields. Were these sheep from then? What had happened to them? Why were they here?

He ran the last few steps to the nearest one. Reaching out to touch it, he realised it was frozen. The sheep had frozen when the snow came. It must have happened quickly for their bodies not to rot away. Their bodies! Meat, they were frozen meat. He could eat meat. Would it be edible? Could he eat these sheep?

Within minutes he had returned from the hut with the axe. He cut through the carcass, hacking at the frozen flesh. The ice hard meat shattered under his blows. A huge piece of the animal came free.

More cutting and hacking made the piece manageable. He staggered back to the hut: axe in one hand and a huge chunk of frozen sheep on his shoulder.

He spent the rest of the day cooking and gorging on the meat. It was surprisingly tasty with no trace of decay. They seldom killed sheep in the pit and when they did only the guards got it. Their wool was far too useful for them to be squandered as food.

In the late evening he lay on the bed, half dozing. He felt full for the first time in days, the unaccustomed food lying heavy in his stomach. Tomorrow he would cut up more sheep and pack it onto the sledge. Tempting though it was, he must not stay here. Just long enough to recuperate and regain his strength for the march ahead. Eden beckoned.

He stuffed the stove with tree bits to keep the fire going until the next day. The heat from the stove and his full stomach lulled his thoughts and he slept well that night.

The day passed in a flurry of activity as he packed frozen meat onto the sledge, returning to the cabin at sunset with a great sense of achievement. He spent the evening eating huge chunks, indulging in the luxury of eating his fill and falling asleep with the glorious heat of the stove,

That night he had vivid dreams of the pit. Floating high in the hall, gazing down at the workers at their Friday night gathering, he watched as they drank and ate. He could see them all as they relaxed. He was with them, yet not part of them. Images of the church intruded and he flew, laughing, towards an enigmatic man standing beneath a huge purple crystal.

He awoke at dawn to a freshening wind that howled beneath the door. He shivered as he relit the cold stove and cooked more meat for breakfast and midday snacks on his journey.

He'd packed the sledge the day before. Masses of frozen meat: cooked and raw. He'd tied wood up in bundles and strapped them on top. That would save what fuel he had left.

Pulling the sledge up onto the ridge was a hard task. Once that was completed, he resumed his journey.

The meat gave him renewed strength and travelling

on the ridge was easier than floundering amongst the snowdrifts that had accumulated further down the valley. The plateau sloped away and he was walking downhill on the flat snowscape.

Something told him he was nearing the end of his journey. Eden was close, he knew it. Where was it?

"Geordie!" he shouted to the sky. "I'm almost there. Journey's end. I've almost reached Eden."

He ended in a fit of laughter. Almost there? What was he thinking of? The journey was easy. Arriving was difficult. Where was Eden. Could he find it? There were no signs saying 'Eden this way'. Only snow to blind him, distract him and misdirect him. Did Eden really exist or was the idea of Eden just something Geordie had put in his mind. Did he even want to reach Eden? Everyone in the pit knew there was Eden. He knew. Geordie knew, but Geordie was dead. He trudged on.

Days passed: turning to a week. Disappointment crept into his mind. He'd felt he was so close.

There was very little of the sheep left and the remnants didn't look very appetising. He ate it anyway, despite its strange taste. The land still sloped down and then it changed again. Strange hills pushing up out of the snow, almost as if some huge being had dumped them there.

Finn marched on and on, repeating the Eden rhyme over and over in his head. His feet pounding out the rhythm as he walked.

'You'll know it when you see it.

It shines in the setting sun,

But you won't see Eden till you know it's there.

It's not for everyone.'

Not for everyone? What did that mean? How could you not see it? It had to be there. Somewhere. Where?

The wind dropped completely. A freezing mist covered the land. He could see just a few metres around him. Frost crackled on his clothes. He wiped it off his goggles. The sun didn't penetrate the mist and although he continued, he had no idea if he was going in the right direction

Not that it mattered. Any direction was better than stopping completely. The momentum he'd built up while travelling was hard to resist. He didn't want to stop.

He could no longer see where he was going and as well as the mist around him, a fog grew in his mind. He felt hot. Sweat oozed from his forehead. He moved erratically, the sledge jerking from side to side as he lurched along. The mist closed in. He could hardly tell where snow ended and the mist began. He tore off his goggles.

He was in a bubble, a huge white bubble. He laughed: a raucous sound instantly deadened by the thick, suffocating mist. Tendrils of vapour clutched at his face and clothes, like flies buzzing about him. He batted them away with his hands.

"Get away! Get away from me!"

Where was he? Where was Eden? How could he come all this way, travel all those miles and not find Eden? The hardships of his journey mocked him.

He shouted, "Eeeeden! Eeeeeeeeeden!"

His words were swallowed by the mist.

The stillness was undisturbed.

"You're here. I know you're here. Show me. Where are you?" His desperate voice wailed up and down, cajoling and angry in turn.

"Geordie! Where are you? You said we'd journey together. Where did you go? You're not here? Why aren't you here? Help me Geordie. Help me! Why don't you show me where Eden is?" His voice tailed off, hopelessly.

He sank down on his knees and raising his arms in the air, brought his fists down angrily in front of him. He pounded the snow in anger as he had on the rim of the pit, all those weeks ago, shouting in despair,

"Help me! Help me! Help me!"

He slumped forward. Great sobs wracked his whole body, which trembled with the emotion coursing through him. Presently, the movements ceased and he lay silent and still, shrouded in mist.

Chapter 9

Blue.

Blue. White.

Straight lines.

Shapes.

Triangles.

Jagged edges.

Blue.

Everything was blue.

Black lines crossed symmetrically. Reflecting shapes. No circles. Blue. He floated in blue, silently, looking closely at the lines that crossed. Black lines: black as ice. He had to get up. He had to cut ice. Ice? He meant coal. It must be his shift. If he didn't get to his shift on time he'd be put on punishment. It was cold? Why was he so cold? Had the heating pipes switched off? Why was his sleeping room so white?

Get up. Come on. Get up.

"In a minute Geordie."

Why hadn't the first bell gone off? Must get up. Punishment shift: didn't want that.

Get up. Up.

"All right Geordie."

But he couldn't move. It was one of those dreams.

Blue.

Blue/white diamonds shone in front of him.

Hexagons. Six sided, shining brightly. Hexagons.

Ahh! That was better. He could move his right arm.

He pushed himself up. The hexagons of shining snow crystals that were millimetres from his eyes, disappeared: replaced by the blue plastic hexagons of Eden's domes. They shone in the rays of the setting sun as it made its way down towards the western horizon.

Eden.

'It shines in the setting sun.'

Eden.

He was here.

"I'm here," his cracked lips and parched throat rasped out the feeble sounds.

He was here.

He laughed. A harsh cackling!

He had arrived.

Get up, go on, get up. You're here. Don't fail now. Move!

Finn clambered to his feet, swaying precariously. His head pulsed. He blinked with the pain, screwing his face up against the hammering in his temples.

Staggering forward, the sledge dragging behind him, he found himself on the edge of the huge hole in the earth that contained Eden.

Finn's laughter rang out across the lonely snowscape for no one to hear. He was here. He knew now. He had been looking for a dome rising up above its surroundings: something huge that you could see from a long distance away.

'But you won't see Eden till you know it's there.'

Of course it was truly there.

'You'll know it when you see it.

How do you see it when it's below ground level? He laughed again, manically. Like all riddles, it was simple, when you understood. Eden was in a huge hole in the ground.

He took another uncertain step closer to the edge and as he did so, the ice gave way beneath him and he slid, in a headlong rush, down the frozen side of the massive space. The sledge slipped over behind him. By the time he reached the bottom, the sledge lying broken beside him, he was unconscious. One arm bent under him at a strange angle.

Finn had reached Eden, only not quite in the way he had expected.

Part two: Eden

Chapter 1

Finn was astonished to be looking down at his own body lying unconscious on blankets beside a metal framed bed. He saw the blood oozing from beneath his long hair and beard. His injured left arm stuck out at an odd angle on the pale green, tiled floor. A woman was bending over him, treating his injuries.

Who was she?

Where was this?

What had happened to him?

Memories trickled back into his mind: the pit, banishment, the purple crystal, falling into Eden. He'd done it. He'd reached Eden. Geordie! Where was Geordie? The pain of reality hit him: Geordie was dead. He had travelled to Eden on his own. He remembered. He'd been on his own for a long time.

He watched as the woman worked on his battered body: cleaning the blood from his forehead and dabbing at the cuts on his swollen nose. The woman's bare, brown arms moved swiftly back and forth as she worked on him. Her long, grey streaked black hair was held back with a rainbow-coloured band.

He gazed down from the ceiling of the small, white painted room as she lifted his head and shoulders and, carefully holding a glass to his lips, gently tipped a brown liquid into his mouth. Medicine?

After cutting his sleeve away and straightening his arm, she placed some leaves on the broken bone, covered them with fabric and fixed it down with tape. She bound flat pieces of wood on either side of his arm with stronger, wider tape. He had seen the pit doctor do this to broken arms and legs so the patient couldn't move them while the bone healed.

Then she did something that Finn had never seen before. Sitting down and holding her hands about five centimetres above his arm, she stroked the air around the break. He stared down at her. What was she doing?

Abruptly he was back in his body, gasping with the pain in his arm. He opened his eyes. The woman's oval face turned towards him. He looked up into her dark eyes.

"Hello. I'm Nisha," she smiled, her even white teeth shining against her brown skin with its patina of fine lines. "I'm so glad you're here. I've been expecting you for so long. You'll soon be well enough to help."

Her voice was light, soft and soothing, in contrast to her startling words. His mouth opened in bewilderment. Expecting him? What was she talking about? How could she be expecting him? No one knew he was coming here. He didn't know her.

Nisha smiled at his blank face.

"It's alright; you don't have to worry about that yet. You broke your left arm when you fell into Eden and perhaps some ribs too. And you have a fever," she added. "Don't try to speak now. What you need is rest. I'll look after you."

He became aware of heat coming from her hands and the pain in his arm diminished. She was looking after him.

Finn closed his eyes and in moments he was in a restless sleep.

Nisha went to a cupboard and took out some clear, pointed, hexagonal crystals, which she placed in a glittering pattern on the floor around Finn's sleeping form. Next, she took a copper tube, with another, longer crystal, mounted on one end. Holding the other end, which was wrapped in cloth, she waved the crystal in a circle over and around the crystal pattern. Then she sat cross legged and closed her eyes.

Time passed and Nisha got up, waved the copper pipe crystal over the other crystals and replaced them in the cupboard. Then she blew out the oil lamp and left.

It was almost dark in the small room when Finn woke to stare about him at the white painted walls. How he had got here? Why couldn't he remember anything?

He was unbearably hot. As he tried to move, a sharp, angry pain shot through his left arm and chest and he was forced to lie still. His head ached. The blood pounded through his body. The ceiling moved back and forth, in and out of focus. A face stared down at him. The pit director. She was talking at him. He couldn't hear the words because the stokers were shovelling noisily as they flung the coal into the furnace flames. They stopped, turned, and pointed at him; their faces contorted in anger.

"Those who work eat. Why aren't you working Finn?"

"Those who work eat. Why aren't you working Finn?"

"Those who work eat. WHY AREN'T YOU WORKING FINN?"

Over and over again they chanted the words, getting ever louder and stepping closer and closer towards him. He quailed before their anger, trying to shrink away. The furnace was making him so hot, yet he was shivering. Cold, why was he so cold?

The director spoke again and now he could hear.

"The food is ours. You can't have it. Look at you, lying there, safe and sound. You killed them, didn't you? Dead! They're dead and it was all your fault."

Dead? Who was dead? He hadn't killed anyone. He tried to reply. His mouth wouldn't move. He began to cry in frustration and then Geordie was there, smiling at him.

It's alright Finn. It wasn't your fault. It wasn't you. You made it. You've arrived at Eden.

You're safe.

And you know what to do.

Finn woke with a jump, looking around. Wondering again, where he was. Then his eyelids drooped and sleep claimed him again.

***

Nisha walked through a series of dim unlit corridors and came to a long dark open space. The huge windows along one side had been painted black. Her hard soled shoes clacked across the wooden floor and up the steps to a balcony overlooking the main space. Pushing through two large swing doors of flexible, translucent plastic she walked into the steamy heat of the rainforest that filled the largest dome. She made her way along the paths that wound their way through thick undergrowth, until she came to a small hut made of woven split plant stems. It was raised on low stilts, with a thatched roof. Climbing the wooden steps, she pushed aside the woven door covering and went into the shadowy interior.

She knelt before a low table and opening the lid of a small round brass pot, she blew on the contents. The smouldering charcoal inside glowed and taking a piece of plaited grass from a box, she held it to the charcoal. When it burst into flame, she used it to light several fat candles at the back of the low table.

The flickering light illuminated the room with its mats and cushions on the wooden floor and the printed wall hangings. The candlelight shone on the crystals hanging from the ceiling and rainbows flickered around the room.

Placing her hands in the prayer position she murmured words and then taking a small stick she ran it around the rim of a small crystal bowl. A low tone began to sound from the bowl and she added her own humming voice to it. The sounds grew louder for some minutes and then slowly faded as she replaced the stick beside the bowl.

She bent her head for a few moments and then, standing, she went to another desk and sinking into a bamboo chair before it, she opened a box, removed a book with a blue embroidered cover and turned to the next clean page. Picking up a pen she wrote rapidly, with great concentration and excitement.

He is here. He has arrived and he has the skills to repair Eden. I know it, I can feel it. Oh, it's been so long. Why did I have to wait so long? The creeping death is spreading. Is he in time? He must be in time. His body will heal soon. His mind may take longer. His spirit is anxious and confused and I do not yet know where his path leads. Yet he is here. He has arrived! He can repair Eden.

Closing the book she hugged it to her chest and smiled.

***

The next day Nisha sat looking at Finn's restless movements. What was going on in his mind? She leant over him, trying to stop him pushing his coverings away.

Don't tell her. She doesn't need to know.

Tell her what Geordie?

You know.

No I don't. Tell me.

How can I tell you what you already know?

Stop it Geordie. I need your help.

Help? I can't help you.

Please help me. You've always looked after me.

Yes, I looked after you. Not now. No more. You're in Eden. She looks after you.

Why Geordie? Why can't you help me?

Tears poured from Finns closed eyes. He thrashed wildly.

You know why Finn. You know.

I can't tell you what you already know.

Abruptly Finn was running along a dark corridor. Lights came on behind him. Quick, shut the doors.

Slam them all, one by one. Keep it in. Don't let it out.

"NOOOOOOOOOooooooooooooooooooooo," his voice was loud and hoarse.

"What is it? Tell me," said Nisha.

Finn sat bolt upright, pushing her away.

"No," calm and clear. He pointed before him.

They looked at him: everyone from the pit.

"Don't listen to Geordie, Finn. Tell her," they chanted. *"Tell her,"* they urged. *"Tell her. Tell her. Tell her. She'll understand."* And they laughed.

"Stop it. Stop it."

They laughed again.

"She'll understand what you did. She'll forgive you for what you did. Tell her. Tell her. Tell her"

"What did I do?"

"You know what you did. Tell her."

"No," his voice was quiet, clear, and authoritative. "No. You can't make me."

He opened his eyes and looked at Nisha.

"They can't make me do it."

"Make you do what? There is no one here but me," soothed Nisha

Finn said nothing.

"It's alright. I'm here. I'm looking after you. You're

safe."

He lay back, turned his head away from her gaze and closed his eyes.

Far away, someone sang. Her voice soothed him and he slept.

He woke again with a start. The words from the pit dwellers echoed in his mind. Tell her? Tell her what? Geordie said he knew, but he didn't and Geordie said he didn't have to. He shook his head in confusion. His blood pounded. His head ached.

He was safe. He was in Eden and he was safe. Geordie had said so. It had been their dream of reaching Eden.

Finn and Geordie, Geordie and Finn.

Together. It surprised him when he had to blink back tears. He'd thought he was used to being alone. He'd reached Eden without Geordie. He'd reached his destination. He was here. What wonders were there for him to see?

Without Geordie!

He could not wait to explore, yet he knew he was not well enough. His head throbbed. He should not have eaten the last of the sheep meat. Its strange taste should have warned him. Though he'd had little choice. What else had there been to eat. He felt bruised and tired, so tired, and he hadn't even told the woman his name. His eyes closed, his breathing became deep and regular and finally he fell into a deep, healing sleep.

***

He spent the next few days recovering, sleeping more often than not. Dreams rushed into his mind, as the fever waxed and waned. Nisha came to see him regularly, to give him the brown liquid. She used the crystal pattern and held her hands over his arm. She cleaned his stinky body like a mother washing her child. She changed the dressing on his arm, fed him, helped him to the toilet. She listened to him talk and shout as his feverish mind wandered. She noted how he always came back to Geordie. She looked after him, sometimes asking him how he felt, otherwise saying little.

Gradually, his health improved.

He woke from another dream. The images vanished. Hidden. Yet his own screams had woken him. What was it? Why was he tormented so? Where had all this come from? Why hadn't it happened to him in the pit or on his journey? Only it had. He'd just not recognised it. It was the purple crystal. He knew.

Nisha bent over him.

"What about your mother? You shouted about your mother."

Mother? The word echoed through his memories.

"No. Geordie. There was only Geordie," the words came out abrasive and harsh.

Thoughts scurried across his brain: whispered messages from his past.

Finn paled and shrank into the mattress as if a weight pressed him down. Nisha looked at Finn's broad face, ashen beneath the beard and tan he'd acquired on his journey across the ice. She looked at his long tousled brown hair. She stared at his averted eyes, at his white countenance, and knew she must wait. He was not ready.

***

Nisha sat at her desk, writing in her journal.

So, he does not remember his mother and says nothing about a father. Who is Geordie? I cannot see a clear picture of him. I feel he is the key. Time is passing. The creeping death has spread. It is moving closer to the doors. It must not infect the Mediterranean dome. What shall I do if he is not ready?

Her face creased into a mask of anxiety.

I did not know he would arrive like this. There must be a reason. Oh Creator, why do you test me so?

Nisha sighed and smiled as she took up her pen.

All is well. All is for a reason. I must have patience. God give me patience. Finn must come to it in his own time. Yet if I allow him too much time, will it be too late? What should I do? He must heal quickly. There is so little time. I didn't know he'd take so long to get here. I didn't know.

She closed the book, slid off her chair and sank to her knees. With a straight back and head held high, she closed her eyes and reached out with her mind. Her silent prayer for help was heartfelt. After sitting for some time, she took a small slip of paper and wrote upon it.

Creator, please grant me the strength and skill to heal him.

She folded it several times and placed it within the small box beside the table. Touching the winged figure on the box lid, she muttered something under her breath, extinguished the lamp and left. She walked along the dark path to the sound of moths' whirring wings.

***

It was three days before he felt able to sit up and take an interest in more than his immediate surroundings. In two more days he could feed himself. Nisha still used the crystals on him and at the beginning of his second week at Eden, with only a little help from Nisha, Finn was able to dress and stand up.

When the room had stopped whirling, he smiled and took a few wobbly, but determined steps across the room towards the wheelchair she had brought.

"Nisha! I can do it."

He felt like a child learning something new, proudly showing his mother how grown up he was. He stopped, memories of a smiling woman crowding into his mind. His face screwed up in pain. Nisha rushed to him, holding him as a mother might once have done.

"Finn! What is it?"

The care and concern in her voice touched his heart. He gasped; the room whirled, his legs lost their strength and he almost collapsed.

The moment passed.

Resolute, he clenched his jaw and leaning on Nisha just a little, he wobbled the few steps to the wheelchair.

His physical body is mending quickly, thought Nisha. How long will the anguish in his mind and spirit take to heal?

I must be patient.

Once in the wheelchair she pushed him along the corridors. Bypassing the stairs they went through the translucent plastic double doors and into the steamy heat of the tropical dome.

Finn was speechless. Before he had crashed down the frozen north side of Eden's hiding place, he had seen Eden's domes. Yet nothing could prepare him for this, his first sight of the tropical forest inside the dome.

How could such a beautiful place exist here amongst the frozen wastes? It filled his heart with awe and wonder. Tears came to his eyes. He had often thought of Eden. He had seen pictures of forests from the before times and had tried to imagine what Eden would be like. Yet even if someone had described Eden to him exactly, he could not have visualised it. To experience the majestic beauty that was this natural world, you had to see it for yourself.

There were tall trees, forty metres or more in

height, trunks wider than he could possibly stretch around with both arms. Luxuriant, thick undergrowth covered every inch of earth. Huge leaves, some almost a metre across, grew from branches green with moss, glistened with the fine mist of warm water sprayed from hidden pipes. Dazzling flowers of every shade shone brightly on all sides. Their exotic scents combined with the smells of growth and decay.

Fruit hung enticingly. They ate what Nisha picked, sharing it, serenaded by the drone of insects and the rustlings of hidden creatures. There were large crystals placed on the ground between the leaves and bushes, like the ones Nisha had used to heal him. Some hung from threads: swaying in the gently moving air. Their shiny faceted surfaces reflected and magnified the beauty of the forest.

And all of this was enclosed in two magnificent, gargantuan, interlocking, geodesic domes, whose hexagonal, tessellated shapes covered everything. Finn estimated it roofed over an area at least fifty metres high, double that wide and a couple of hundred metres long. Keeping everything protected from the cold outside.

After his years in the pit and his journey across the

white wastes, Finn gulped down this feast for the senses.

Something brushed his cheek. He jumped in alarm and raised a hand to push it away.

Nisha laughed: a tinkle of amusement.

"It's alright Finn. It's only a butterfly."

"Butterfly."

"A winged insect. They're beautiful. Look."

Finn eyes followed her pointing fingers to where the pale blue butterfly was now perched on a flower. Its long angular legs clutched at the petals, whilst its tongue unfurled and probed the centre for nectar. Others flew between the plants.

Everywhere he looked there were wonders.

As they turned a corner, Finn immediately recognised the scene before him.

"Nisha," he said excitedly. "It's the pond: the pond in my dream. It was you. You saved me."

"I saved you?" Nisha looked puzzled.

"It was a dream. I had a dream," Finn rushed into his story. "It was when the first storm came on my journey. I hadn't opened the vents in the tent and the snow was frozen over them. I would've suffocated. In my dream I was drowning in a pond, this pond, and you were shouting at me. Then I woke up and realised what was happening. You saved me."

"I don't remember doing that. It must have been in my dream too," said Nisha. "Do you often have dreams like that?"

Finn nodded and began to talk excitedly about his journey, the church, the pit, the weather, everything except his dreams, the purple crystal light in the church and especially, not about Geordie.

Despite the energy sapping heat, Nisha had no difficulty walking up the steep slopes whilst pushing the wheelchair. She might be old, thought Finn, but she's strong. He admired the towering bows of the boat that greeted them without understanding at all why it was there. He gazed at the colourful statues and effigies, paintings and pictures that were worlds away from the harsh, black and white pit.

Nisha pointed out so many wonders to him, although she made no comment when they went past her hut.

He marvelled at the clouds clustered around the huge trees that spread their crowns just beneath the tracery of metal that held the plastic hexagons in place.

They continued their journey along the paths that wound up and around, the noise of the waterfall growing ever louder. Finally they reached where the waterfall burst from rocks above them and plunged down beneath the bridge they stood on. The noise was deafening. As it crashed down from its source above, Finn felt the power of the water's energy as it rushed under the bridge, rushing down towards the pond at the lowest point of the dome.

In the pit they pumped water up from the deepest part of an old abandoned shaft that had flooded sometime in the past. After purification it was fit to be used. Their waste water went to another branch of the same shaft so the two didn't mix. All that was practical and the pumps used very little energy. This was different. He shook his head in amazement. This water pouring from the rocks was so wasteful of power.

"This is the Mediterranean Biome," said Nisha as she pushed him through the plastic doors.

"Biome?" queried Finn.

Nisha explained. Biome meant a particular type of growing area. It was noticeably cooler here. Comfortably warm, with less humidity. She showed him the places where she grew food. She told him what the plants were: tomatoes, leeks, beans, onions. Some he'd never seen before.

He wondered at the meaning of the life-size metal sculptures. The raging, human-headed bull, and the dancing people. He examined the olive trees with their small green fruit. He held leaves in his hand and felt their textures. He sampled the delicious fruit and vegetables and asked Nisha many questions about the domes: most of which she could not answer. He smelt the perfumes of the colourful flowers. It was so unlike the stark pit with its plants grown only for food. His mind was overwhelmed with the beauty of it all.

He tried to imagine the paths covered with crowds of people looking at the plants and the steel webbed construction. He understood why Geordie had wanted them to get here. This was beauty beyond description. This was what the world should be like. What had happened to change it into the white wilderness that surrounded them? Not for the first time since leaving the pit, his eyes overflowed with tears. Nisha stood beside him, holding the hand he had held up to her. She smiled. Finn stared up into her lined brown face, at her reassuring smile. He was a small child; she was an adult. He could safely leave everything to her and all would be well.

"I didn't know it would be this beautiful. Thank you for bringing me in here. Was it all like this? The world before the snow, I mean." Without waiting for a reply, he continued. "When can I meet the others, Nisha?" she stared at him blankly. "Your companions. The others who live here."

"Companions?" Nisha's voice was puzzled.

"Yes," said Finn. "The people who live here with you and tend to Eden. I could hear one of them singing when I was ill. She has a beautiful voice. I thought I knew the song, even though I couldn't hear the words."

"Others?" Nisha was puzzled. "There are no others, Finn." She looked at his startled face. "I have no companions. I don't know where the singing came from. I live here on my own. You and I are the only living souls in Eden. Did you not know that?"

Chapter two

He knows now that I live alone. He does not understand who tends the plants, trees and bushes. I cannot tell him, yet. He is not ready. Patience, Nisha, patience. Show him the creeping death tomorrow. Let him see it and feel the cold for himself. He must know where Eden is dying.

Who did he hear singing? Was it in his dreams: the dreams of which he told me nothing?

Nisha smiled wryly.

Is it a part of what he hides within him?

I know he was sent to me for a reason. He has the skills to repair Eden. Must I heal him, too? Please God we have enough time for him to do what he must, before I have to send him on his next journey.

***

Alone! Nisha lives alone? He had thought Nisha was the one given the task of looking after him and he would meet the rest some other time. He had thought they were all so busy looking after Eden, they had no time to come and see him. He had thought there would be lots of people who had come to live in Eden. He had thought there would be companions to talk to, laugh with, cry with, but there was no one. Except Nisha.

There was no one else to do everything needing to be done at Eden. How could this be? Eden was huge. There must be equipment needing maintenance, plants to be tended, crops gathered and seeds to be sown. Who would do all this, if it was just Nisha living here? What provided the heat to keep Eden warm in the freezing white waste of snow?

Finn lay back in his bed. He no longer needed to lie on the floor. Nisha said he had to rest and regain his strength. Yet questions crowded into his mind and sleep evaded him.

It must have been Nisha who dragged him, unaided, in from the cold when he fell into Eden. For the first time since arriving, he wondered where his sledge was. Nisha would have put it somewhere safe. Why didn't she tell him she was alone? But then, why would she? Living alone was what she did. He was the stranger. He was the guest.

Nisha had things to do, chores that could not wait,

she said. He lay on his bed, thinking, until the light from the small window behind him became dim. Nisha had said she would come soon, to light the lamp. It had surprised him that Nisha had lamps like the one he had used on his journey. He had watched her cleaning the glasses and filling their reservoirs with a pale green translucent liquid.

Something stopped Eden from freezing. Something heated the domes and powered the water and steam sprays. Something warmed the soil and the air. Where did the power come from to keep Eden warm? How did this amazing natural world exist in the cold? Eden must have electricity. Did Nisha know this? She seemed to just accept that Eden worked and did not question how.

He had thought getting to Eden would be the answer to everything. Now there seemed more questions than ever. He hoped Nisha could answer them when she came with the lamp. Only when she arrived, fatigue had claimed him. She pulled the covers over his sleeping form and crept out.

***

Finn floated, high above Eden, looking down upon the domes. The wind was blowing huge clouds of ice and snow, yet he felt no cold. A massive white figure made of snow, with rounded body, arms and legs, a scarf around its neck and a hat on its head, was standing beside Eden. It blocked out the stars in the night sky. It put its hands on its body, its elbows sticking out, and opened its mouth in an enormous laugh. Finn felt a growing fear grasp him. The snow creature, three times as tall as the domes, bent. Its huge mouth opened in a malevolent smile, showing sharp icicle teeth ready to take an enormous mouthful from the domes. He wanted to stop it happening, but he couldn't move. He shouted, "Stop! Don't!"

The snow creature paid no heed. Its huge mouth smiled and bit into the domes. Finn screamed and sat up in bed, "No! No! NO!"

Moments later Nisha came hurrying through the door dressed in swirling night clothes, her long hair plaited and a lamp in her hands. Her face was tight, anxious and concerned. She looked older, the lamplight making the lines on her face look deeper than they actually were.

"Finn, are you alright? You were screaming."

"I had a horrible dream."

She sat on the bed and listened as he told her what

he had seen. She laughed at his anxious face.

"Don't worry Finn. I know what it means. It shows what is happening to Eden. Part of Eden is broken and needs to be mended. The snow and ice are eating away at it. You wanted to stop it, but you could not. When you are healed, you can repair it and complete your task."

Yet he had felt something else; something else hiding behind the snow creature. He hid the feeling.

"Nisha," began Finn. "Why are you on your own? Who does everything if you are here alone? How does Eden keep going with only you to do everything? I don't understand? Please tell me."

Nish sat down on the bed. "My mother died when I was born, shortly after my parents came to Eden. My father died too, many years after. They are buried with the others who were here before us."

Nisha stopped. Her whole head was enveloped in the lamp's golden glow and her eyes shone with tears for what had been. "How long the world has been frozen I do not know. My father told me little of that. My mother's death affected him and although he taught me all he knew of crystals and healing herbs; he did not talk about the world. I do know Eden is a storehouse of the natural world. The white wilderness will not last forever. Eden needs you, Finn. I need you. Tomorrow, I will show you what has happened to Eden. Now let me do some healing on your arm. It will relax you."

Finn began to feel the familiar healing warmth from Nisha's hands. He stared at the ceiling, his thoughts wandering. He was to repair Eden. Was he really that special? Did he want to be special? Did he have a choice? He did not doubt its truth. Something within him said it was so. Should he believe that he could do this? Eden was not what he had thought it would be. It was more exciting and more scary than all his imaginings.

Nisha sat beside him till he fell asleep.

***

The stench of death and decay hit him as Nisha pushed his wheelchair through the doors into the last biome. A silent wave of cold crept over them. A short distance from the doors, a slimy carpet of dead leaves covered the soil with patches of white fungus poking through it.

Further back the white patches had joined together and covered the earth like the snow outside. Lifeless, leafless trees and shrubs stood stark against the white, in deadly contrast to the other life-filled domes. In places he could see crystals. They were different to the ones in the other biomes. These were shattered into pieces. And not just shattered. The pieces were blackened as if something had burnt them.

He stared: speechless. A feeling of bleak despondency crept stealthily into his mind, as the cold had sometimes seeped into his bones on the journey to Eden. Nisha wheeled him out from the dreadful place of death and guided his chair back along the short corridor to a wooden bench in the temperate biome.

"I have lived at Eden for all my life, over fifty years Finn," explained Nisha. "The books I have found here, say the white death biome was once a desert. The people who lived here long before me, they changed it when the snow came, so it was temperate and had seasons."

"What are seasons?"

"A cycle when the weather changed from hot to cool, then to cold and to cool again and back to hot. I ran here when I was young. I ran through the seasons as they changed." Nisha's voice became more youthful as she entered her memories. "My father brought me here to pick leaves, roots and bark when he was teaching me to make the medicines. It was such a beautiful place then. We were so happy." Finn sat motionless. After a moment, Nisha continued.

"This is where I remember him best," her voice faltered for a moment, and then, as if realising that Finn was sitting next to her, she shook her mood off. "Two years ago, there was a storm unlike any other I had known before. It was not just the snow and the wind howling across the domes, the clouds were thicker and heavier. Huge shafts of fractured light flashed down from the sky. For seconds at a time, night was day. A terrible crashing followed. The flashing lights concentrated on this biome. I was terrified. I hid until it stopped and daylight returned.

I noticed nothing until it was too late. I didn't see what was happening because it was winter, the cold season in this biome. I thought nothing had changed.

Then I realised that spring had not come. It was not getting warm again. It stays very cold now, especially at night. The only thing that grows, is the white fungus. It thrives on the dead plants and covers everything. There were no flowers. I had no seeds to collect. The plants died. I tried moving some to the Mediterranean biome. Very few survived. All I have left is what herbs I had dried and what still grows in the other biomes.

And then the white fungus began to grow. It spread from the far end of the biome and it grows closer to the doors every day. It likes the cold here, but I feel it will spread in the humidity of the other domes.

I fear it will kill all the plants and Eden will die. We have to stop it here. If you can make this biome hot again like the desert it once was, the heat will dry out the soil and the fungus will die. Even the spores would die. We could take it outside and burn it." Nisha turned to Finn. "Help me, Finn. I know what must be done. I cannot do it. I do not know how. You understand the technology. You can repair it. Change it. Find out how to make it hot again. It will stop the fungus. You must help me return Eden to what it was. You were sent. I prayed and asked for so long, and you were sent. You can do it. I know you can."

Nisha's shining brown eyes were full of hope and expectation.

***

That evening, after Finn was asleep, Nisha went to her

hut and wrote in her journal.

Now he knows. I have told him all I can, for the moment. All else I must keep from him until he is ready. If I told him now, he would not understand. When he finds out he may be angry with me. What else can I do? It is a chance I must take. He has seen how Eden is in danger. He MUST repair the heating and kill the fungus. And yet, and yet there is something within him that seeks to run, to escape. I pray that it does not stop him from doing his work. He was brought here to mend Eden. He must be able to fulfil his purpose.

Putting her pen aside, Nisha sat with closed eyes for a long while on her mat on the floor.

***

After they had shared breakfast, Nisha removed the splints from Finn's arm. She cautioned him to move carefully and told him that he must continue to have healing or it might not mend correctly.

Later, Finn walked slowly along the paths, trying to understand what was happening in Eden. Nisha had told him to.

"Go Finn. Look at Eden. Understand it. Find its secrets so you can repair it. You are ready for the exercise. Go. I have work I must do."

She had smiled and given him a gentle push.

Finn had returned the smile and walking tentatively, went out into Eden. He wandered slowly along the paths, trying to make sense of it all. He could always see what was wrong in the pit and then he would fix it. Eden was more complicated.

He sat on a bench and closed his eyes.

A strange fluttering noise jerked his eyes open. Something was in the air. He stared in astonishment. It was birds! Birds flying in the air! They had feathers and wings just like the hens in the pit, only these were small birds with small bodies. The hens couldn't fly of course, they just rooted around in their enclosures, eating the compost worms they were fed on and laying eggs for the guards.

There was another, smaller bird in the bushes close to him. No more than ten centimetres long, the small rounded creature with bright eyes and sharp beak was hopping from branch to branch. It was pale brown with a striking red front. Unafraid, the bird hopped onto the bench beside him and putting its head to one side looked at him questioningly.

Fascinated, Finn stared at the bird. Time slowed.

The bird's head took an age to move from side to side. Like a series of photographs, there was one picture, then another and another: each a millisecond later. He blinked. The bird flew and the pictures stopped.

Finn still sat, staring where a branch cast shadows on the wooden slats of the bench, its leaves arranged asymmetrically on either side of its stalk. He noticed the pattern the way he always saw clear patterns in everything. The patterns that had helped him solve problems in the pit.

Machines had patterns. No life, but patterns and purpose. He could see that the life in Eden had patterns and purpose too. If he followed them, would he find the answer? What was the key to this place? Machines he was used to. He could follow their complexities. Could he make this place work, with its mixture of machines and the natural world? The creeping death was spreading fast. Nisha said there was no time. Yet he needed time.

He wandered off into the farthest reaches of the Mediterranean biome. He stumbled through the undergrowth that Nisha had not cleared to grow crops. Despite its wildness it felt as if it was tended and cared for, yet kept wild.

He pushed back a branch, releasing another that whipped across his eyes. He gasped and took several tottering steps sideways into the undergrowth. His flailing arm hit a ball shaped thing hanging from a horizontal branch. There was a moment's silence and then a high-pitched whining began, like a fast-running electric motor gradually gaining speed. Through his tear washed vision, he saw a myriad of small black things rushing towards him. One landed on his outstretched right forearm. Liquid fire was injected through his skin. He jerked his arm back involuntarily. Fire was inserted into his right leg; More in his left arm. Thousands more wasps poured towards him, landing on his unprotected flesh.

A scream was wrenched from his lips. He pushed violently at the wasps. The stinging sensations stopped. The whining, buzz diminished. He looked up. Ahead of him, half a metre away, was a curtain of the creatures. They were trying to get at him, yet could come no closer.

What had he done?

The thought flashed through his mind, even as he tottered away from the angry creatures.

Nisha's soothing herbs took the sting from his

flesh. He didn't tell her what he'd done to the wasps. She made no comment when he said he'd accidentally disturbed their nest. As she treated him, he wondered over what he'd done? How had he done it? He'd done it, that was a fact. The problem was, he had no idea how he'd done it, and, crucially, no control over it.

His next day of wandering he stayed clear of the wild parts of Eden and that evening when Nisha asked him what he thought, he frowned.

"I don't know yet, Nisha."

She made no comment.

When she asked again, after the second day of his wandering, his reply was the same. She looked at him anxiously and said nothing.

On the third day it was getting dark and Finn had still not returned. Nisha went looking for him.

She found him crouching on the path just inside the Mediterranean biome. At the sound of the doors opening, he turned a tear-streaked face towards her.

"I can't do it Nisha. It's gone. Something's happened to me. I know there are patterns here. I can see them, but they won't fit together. I don't know how to do it.

I could always see the patterns in the machinery in

the pit. I was a tek. The best they'd ever had! I could solve any problem in the pit." He looked down at the path. "Something's happened. I can't put it all together."

A strange look of half understanding slipped onto his face.

"It's the crystal, Nisha. The purple crystal in the church."

What purple crystal? Thought Nisha. What haven't you told me Finn?

"It's changed me. It's taken away my abilities. It's stolen my talent. I can't do it." His voice died to a whisper. "I don't know how to fix things anymore."

He raised his arms and brought his fists down hard on the path, like he had when he'd reached the top of the ice cliff in the pit and realised that there were no others. He gasped with the pain in his hands.

Nisha stepped closer.

"Stop!" Finn edged away from her. "Don't touch me! LEAVE ME ALONE!" His voice was strange, high pitched, childlike.

Nisha stopped in surprise.

Finn stretched one arm out in front of him protectively, fingers spread like talons. His eyes stared through Nisha at something beyond her. He held his body as would a child.

She stared at him. He was no longer a young man: strong and powerful. He was a fearful child. His eyes, darting from side to side, were wild and haunted. Nisha reached out to comfort him. Finn whacked her hand away. She gasped and pulled back.

Finn crouched as if he would melt into the floor. A look of grim, desperate determination spread on his features; his teeth bared in an angry grimace. Like a cornered animal, thought Nisha.

"I won't. I WON'T GO. No, No, No, NO, NO," Finn's voice rose to a shriek.

His head jerked back and he screamed. His cry of anguish reverberated around the domes. The metal sculptures vibrated and hummed till the sound was lost in the roar of the waterfall from the tropical biome.

***

Nisha sat before her journal in her sanctuary.

Oh Finn. What happened to you in the pit? What did they do to make you scream in pain like that? How did you become that frightened child? What is it that scares you so? Why didn't you tell me about the purple crystal in the church? I need to know how it changed you. What are you hiding?

What happened to you Finn?

You have told me many things of your life in the pit and your journey, yet almost nothing of your friend Geordie. You think I have not noticed how little you tell me of him. What do you not wish to see? It blocks you seeing how to heal Eden. It must be something to do with Geordie.

I must act quickly. Eden needs you.

I will add the truth finding herbs to your healing drink.

***

Finn stood on a path in the tropical biome. For three more days, at Nisha's command, he had wandered in Eden. For three more days he had tried to understand how Eden worked.

Why had he become a child and screamed when Nisha went to help him? He'd had no memory of it until Nisha had told him what had happened.

And now... and now...

He still didn't understand how to repair Eden. The more he looked the less he understood. He felt the greenness enclose him. Enveloping him, like a trap.

Tears of exasperation filled his eyes. He shook his head in frustration.

What was that?

A movement on the branches drew his gaze.

Fluttering wings. Birds. Looking at him. Beaks moving in unison. They screamed their message. "Weep, weep, weep."

Mocking laughter dripped from their beaks. "Can't do it. Can't do it. Can't do it."

The humming whine of the cicada buzzed in his ears. "Nooooooooooooooooooooooo. Goooooooooooooooooooooooooooooooo."

The waterfall shouted,

"Sttttttttttooooooooooooooooooooooooopppp."

He stared wildly about him. What was happening? This was not real. Still the messages bombarded him. He clamped his hands over his ears, but the sounds were in his head, repeated over and over again.

"Can't do it! Weep. Can't do it! Weep. Can't do it!"

And he couldn't.

***

"I can't do it Nisha. I was always able to see the patterns in the pit. I could SEE how the machinery worked. Geordie said it was a gift. Now it's gone.

It doesn't make any sense to me. I don't know what to do."

His voice betrayed his desperation. He felt cut off, abandoned, shut down. His ability had vanished. His gift had deserted him.

"It's like a huge puzzle and I don't know where the pieces fit."

Puzzle? He remembered doing a puzzle. The pieces were old and worn. There were bits missing. Someone made new pieces, for him, from mush card. He could see their hands as they coloured them. Who had done that? The vision dissolved before he could see who they were. Someone had cared enough to do that for him. Cared for him. Him? Who was it? Who had it been?

He sighed. It was no good. He would never remember.

Finn slumped onto his kitchen chair. He thrust his hands beneath his thighs. Resignation hung like a cloud above him. Defeat was written upon his face. He kicked at the floor.

"Finn," began Nisha

"No," said Finn. "Don't. I can't do it. I've failed you. I'm no use."

Nisha looked at him. What was happening? What should she do? To save Eden, she must save Finn from his despair. His shine and glow, always with him, even in his sickness, had faded. Like Nisha's lamp turned down low, he cast scarcely any light.

"Finn!"

He didn't move.

"Finn, look at me!"

The sharpness of her voice jerked him from his misery. His lackluster eyes looked into hers.

Where was his enthusiasm? Where was his confidence? His self-belief had deserted him.

"Finn, I used all my skills to keep you here, in this world. Eden needs you. I need you. I know nothing of mechanical things. Eden needs you to repair its machinery. When I asked for help to keep it safe, you were sent."

Finn shrugged.

"I can't do it Nisha. I don't know how it works," Finn's voice dropped and Nisha could scarcely hear his last words. "I don't understand. I'm sorry."

Something smiled. Nisha gasped and looked around. Something was there with them. Something intangible. Something pleased with itself. She could feel it.

She shook her head.

Something didn't want Finn to succeed!

***

There was a presence in the room. I could feel it. Finn did not. It was affecting him.

What am I to do? He has given up. I have used nearly all my herbs that can help him.

There is something buried deep within him, unrecognized and unknown. The presence I felt wants to keep it that way. It wants the fungus to destroy Eden.

I cannot allow that. I must protect Eden. I must protect Finn. He is my only hope.

Oh Finn, what happened to you?

He cannot acknowledge it, so he blocks it in his mind. It stops him seeing the patterns.

He has given up. What am I to do?

The creeping death comes closer each day. He has seen it. It filled him with horror. He talks of blocking the doors. That, he knows, will not work.

Heat will kill the fungus. Yet even if Finn can stop the creeping death, only new seeds and new crystals can give focus to the energy and allow the new seeds to grow.

Time is running out.

I write this calmly. Yet what if the creeping death spreads and engulfs Eden. What if I can't grow food? Where would we go?

What is this presence that wishes us ill.

Nisha paused. She put down her pen. Worry lines clustered as she frowned. She shook her head as a wet dog shakes itself. A smile crossed her features and she picked up her pen.

NO! Courage Nisha. I will program crystals for our protection.

Finn was guided here to repair Eden. There is something locked within him. I know it. I can feel it. If I can release it, all will be well.

Help me, Creator of all things. Help me find the way. Show me what I must do?

She replaced the pen and closing her journal, she went to her mat and sat closing her eyes. Her breathing slowed and deepened. Her whole body sank down. As her body relaxed, the worry lines dropped from her face. She slipped away from her cares and was at peace.

Chapter 3

Finn leant against the rail with the waterfall crashing down behind him, staring at the tropical biome spread before him.

What was that? Something moved at the edge of his vision. There was a figure by the pond. Was it Nisha? No! Nisha was in the Mediterranean biome, tending the tomatoes and other plants. She was going to be there all afternoon. She'd told him so.

As soon as he tried to focus on it, the figure was gone. All he could see now were leaves. He must have been dreaming. He and Nisha were the only ones to live in Eden. Nisha had said so and he believed her. He saw it again. A figure. Clearer this time. A shining green figure. A person.

There *were* others at Eden.

Nisha had lied to him. As the words formed in his mind, he staggered back as though something had hit him in the chest. He felt a cold hand clasp his heart as he sank down on the path. *Nisha had lied to him.* Why would she do that? If *that* was a lie, what else had she lied about?

Anger rose within him. He couldn't trust her. He must leave Eden. He must go somewhere else. Far from Eden.

Quickly he went down to the pond. He searched the undergrowth for the figures he had seen, but found nothing. They eluded him. He stamped off to the Mediterranean biome.

"Who are they?" he demanded as he rushed towards Nisha. "Who else lives at Eden? You said you were alone. That's not true? Who else is here that I don't know about? Why do they always disappear when I try to get close to them? Why are you deceiving me? Tell me the truth!"

Nisha stood up and wiped her right arm across her sweaty forehead, leaving a streak of earth. A trowel hung in her left hand. Her green Eden apron was muddied. A puzzled frown displaced her smile of welcome.

"I am not deceiving you, Finn. We are alone. There are no other people here. What have you seen?"

"People. Figures tending to the plants. I SAW

THEM. They disappear when I get close. Who are they? Why did you keep this from me?"

A smile of understanding replaced Nisha's frown.

"It's the guardians Finn. The nature spirits. The Devas that look after the natural world. I can't see them. I feel them and know they are there. I didn't say anything to you because I didn't know you could see them. I didn't know you had that gift."

"Spirits! But..." There were no such things. There couldn't be. It wasn't scientific. Yet the purple crystal shone in the darkness of his mind. That had been real. NO! NO! NO! It cannot be. Eden was supposed to be a place of wonder. This was not one of the wonders he wanted.

"I don't believe you. Geordie would have told me if there were spirits. Geordie taught me everything. Geordie would have known. My life in the pit with Geordie was simple. You are complicating it. It's not meant to be like this." Finn shook his head in frustration. "Geordie said I would understand it all when I got here, but I don't."

Nisha frowned again.

"Geordie, Geordie, Geordie, you're always talking about Geordie, yet you never tell me anything about him, Finn. Who is this Geordie, this seer, this all wise being? If he was so good, why isn't he here?"

"He's dead. I told you. He saved me. He cared for me. If it wasn't for him, I'd be dead."

"What do you mean? Why would you be dead? Tell me? You must tell me. What don't you want to say? How did he save you?"

He backed away, holding his arms in front of him for protection.

"Stop it. Leave me alone."

Something awful and terrible was within him: hovering on the brink of his conscious mind.

"Tell me?" Nisha advanced on him. "Why did he have to look after you? What are you afraid of?"

"No, STOP." A low moan escaped him.

"Finn, listen to me. Whatever it is, let it out, let it go."

She reached out and touched him on the arm. With a cry, she jumped back, as if hit by an electric shock. She stared at Finn in amazement.

"He's a spirit, Geordies a spirit. He was a spirit. He was already dead," She stared at his confused face. "Oh Finn, I'm so sorry. How could you have known? I never meant..."

He gaped at her, horrified.

He staggered back and collapsed onto the earth. He put his hands on either side of his head and rocked back and forth.

"Leave me alone. It's not true. You're lying. Why are you doing this to me?"

What was she talking about? Geordie a spirit? He didn't understand. Oh Geordie, help me!

"Geordie was a spirit," she repeated firmly. "He was tied to the pit. He was held there."

Finn stared at the path, stunned. No! Geordie was real: as real as anyone in his life.

"You must have been the only one who could see him," Nisha's relentless words shattered his world, breaking down the illusions he was trying to cling to. "Did you never wonder why no one else ever spoke to him or referred to him. Why he didn't touch you,"

No! Geordie was Geordie.

"He's gone now," said Nisha. "He needed to help someone. You let him help you when you needed it. Then you let him go. You saw him die, didn't you?"

Yes, he could see the rocks fall on Geordie and crush the life from him.

He could see it.

"I don't understand?" he whispered. "How could I see him die if he was already dead?"

"It happened again. He lived through it again, and then truly died and left this Earth. It was what you and he had to do. You know this. Why did you bury it? Think Finn. Why did he have to look after you? Where were your parents?" Her sharp questions pierced the careful story he had told himself.

Finn jumped up in front of Nisha.

"This isn't true, it can't be. You're lying," He waved his arms at her. He jabbed at the air, emphasising his words as he shouted them out, getting louder and louder. "What are you trying to do to me? Geordie was my friend. He looked after me," Finn was panting for breath, his eyes wild, his face red. "I thought you were my friend. I felt so cared for and loved when I first arrived here. I THOUGHT YOU WERE MY MOTHER!"

Finn stopped, his hand darting to his mouth, horrified at what he'd said. The words had come out so fast: tumbling out, one after another in his haste to rid himself of his anger and despair.

I thought you were my mother.

I THOUGHT YOU WERE MY MOTHER.

The words repeated themselves within him. How could he say that? He had no mother. No memories of a mother. How could he have had a mother? Yet everyone had a mother. No! No! No! Not him. He had no mother. He deserved no mother. He deserved no one to hold him, to love him, to care for him and look after him.

HE DESERVED NO ONE.

Finn turned and ran as fast as he could, away from Nisha, away from himself, into the gathering darkness of the tropical biome and stood there before the switched off silent waterfall, gazing intently across the cool night time landscape, his whole mind concentrated within himself.

He had always known he had no mother. That was a fact in his life.

Where had those images of Geordie dying come from? He had not known they'd been there, submerged and hidden somewhere in the back of his mind. Why hadn't he wanted to find them? Why had he hidden them from himself?

There was only Geordie after his father died. Now he had seen a vision of a woman that he knew was his mother.

HE KNEW.

What else was buried in his mind?

Chapter 4

"How do I find the rest Nisha?"

Nisha was waiting for him. She smiled as he opened the door. Accepting his running away, accepting his return. Knowing how hard it had been for him to understand that Geordie was a spirit. Knowing that he would return to find out about his mother.

Nisha smiled at him. "I am not your mother Finn, but I am your friend."

She held out her arms and he went to her and she held him and comforted him as his friend. He'd had no real friends in the pit. Just people he knew: some closer than others.

Like Tracie in the pit. He knew the others had dared her to kiss him. And Esmerelda? Had she been his friend? He'd only ever seen her when she worked. She'd always gone back home to her family. Until that day she'd died.

Who did he go back home to?

Only Geordie. Geordie, who loved him and cared for him, Geordie, who taught him what to do and how to do it, Geordie, who could never touch him and hold him close. Geordie was the only one who'd cared for him.

He sat cross legged on the floor of his room where he felt safe. He held the purple crystal Nisha had placed in his hand, feeling the warm, smooth surface. It was the same colour as the crystal in the church, yet it didn't feel the same. When he'd tried to touch the church crystal, it had felt cold and remote. Nisha's crystal felt warm and close.

"Close your eyes, Finn."

Nisha's commands, the steady even tone of her voice, were relaxing. He could feel something pushing up inside him: something trying to rise to his conscious mind. He could hear someone singing as he had before. The song was a lullaby. He was safe and loved. He knew it. He was strong: strong enough to face the truth.

"Finn."

A voice that was not Nisha's called him.

The voice slid into his brain as a key entered a lock. He could feel its subtle twisting. The slight grating as the tumblers clicked into place, and the door began to move. Slowly, it opened. Slowly it relieved his distress. Letting out the childhood memories he'd kept behind the wall he'd constructed. He stared within him, at the path leading to knowledge and understanding.

He looked up, and as had happened in the church, a blinding light flashed across his brain. He crumpled in fear.

"It's alright Finn, you're safe."

Pictures filtered into his mind. Brown and cream images flickering across his consciousness. Like the ancient sepia photographs of the before time workers on the walls of the hall in the pit. One by one, the pictures, soundless scenes of his unknown childhood, clicked rhythmically into his mind.

"I can see pictures, Nisha."

"Tell me what you see, Finn."

A tender eyed woman holds a baby; a man smiles.

Finn gasped in recognition of his father's youthful face.

The mother rocks the baby.

He sees her mouth moving. The song! The song he'd heard. A lullaby.

A toddler (Little Finn) walks across a dark wooden

floor. Loving parents laugh and cuddle the child.

Tears stream from Finn's eyes and he cried out, reaching to touch the figures. The images move on and the moment is lost. Where did they go? Bring them back. Please bring them back. Give me that love. I want it. What happened to them?

More pictures. The child grows and Finn recognises his own features developing.

The child coughs, lies in bed, pale and stiller than the still of the picture. The mother, (His mother!) dressed in white, sits beside him, holding him, cooling his fever with a wet rag.

She talks to his father. His father says no.

His mother stares at the floor.

The pictures move on.

He sees her working: nursing sick people.

The sickness spreads.

Adults lie in a separate room, recovering.

His mother is talking to the man, obviously in charge. He shakes his head. She remonstrates. He shakes his head again, not unkindly and points to a small box, where a few, a very few, doses of the medicine lay.

Oh Mother what did you do? What happened to you?

Where did you go?

It is dark and she, (His mother) **takes medicine from the box and hurries away.**

She (His mother) **gives the medicine to Little Finn.** She gives it to HIM.

She sits with him, hope written on her face.

The pictures slow. He can see each and every line on her face, the stains on her white tunic, the long, sensitive, tapering fingers blunted by hard work and privation. There is white in the brown hair that escapes its covering.

The picture changes.

Mother?

Men in uniform hold her. More hold his despairing, distraught, Father.

Another picture.

She, (His mother), **is dressed in heavy clothes.** (NO!) **There is one pack upon her back.** (NO!) **She walks between the ranks of workers.** (NO!) **Their eyes blaze with hate, their fists shake, their mouths mime the words he knows they shout.** (NO!) A cry escapes his lips. (NO!) The tears stream again. (NO, NO! NO! NO! NO!) He reaches out at the images to stop them, stop them, stop them, from banishing her. (His mother)

They drag and push her: taking her to the doors, to the outside.

He catches one last glimpse.

Pale, terrified, staring. Her last backward glance, a grimace, softens to a smile as their eyes meet. One hand was raised, waving goodbye.

The picture stayed frozen for an eternity. "Mother," he whispers. Too late.

The doors slam shut and she is gone.

Beyond the doors, he can hear the footfalls on the gantry, as they take her to the snowbound surface. Perhaps she will stumble a short distance in the numbing, life draining cold and raging ice storms.

He sees his father standing beside Little Finn, (Himself). His father's eyes are looking, yet see nothing. The shock has robbed him of his senses.

Little Finn was gone too. He saw the images, recorded them in his brain, yet did not know that he did so. They were locked away in his unconscious. Little Finn was gone: Older Finn had not yet begun to process his world.

Neither of them knew the other was there. They both had to survive.

Nisha, softly saying his name, brought him back to Eden.

His tears poured. So many tears for his lost past. So many tears for the lost love of his parents. Nisha held him, comforting him.

***

Only after they had eaten and Finn was asleep, did Nisha go to write in her journal.

Brave Finn. Courageous Finn. Hero Finn. That was not an easy thing to do. Small wonder you had buried it. Perhaps you had no choice. Little Finn and Older Finn had to survive. And now you have found your child again.

The presence was not strong enough to stop you. I can still feel its disconcerting company. Is this enough? Will you be able to see the patterns? Can you repair Eden?

It was still dark when Nisha replaced her book within its box. She sat cross legged with closed eyes until the dawning light brought her back to Eden.

Finn slept for most of the following day. That evening, when they had eaten and cleared away, Nisha said, "After all that work Finn, it's time to play."

She produced a folded rectangular board. She

opened it into a square and placed it on the table. A fleeting memory of laughter and love flew into Finn's mind as she opened it. Who had he played with? Finn stared at the squares with the brightly coloured snakes and the brown ladders. Who had he played this game with?

He heard a voice asking, "Is Finn coming to play?"

He saw them playing happily together. He heard her laughter. He saw the bright smile on her dark face. He felt the crinkliness of her hair on his cheek as they touched heads. He remembered their forgotten friendship.

"What is it, Finn?" asked Nisha. Concern had replaced her smile.

"Cher Lee," he said. "When I was little, I played with Cher Lee in the pit. She was my friend. I had a friend. I remember."

***

So he remembers his friend, Cher Lee. Yet he told me Geordie was his only friend. He thinks we have found it all. He does not realise there is more within him, more to be uncovered. It is taking so long. The creeping death is approaching the doors. Still he cannot see how to repair Eden. He does not see the patterns and I am no help to him.

Linda will be here soon. He is not ready. Before she arrives, he must repair Eden and I must explain to him what I need him to do. He must understand. He must.

Chapter 9

Desperation inspired her to choose a new combination of herbs. She had few of the originals left. She ground the leaves to a paste, murmuring to herself, as she did so. Words that implored guidance be given her. He must remember.

That evening, she put it in his drink.

She watched him drink it. Although he was good at hiding his feelings, she knew he suspected. There was a slight bitterness to the taste she was unable to hide, despite the strong mint and ginger she'd added. He could still detect it. Yet he drank more. Why? Did he know? Did he suspect and yet co-operate with her to do what she wished?

"What did you put in the drink Nisha?" he smiled wryly. "What are you doing?" His voice was calm.

"You know Finn. You know what I am doing. I am helping you. You must see all that you have hidden. You must know everything."

The mixture began to bite into his mind. Unease built within him.

"Why are you doing this?" he asked, still calm. Only now there was an edge to his question.

"Finn. It is necessary. You have to see everything. You know this, don't you?"

Yes, he knew. It was not just her potion doing this to him. There was something within him which collaborated with her, helped her.

He stood up, his clothes catching the cloth on the table, scattering the meal that lay there.

"I don't... I can't... Stop it... I can't do it... I can't," His voice faltered and he uttered a last word in a breathless whisper. "Please."

He gasped for breath. One hand clutched his chest, his other reached out, grabbing at the air. He stumbled forward, pushing the table over as he went, Nisha moving nimbly out of his way.

"No. I can't. Stop."

He fell to his knees.

"What did you do? What is it?" Nisha's questions came from far away.

The fear bubbled up inside him, water rushing towards him like the waterfall in the dome. His tears overflowed. Eyes streaming, he sobbed.

"What is it, Finn? Tell me," she demanded.

"It's dark... Dark... DARK." Finn's voice was full of fear and trepidation.

Nisha looked at the pale sunlight slanting through the window.

He fell forward into blackness. Why was it so dark?

His head throbbed intensely. Carefully he sat up. The pounding in his head receded.

A dim light shone on faces looking at him from the blackness. Who were they? Why were they looking at him?

"Go away," he commanded. They didn't. They watched him.

"Why are you looking at me? Who are you?"

The faces in the dark stared at him, wondering at his strangeness. Why did they think him strange? Was he not one of them? Was he not a child of the pit as they were? No, no longer a child, he was almost a grown man. Yet they looked at him, out of his past and he hadn't grown at all.

He stood, turning away from the faces. Ahead was darkness: Dark as only an unlit corridor in the pit could be. Yet he could see something. Pinpoints of light beckoned him. Beacons of hope. He plunged into the dark, escaping the gaze of the faces. The lights went out behind him. He raced to the patch of brightness ahead, then the next and the next, along the corridor to the light at the end of the tunnel. One by one he reached each small light bulb oasis.

Until, until...

He saw a figure running before him, always in front, always running to the next pool of light. He reached out to grasp...nothing. He laughed. It was a dream. You cannot fool me. If this is a dream, you are not real.

Yet he raced along the corridor: the figure still out of reach.

He gasped. An involuntary cry of pain, despair and torment, overflowed from his lips. Tears rushed down his cheeks.

"What is it, Finn? Tell me. You must tell me or I cannot help. Tell me what you see."

Another cry escaped him.

"I can't,"

The anguish forced more tears. Squeezing them from his eyes, his soul?

"Stop, stop!" his words came in a harsh whisper.

"No... I can't. Please, no." he pleaded.

He gasped again. The forced inhale helped a little calm to return.

Nisha' voice came from far away, "Let me help you, Finn." The voice receded.

"Don't go. Stay. Please stay."

"I am here Finn. You are not alone. I am with you."

He nodded as if Nisha could see him standing there, in the corridor of his despair.

"What can you see Finn? Tell me what you see."

"A dark corridor. A pinpoint of light at the far end. Help me."

Finn gasped again, as another wave of torment roared across his mind. He cringed before its power.

"What is it, Finn? What can you see in the corridor?"

"Nothing, I can see nothing." The tension drained from his body. He relaxed. There was nothing to see, nothing to do. He could leave this place of desolation.

He went to turn away. Something held him. He couldn't move.

He gasped once more.

"It won't let me go."

Fear rushed upon him, weakening his resolve.

"Arghhhhhhh."

He must hide; hide from the monster that waited for him.

"What is it Finn," Nisha's voice was demanding. "Tell me!"

Geordie was standing in the light, pointing to something on the wall.

"Geordie. NO!"

"What is it, Finn?"

Finn's voice was a whisper, "It's a brass memorial plaque. There's a picture of Geordie and an inscription."

"What does it say Finn?"

Slowly, haltingly, the words came.

"In 1978, John (Geordie) Nichols, the foreman, led ten men to safety after a rock fall. To save them, he had to leave Frank Pearse, his mate, trapped at the pit face. Having rescued the others he returned for Frank. They both died in further rock falls."

Geordie was a hero.

"Finn, listen to me. This is why Geordie's spirit was still in the pit. He felt such a strong sense of guilt that he'd failed his mate, he stayed there. Waiting all those years to help someone else and then you came along.

Geordie wasn't a real person, Finn. He was the spirit of the man he used to be. His spirit was tied to the pit. You were sensitive. You had the gift. You could see him."

"Then why did he show me the plaque, Nisha. Why couldn't he just let me stay in the pit and be happy?"

"You had to leave Finn. I was calling you. Geordie knew that. He had to break the spell. He showed you the truth."

A sudden realisation dawned on Finn.

"I couldn't cope with it. I had to get away from him."

"Yes Finn. He knew. It was time for him to go, too."

"And that's when I saw the rocks fall. I saw him die. He was gone and I had no one."

"Yes Finn."

"No wonder they all avoided me when I was young. They thought I was talking to no one. They thought I was touched. Mad! They couldn't see Geordie. Only I could see Geordie," Finn laughed. "And I was young enough to believe he was a real human being. Some of the other children played cruel tricks on me because of it. I remember Nisha, I remember. I learnt not to speak to Geordie when anybody was there. He would talk to me. All the time I was learning." Finn rushed along with the explanation.

"That was when he told me stories of Eden. And he said that one day I would leave the pit and go to Eden. He taught me the rhyme. Then the teachers realised I was clever. Geordie had taught me well. I could do things other children couldn't. I was selected to be educated. I was taught by Geordie and the teacher. No wonder I excelled. Yet somehow, I pushed the true knowledge of what Geordie was, into an unused space in my mind." Finn paused. "If he hadn't shown me the plaque, I might have stayed in the mine all my life, not knowing the truth of what had happened. Geordie confronted me with that truth on the upper levels where workers weren't allowed. Geordie saved me."

A sudden cry of pain burst its way through Finn's half-closed lips.

"What is it, Finn? Is there more? What can you see now?"

Finn screwed up his closed eyes.

"A child, a boy, standing alone in the middle of a room."

"Who is it, Finn? Who is it?"

A tortured cry escaped Finn and he turned his head

from side to side, as if trying not to look.

"Who is it, Finn?"

Finn lay still.

"It's me, Nisha."

"What are you doing Finn? What are you waiting for?"

"They are coming to take me to the place for children with no parents."

"An orphanage Finn. Why? Where is your father?"

"Father is dead." Finn's voice was dead too.

"Dead? How do you know Finn?"

"Simon told me."

"What happened to your father Finn?"

"After Mother was banished, he didn't care what happened to him. He grew careless. There was an accident at the coal face."

"You were on your own in the room, Finn."

"Yes."

"How do you feel?"

"Lost. Alone."

Finn cried out; shaking his head from side to side.

"No! No! No! You can't do it. No."

"What can't they do, Finn? Tell me what you see."

"They came to take me. I screamed, I fought, I

scratched and bit. I hit them with anything I could find. After a while they stopped trying and left me."

"They left you?"

"Yes. They left me alone. They couldn't stand my cries. Sandeep said it was like having skewers pushed into him. I wouldn't stop and they couldn't take me." There was a hint of triumph in Finn's voice.

"How did you feel Finn?"

"Proud. Alone. Abandoned. No one to care for me. Alone, alone, alone." Finn rocked from side to side. Tears coursed down his cheeks.

His desolation overwhelmed him.

"It was me. It was my fault."

"What do you mean Finn? What did you do?"

"She stole the medicines to give to me. The ant…ant…ee…bi…otics," he stumbled childishly over the word, "The medicine to make me better. It was my fault I got ill."

Memories of playing with Cher Lee flooded his mind, as if a tap had been turned on. Finn smiled as the memories flowed into his conscious mind. Then his face crumpled into sadness.

"I crept out to see Cher Lee. Mother said not to. Cher Lee had the sickness. I wanted to see her. I wanted to tell her I was her friend."

He was aghast at what he had done. He had caught the sickness and it was his fault. He had killed his mother.

"Did you see Cher Lee, Finn? Did you tell Cher Lee you were her friend?"

"Yes. No. She was dead. They let me see her to say goodbye and they gave me Bear."

"Bear?"

"I gave Cher Lee my toy bear when we used to play together. She called it Bear. Her mother gave it back to me. My mother put it in the flames to burn. She said it had the sickness on it. She was too late. Next day I had the sickness. You know what happened then."

"Yes Finn. Tell me what else you remember, Finn."

"I was following father back to our gallery. He wouldn't hold my hand. He shouted at me. He said I killed mother. She wouldn't have stolen the antibiotics if I hadn't got ill. If I hadn't gone to see Cher Lee, I wouldn't have caught the sickness. I did it. I killed her. He said get away. He said, you are not my son."

The accusation was almost more than he could bear. This was the father who loved him. Who had taken care of him? His mother was gone and his father didn't love him anymore.

"Father."

The tears poured. As if every last drop of remorse was being squeezed from him. Every part of his body ached and he cried out.

"I killed my mother."

"No, Finn. Your mother chose to help you. She chose."

"But Father said I did it. I went off and caught the sickness. He didn't love me anymore."

"Forgive him, Finn. His heart was broken. He was lost and alone. He did not speak as the loving father he really was."

"But my mother was angry with me for going to see Cher Lee."

"Yet still she helped you, Finn. She chose to help the son she loved. She knew what would happen. It was her choice. She loved you above her life. She wanted you to live," Nisha's voice was insistent. "Do you hear me, Finn?"

He nodded, "Yes, I hear you."

"Your mother loved you, Finn."

"But I disobeyed."

"Finn, you were a child. You did not understand the

consequences of your visit to Cher Lee. Cher Lee was your friend and she loved you. You were responding to that love. And your mother loved you too."

"My mother loved me?" Relief was in his voice.

"Yes, Finn. So very much, she was willing to risk dying for you. She wanted you to live so much, she gave up her life for you. Don't forget that, Finn. Ever. You were loved by your mother and you are loved by me."

"You love me, Nisha?" Finn's voice was hopeful.

"Yes Finn. Not like a mother, Finn. I love you as my friend. You have great strength and integrity. You are clever and resourceful. You think of things that would not occur to me. Things I do not see, unless you focus me on them. We are complimentary. You have a future, which is what your mother wanted. Your mother gave you your future. Be the son she wanted you to be, Finn."

Nisha reached down and placed a hand on his shoulder. Finn opened his eyes and looked at Nisha.

"Why couldn't I remember this before, Nisha?"

"It got stuck. It hurt so much. You blocked it all off and started another you instead. It's like you split off from Little Finn, the child. You left him behind in the dark. Scared, frightened, so afraid of what he'd experienced. You forgot Little Finn and grew up."

The realisation of what he had done, hit him. Regret was in his voice. "I buried that poor little boy inside me. Alone in the dark. Unable to cry for his mother. Unable to do anything. Like a prisoner in a cage."

"Finn, you did what you did to survive. Your mother would be proud of you. Now you can get to know the child within you that you once were. You are whole."

Why here, why now, he thought? Like a cork long held beneath the surface of water, a thought bobbed to the surface of his brain and he knew the reason why. It was time. Like a thorn that was buried deep in the flesh, invisible from the surface, it had poisoned his system and had been hurting, always hurting. However much he had hidden it from himself.

Now he knew. It was like opening a door in his mind to a past world. He stood in the doorway of his mind and turned to survey where he had lived in the pit. It seemed somehow cramped and small. He had not realised this before. Slowly he turned and faced the new panorama that beckoned him. There were new and glorious things to see. It was his life to be.

Finn lay there: exhausted and triumphant!

***

Next evening, after resting all day at Nisha's command, Finn walked up to the waterfall. With the its roar filling his ears, he looked out over the tropical biome. As the clouds covering the setting sun moved away, its horizontal rays cut across the waterfall and there was a vivid rainbow.

A memory of tiny rainbows slipped into his mind. He saw again the ice frozen onto the trees in the valley near the hut on his journey from the pit and the sun turning the frozen fragments into tiny rainbows.

The sun set, the rainbow vanished and dusk crept across the biome. Then, as night turned Eden to shadows, he saw the lines shining in the darkness.

Exhilaration shot through him. He could see them: lines of energy connecting all of Eden. Not only could he feel the power, as he had in the pit, he could see how it all fitted together. Just like the pieces of the jigsaw puzzle he had played with in the pit.

A picture formed in his mind and he watched Father make a puzzle for him from scrap mushcard. Finn had fitted all the pieces of his childhood together and he could see the whole picture, just like the puzzle. He smiled.

Part 3-London

Chapter 1

Finn had started to explain to Nisha the technical details of checking the relays and electrical circuits in the temperate biome. Only, when she looked at him across the table, spread with their evening meal, her puzzled gaze showed she had no understanding of anything he'd said.

Finn laughed at his own foolishness

It didn't matter. Nisha didn't need to know how he did it, so long as he did it.

They laughed together.

"It's okay Nisha, I'm fixing it."

They continued eating.

He didn't explain the long hours it had taken him to trace the wiring of the temperate biome or how long it would take him to replace the cables and fuses burnt and damaged by the lightning storm. She knew he understood everything, having faith he could repair it.

He only casually mentioned, in passing, the

storeroom he found with everything he might need to repair Eden.

***

Oh the joy there is within him. He is fulfilling his purpose: doing what he came to Eden for. He does not need to explain what I do not understand and I do not yet need to tell him of his future.

He is like the child I would have wished for, if things had been different.

She stopped: a whisper of regret surfaced in her consciousness.

Mine is a good life. I am doing what I must. I am fulfilling my purpose. And yet…And yet…I will miss him so much. We must enjoy this time together even though it will not last long. He will soon discover what I can no longer keep from him.

***

As the days passed, Finn alternated between working on Eden's systems and the exercise schedules he and Nisha had worked out. He was still weak and puny. His muscles not yet recovered from his sickness.

"Finn, you must become strong again," Nisha had said with a smile. "You have so much to do. You must grow strong to do it all and you need some quiet time.

You are working too hard. Won't you come and meditate with me?"

She stopped at Finn's expression.

"At least come for a walk in Eden. Take it slowly. Feel the trees and plants around you. Listen to the hum of the insects and the songs of the birds. Let the Deva spirits heal you. You might see them again."

Nisha smiled at him. He returned her smile, nodding his agreement.

Every day he exercised. Sometimes with Nisha: sometimes on his own. Walking round and round the paths, carrying an increasing load on his back. He graduated to running, his muscles worked hard, protesting, and rebuilding their strength, pace by pace. Then he found the bicycles in the storage rooms beneath Eden, that Nisha had not known were there.

Round and round they rode, laughing and shrieking together as Finn found his energy and enthusiasm once more. And finding himself, also, thinking of the abandoned gym in the pit. Who needed to exercise in the pit, beyond the everyday tasks of feeding the furnaces, cutting the coal, growing their food and all the thousands of necessary tasks to keep the pit functioning? Yet he had found the gym a good place to be alone in the pit, using the cycling machine to build his stamina in a way that feeding the flames did not.

***

Finn had to tell Nisha he was going outside to examine Eden's structure. He needed his warm clothes that she had washed and put away for him. He didn't need to tell her about the solar panels he would find.

The feeble sun was already climbing from the east into the brilliant blue sky. This was the first time he had been outside since he fell into Eden. Climbing the small hill to the south of the domes had him breathing hard. There were ragged remnants of cloth, tied to the tops of tall posts on the top of the hill. They flapped beside him in the breeze as he looked out across the huge hole that Eden was built in.

Then it struck him. Why was it not full of snow and ice? In the pit, the guards regularly steamed away any drifts of snow and ice that threatened to cover the winding gear and other pithead buildings, flushing it down the shaft where their clean water was stored. No one did that at Eden. Yet the buildings were clear and the ground scarcely covered. He shook his head.

Eden should not exist, yet it did.

Then he noticed the small black squares attached to

the joints where the hexagons met on the dome. What were they? He made his way back down the hill and examined the nearest one. About thirty centimetres square, neat silver lines divided the sturdily made flat black plastic into rectangles. What was its purpose? There were hundreds of them scattered all over the domes on nearly every joint. Bending down he could see a wire from the nearest square going through a hole in the metal strut into Eden.

Oh, of course. Solar panels. He'd read about them in the pit. He went back inside and climbing a staircase fixed to the inside frame of the dome, he examined the metal framework beneath the joint. Yes! The wire coming through the small hole in the metal joined others and ran off through the plants. Was it these strange square devices that supplied electricity to Eden? If they did, all he had to do was replace the damaged wires in the temperate dome and Eden was repaired. The dome's temperature would rise and life would return.

It was when he traced the main power cable to the stairs leading down into the depths below Eden that he knew he must tell Nisha. She had to see this with him.

Chapter 2

With mounting excitement, Nisha followed Finn as they tracked Eden's main electrical cable along the labyrinthine corridors and down the stairs. As they descended into the subterranean depths beneath Eden, everything changed. The stairs were rough unpainted wood. The corridors' walls and ceilings were lined with mismatched cladding. Lights were fixed haphazardly to the walls, the cables carrying the power hung in loops between them. This was not Eden's original building. This had been added after winter had come.

Feeling an increasingly strong electrical vibration, Finn knew they were close to Eden's powerhouse. At the same time he could feel that all was not well with it.

Rounding a sharp corner, they found what he was looking for. A red door with a yellow lightning flash clumsily painted on it. Finn pushed open the door and they walked into Eden's electrical heart.

It was a white painted room, a cuboid, its sides about four metres long, six wide and the ceiling roughly two metres high. Almost filling the room was a ring of twelve hexagonal containers made from a clear moulded plastic. All the hexagons held a cube, labelled 'fuel cell', made of layers of metal and plastic. What was a fuel cell? He'd never heard of them. Did it supply energy? Each a metre tall, they were set around an enormous clear quartz crystal, held, point upright, in a sheath of the moulded plastic.

Each cell was mounted on a clear plastic pedestal in the centre of its hexagon. Wires and tubes fixed beneath them ran in and out of the base of the hexagons. Three hexagonal, clear quartz crystals were mounted in plastic cradles around each fuel cell, with their pointed end towards the cell.

Finn walked slowly around the outside of the circle, gazing at the display in wonder. The wires and tubes attached to the fuel cells snaked in and out of the cubes, joined together and disappeared into channels cut through the walls. The cable they had followed down the stairs was joined by a mass of others. A large pipeline, labelled hydrogen, came in through the floor.

He had no idea how any of this worked. Something within him said he did not need to know.

On the far side of the array he could see his problem. There were flashing red lights on two of the fuel cell cubes. These crystals in their cradles around the glass hexagons, were burnt, just like the crystals in the temperate biome.

All at once the answer to the enigma of Eden was in plain sight. Why hadn't he realised? The crystals weren't just to channel the energy. They did more, much more.

He hadn't understood. It was like the purple crystal in the church. The power of the purple crystal kept the coloured glass windows in the church from shattering and stopped the wooden roof caving in. And that's what was happening in Eden.

The books he'd found about Eden said its plastic roof was only supposed to last for 25 years. How long had it lasted? He had no idea when the Earth was plunged into winter. The roof should've collapsed a long while ago. It didn't because of the power of the crystals. They made sure the electricity flowed. Adding their power and focusing it on the fuel cells, they enabled Eden to exist where it had no right to. Their power kept the snow from covering Eden.

And Nisha knew. Not about the blown fuses and burnt wiring, that was his domain. Nisha had known all along what the crystals did. A prickle of uncertainty crept across his scalp. Why hadn't she told him? What was she afraid of? What was she hiding?

He turned and looked at Nisha. He gasped, because her staring face told him everything.

His mind leapt to the conclusions he now knew were inevitable.

He had to leave Eden and Nisha hadn't told him. He'd had to find out for himself. He had to leave and fetch new crystals from somewhere, somewhere dangerous. And she didn't want him to go. Yet he must go, because if he didn't, Eden would be incomplete and Eden must be complete. This was what she had been hiding! This was what she was afraid of!

He could fix the burnt wiring. He could replace the blown fuses. He could fit a lightning conductor, like at the pit, to stop the lightning striking again, but the crystals, he couldn't repair the crystals.

Nisha's face turned ashen, worry written in every line.

Tears dribbled from the corners of her eyes.

She stood; feet glued to the floor by her conflicting emotions. Her hands reached out to Finn, but he backed away.

"It's the crystals, isn't it, Nisha?" his quiet tone broke their silence.

"Yes." Nisha's voice was a whisper.

"They keep the domes from collapsing, don't they?"

"Yes."

"They keep the electricity flowing."

"Yes"

"Otherwise there isn't enough power. Is there?"

"No"

"Even now I've repaired the wiring, there still isn't enough power?"

"No."

"And I have to leave Eden and get new crystals. I have to go somewhere dangerous. Do something risky. And you're worried I might not come back, aren't you?"

"Yes."

"And you couldn't ask me. Could you?"

"No."

The words came from her lips with great effort.

They whispered to Finn of the struggle within her. He waited patiently as she struggled to express herself.

"I've never had children. There was no one to be my mate. I pretended to myself I didn't mind. That it didn't matter. But it does. You are the son I wished for. I thought I had accepted you would go. I even wrote about it in my journal. I didn't know if you'd understand. I didn't want to say until you found out and I had to tell you. I'm sorry Finn."

She lurched forward, breaking the seal of her feet on the floor. This time Finn didn't draw away. He took her hands and they stood there together. They felt each other's emotions, shared their feelings of fear and pain. They had shared so much together in a short time.

Finn dropped Nisha's hands, grasped her in his arms and crushed her to him.

"I'll return Nisha. I promise. I'll get what we need and I'll come home."

And Nisha nodded: a strange lopsided smile on her lips. He pushed her from him: holding her at arm's length.

"I have to sterilise the soil and stop the fungus? But I can't because there's not enough power with these burnt crystals. I don't know how to do it and you certainly don't, do you?"

What had made him think of that now?

"No," said Nisha, but this time the relief of tension between them made her laugh.

Then the answer burst into his brain, almost as if it had come from Nisha's mind through their touch.

"I know, Nisha, I know. A temporary repair. Can you take some crystals from the other domes. Just a few. Not enough to weaken the energy web."

Nisha nodded.

His mind raced on. He dropped his arms.

"If I change the computer program for the temperate dome back to its original desert mode, it'll turn into a searingly hot desert again, sterilising the earth and killing the fungus. It'll only take a few days. I think there's enough power to do that."

Nisha nodded once more.

"If we take the crystals at night, I can see the energy lines and make sure they still flow after removing the crystals," he said. "And then I must leave Eden and fetch new crystals to replace the burnt ones."

"And seeds Finn. I need seeds to replace the plants

that died."

It was Finn's turn to nod.

"Where do I have to go Nisha?"

"London, Finn. You must go to London."

"London? Where is London? Is it far? How can I get there? Oh!" Finn smiled. "You have a plan, don't you Nisha?"

Nisha nodded.

"Linda will be here soon. She will take you to London. London is dangerous. Linda escaped it. She says little about it, yet I can feel her pain, her fear."

So, he must exchange the safety of Eden and the love of Nisha, for the dangers of the wilderness again. He must go with Linda: whoever she was.

Nisha studied Finn's face anxiously. "You know you have to go Finn?"

Finn sighed, "Yes," his words came slowly. "I don't want to go, Nisha. Eden is my home now. I don't want to leave my home. You know that. You saved me. You healed me and I'll never want to live anywhere else," he paused. "I know you don't want me to go. I can't stay, though, can I? We need the crystals and seeds," he paused again. "Something else calls me." Finn shrugged. "I must go. I have no choice."

It was not just the crystals and seeds: something else really was calling him. He didn't know what it was. Perhaps he would find out in London. Perhaps, but whatever it was, he had to go.

***

So he knows. All my fears are out in the open. He knows and he is not angry with me for keeping it from him. He understands he had to find out for himself.

London will be dangerous. I will program a crystal to help keep him safe.

Another thought crept into her mind. Nisha smiled.

He will have help with his task. All will be well.

Chapter 3

The hiss of the sledge and the patter of the dog's feet hitting the snow were the only sounds, apart from an occasional command from Linda and a yelp from one of the dogs. Finn lay shrouded in furs and blankets on his sledge as they sped towards London.

Linda had solved the problem of how to use her dogs to pull the sledges. She'd allocated eight of her sixteen dog team to each sledge. They'd travel slower than she usually did and the dogs would need more rests. Finn went in front, with the more experienced dogs pulling his sledge. Linda followed so she was able to issue commands to both teams. Finn held the reins to his dogs, but Linda gave the orders.

Linda, flat nosed, heavy browed, strong, muscular, had stood in the doorway of their living quarters, a bulking presence. Dark eyes, weather aged skin, thin lips, a fur fringed hood edging her lined round face. For a moment Finn felt she was more animal than human. There was an instinctive awareness and intensity to her. She took in all around her, it was an unconscious, intuitive insight.

Linda was a survivor.

As Linda closed the door, Nisha rushed towards her, arms outstretched. Linda stood there accepting the hug, a slow smile spreading on her face as if she had suddenly remembered something she had forgotten and slowly her arms rose to return the hug. She closed her eyes and laid her head against Nisha's.

"Oh, Linda, it's so good to see you again. You're later than usual. I wondered and here you are. Come and eat. I've prepared your favourites," Nisha began to take Linda through and then stopped as she saw Finn waiting.

Nisha blushed. Finn stared. For an instant she had not been his Nisha. Had she really forgotten him in that moment of her greeting with Linda? Nisha turned Linda to face Finn.

"Linda, this is Finn. He is from the Pit. You know the Pit. We have talked of it before. He can tell his story later. Come and eat."

She smiled in apology and swept Linda past him. Finn followed; his thoughts jangled. He recognised the jealousy within him, where once he would have been unable to acknowledge it. He looked at his jealousy from a distance. It had no right to be there. Yet it was there. He had felt that Nisha was his. His Nisha. Nonetheless he had to accept that she obviously owed something to Linda too. He toyed with his jealousy, poking it, turning it this way and that, looking at it with sideways glances, trying to understand where it had come from.

Why had he thought Nisha was only his? He did not own her. She was as free as he was, to do as she wished, as she thought. Only he had felt their bond was above all others. Was Nisha jealous of Geordie? Finn had not thought of this before. Geordie was gone, but he remained within Finn's memories. Nisha could not share them, ever, even though they had shared his release. Finn smiled ruefully and leaving his jealousy at the door, followed Nisha and Linda.

As they ate, Nisha had chattered. She flittered here and there in her conversation. Linda said little. She concentrated on the food, methodically taking a little from each dish to fill her plate. She ate slowly, noisily, allowing Nisha's conversation to ebb and flow around her, only occasionally interjecting a word or two into the pauses that Nisha left for her. Nisha told her of her harvests, her successes and failures. Of plants that had yielded unexpected results. Of how she was looking forward to sending her medicines and herbs to the others that waited, in their scattered communities, for her healing compounds.

So there are others, thought Finn.

And all the while she did not mention Finn. Only after the end of Nisha's explanations, did Linda speak.

"What of him? What do you want for him?"

Nisha stared at her and laughed. They both understood that Nisha wanted something for Finn.

"He needs to get to London," she said quietly. "I need something for Eden. I want you to take him there for me. Will you?"

Linda sat silently in her chair for a long time; they could almost hear her thinking. Finally, speaking slowly and deliberately, she leant forward and put obstacles in the way of taking Finn, and quietly, one by one, Nisha demolished her arguments.

"London's dangerous."

"Leave him at the outskirts. He can walk in."

"He needs a tent. I can't share."

"He's got one," said Nisha.

"It has to be white."

"It is white."

"I don't have enough food."

"I'll give him food."

"I have no room. You want me take him with everything I pack? No."

Linda sat back as if this was the end of the matter.

"He has something to trade," said Nisha.

"Trade?" Linda's eyes lit up. "What?"

"Finn has a sledge. It's yours if you take him."

Nisha deliberately avoided looking at Finn. He said nothing.

"Show me."

She'd examined the sledge minutely. She looked at the repairs Finn had made. Tested them and nodded.

"Maybe. It'll be hard. Slow me down."

She stood and thought.

"Okay. I split dogs. He look after himself."

"He will, Linda. Deal?"

Linda nodded. She had no more arguments.

Nisha put out her hand. Linda grasped it and they shook.

"I leave two days. Not ready. I go."

Nisha and Finn nodded together.

Later, after the meal, when Linda had fallen asleep on a bed on the floor, Nisha beckoned to Finn and they walked into the Mediterranean dome.

"I'm sorry Finn. I didn't want to say about your sledge until you'd actually met her. You do understand, don't you Finn?" Nisha looked at Finns set expression. She sighed. "You wouldn't have said yes if I'd asked you before, would you? I wanted you to meet Linda first," as Finn still said nothing, she continued. "Linda travels between the groups. She and her dog team are the link that keeps all of us in contact and able to share our talents. I share my healing. Linda takes my herbal remedies to trade. I have known her for so long. She is like a child, I know. It doesn't matter, Finn. She helps me. She is a companion. I have few companions. Please do not be jealous. She will take you to London. You only have to give her your sledge."

"How do I get back from London without my sledge?"

"Trust! You must trust and feel what to do. You will be looked after."

Finn had grimaced, but nodded.

***

And now their sledges hissed through the snow

towards London. Their pace sustained by the eight dogs that pulled each sledge. Malamute husky dogs, Linda had said when he asked. They were big and muscular with short, curly tails and thick, grey and cream, double layered, insulating fur.

Their eyes were strange. Brilliant blue irises set in sky blue where the white should be. They pulled the sledges, seemingly without effort, fifty kilometres a day if necessary and their muzzles smiling with pleasure at being able to do what they loved. It was what they'd been bred for and they pulled Finn into his unknown future.

On his journey from the pit he'd rarely managed enough speed for the runners to hiss. Only on short steep slopes, when he had stood at the back of the sledge and it had careered downhill. The wind had cut into his face and he had breathed the freezing air rushing into his lungs. For those few brief minutes of exhilarating speed, he had felt out of control. He had not been the master of his fate. He had let his cares go. He had been free. The feeling had been overwhelming.

Like the urge he had felt, just before he'd discovered the church, to surrender to the weather. To let his life end, lie down in the snow and die. The speed had been like that. It hadn't mattered that he might hit something. It hadn't mattered that he might shatter his only means of survival. At that moment, all he wanted was that feeling of elation. He had not dared to do it often. Sanity would return and he would continue at his normal pace.

This was different. No danger. No exhilaration. Just controlled speed. The dogs made all the difference. Strong, enduring, they ran patiently for Linda, maintaining a steady pace to take him onward to London.

Using just a few gruff words, Linda had perfect control over both dog teams. Although Finn held the reins, he had no more control over the dogs than he did over the sun's path across the sky.

His mind wandered back to his disposal of the burnt crystals.

"You must crush them, Finn. Now the temperate dome is fungus free, you must collect them and destroy them to make sure the presence cannot use them to cause Eden more trouble." He had looked at Nisha in surprise. "After you have crushed them to a powder, they must be buried in the ground with salt. Take some from the kitchen. That will cleanse and earth them. They will be of no more use after that. Take them far from the domes. Somewhere they can do no harm. I will give you a crystal to protect you."

He had done her bidding; crushing the burnt crystals inside a thick bag, hitting them time and again, with a large hammer, until they were reduced to dust. He had mixed in the salt, dug down through the ice and buried the bag in the frozen earth, as far from Eden as he could walk and still return in a day. Yet even as he buried the bag, it felt as if someone was watching him do it. The feeling slowly faded as he returned to Eden. He shivered as he remembered it.

He was jerked back to the present by the crack of Linda's whip as she steered the dogs from running into deep snow.

Chapter 4

That first night set the pattern for those that followed. Linda picked a campsite in the lee of a small hill. The tops of snow-covered trees almost completely hid their tents, the dogs bedded down around them.

"Why did we come this way, Linda? Why didn't you follow your tracks to Eden?" asked Finn

"Never go same tracks. Snow pirates."

"Snow pirates! Is that why we're hiding, Linda? What if they find us?"

"Dogs know. Tell me. Then go. Quick."

"How do the dogs tell you?"

Linda's face showed her struggle to articulate her thoughts.

"They tell me here."

She pointed to her head.

Finn nodded. She understood her dogs, instinctively, he thought.

After eating, Finn lay in his tent, wakeful, puzzling

over what he'd found on the computer before they'd left Eden. There were many programs to control everything that made Eden work. One pumped water up from the sea by an underground pipe reaching deep beneath the ice. Another split hydrogen from the sea water using electricity from the solar panels. The hydrogen was burnt in the fuel cells to make electricity and keep Eden running at night when the solar panels didn't work. Waste hot water from the fuel cells ran down into a tank below Eden. The hot water was pumped through Eden at night to keep it warm and then it was misted over the plants in the Tropical biome to keep it humid. The computer programs controlled it all. It was a beautifully designed system.

Finn hadn't told Nisha any of these technical details. What he did tell her about was Project Amon Ra.

"Nisha, there's something on the computer called Project Amon Ra?"

She'd looked at him blankly.

"What is it, Finn?"

"This page keeps coming up whether I want it to or not. It has a spinning yellow disc above a yellow pyramid on a blue background. But when you click on

'Welcome to Project Amon Ra', it says the page is no longer available and to contact the page's author. And I can't."

Nisha thought for a moment.

"You will, Finn. It is important; I can feel it. Remember it."

He couldn't forget. It kept coming into his mind at unexpected moments. It wouldn't leave him alone: like tonight.

Maybe something in London would help him understand.

He slept.

***

Tracks! There were tracks in the snow ahead. Linda stopped the dogs and strode over to Finn.

"Go fast. No stopping."

"Why?" asked Finn.

"No other way. Dangerous."

"Dangerous? Why?"

"Snow pirates. Do as I tell."

Finn nodded. Linda was in charge. She did this all the time. She must know what she was talking about.

He felt the protection crystal Nisha had given him when he buried the burnt crystals. He could still see her serious face as she tried to impress its importance on him. He had smiled and slipped it into his pocket just to please her.

Would it keep him and Linda safe?

At Linda's command, the dogs pulled. They gathered speed: travelling much faster than before. It was exhilarating. Finn almost shouted out with excitement. Only the thought of the snow pirates stopped him.

The sun moved across the sky as they climbed a gradually rising slope. Huge snow mounds, on either side of the trail, hemmed them in. The dog's pace slowed.

Without warning, Linda uttered a sudden muffled command. The dogs stopped.

"What is it?" asked Finn as Linda strode past him.

"Wrong," she muttered.

Finn looked ahead, beyond the mounds of snow that hemmed in the narrow track. The trail disappeared to the left, passing a massive, dark rock, sticking out of the snow.

He could see nothing. He didn't doubt Linda's intuition. She knew.

He followed Linda, keeping to the left, as she did.

Reaching the sharp edge of the rock, she looked carefully around it. Finn crouched beside her and peered too.

The trail widened out to a flat space. Scattered treetops poked through the snow crust. The trail split into many branches. Each made their individual way amongst the treetops, according to the whim of each sledge that had passed.

Were there that many others?

Linda surveyed the area for an age. Finally she nodded.

"Go."

Slowly, the dogs pulled the sledges around the sharp corner and began to accelerate across the flat space ahead. Suddenly, Finn's dogs stopped and his sledge swerved to a stop.

Ahead were the remains of a camp. Torn tents, a broken sledge and other pieces of smashed equipment lay scattered before them. All around, the snow was trampled flat.

"Snow pirates?" asked Finn.

Linda nodded.

"Is it safe to be here?"

She nodded again, "Got what wanted. Gone now."

Linda walked over to the remains and rummaged amongst them. Finn followed, asking questions. Only some of which she answered.

"Do people often get attacked?"

There was no answer.

"Where are all the people?"

"Slaves."

"Slaves! Where do the snow pirates take them?"

"London."

"Why?"

"Trade."

"Blood!" he pointed at the frozen pool of red. A cold shiver passed through him.

"Do the pirates kill?" he asked quietly.

"Maybe."

"Where are the bodies?"

Linda stopped and looked him square in the face. "Food."

"Food!" Finn's voice was a horrified screech.

"Cannibals. No trade. No food. Must eat."

People! Food! He stood still, shocked. In the pit, people were buried in the compost and left until their flesh was eaten by the compost worms. Then the bones were unearthed, crushed and added back to the compost. They became part of the cycle of life and death. It was fitting and respectful.

The thought of people being eaten as food was repulsive.

He wandered away from Linda, trying to distance himself from the thoughts crowding his brain. He looked around: seeking distraction.

"Linda."

Linda turned.

"What?"

Finn pointed to where he could see a faint pink glow amongst the ice and snow.

"There."

Linda looked at where he was pointing. A puzzled expression came over her face.

"Nothing."

"There is. Look."

He walked over to the inert body lying there.

Linda tilted her head, screwing up her eyes. "Dead. Leave. We got food."

Finn ignored the thought that Linda might be a cannibal too.

"It's a girl." How did he know that? The figure was shrouded in thick clothes. "She's not dead. She's glowing."

"Glowing. What you mean?"

A sudden thought struck him. She doesn't see it. I must be careful.

"I mean she's breathing. Look, her chest is moving. She's alive. We have to take her with us."

"No."

"She's alive."

"She'll slow us down."

"We have to."

"Why?"

Finn kept trying.

"You can't leave someone out here. She'll die."

"Not my problem."

"I'm not going without her."

"You stay then."

"You made a deal with Nisha."

"Not for girl."

"She's a human being, like us. We can't leave her."

"You want snow pirates get us?"

"No. Nisha said I'm protected. She gave me a crystal. Please Linda."

Linda stopped and looked at Finn. She sighed. A deep outpouring of breath and emotion.

"Okay. She yours. Rides your sledge. Sleeps your tent. Eats your food. Snow pirates come. I go."

Finn smiled at Linda's instructions.

"Okay, Linda. Deal?" He held out his hand.

A slow, grudging smile spread across Linda's face and she nodded, clasping his hand as Nisha had done hers in Eden.

Finn picked the girl up. She was light as a feather. Carrying her to his sledge, he removed its contents and placed her in it. He packed everything, except the tent, around the girl. He put the blanket over her and covered everything with the thick tarpaulin. Slinging the tent across his shoulders he stood on the platform at the rear of the sledge.

As soon as he was ready, Linda flicked her whip and his dogs ran, making light work of the girl's extra weight.

***

By the time they reached Linda's next camping spot, the sun had almost set. After pitching his tent, Finn unpacked his supplies from around the girl. She moved restlessly and her eyelids flickered, as if she was dreaming. Finn lifted her from the sledge and put her inside the tent, out of the freshening wind.

He heated some soup on the stove, put some in a bowl, grabbed a spoon and turned to look at the girl. He was surprised to see she was awake, half sitting, staring at him.

Finn smiled, "Hello, my name's Finn. Are you feeling better?"

The girl didn't move. Her large, dark eyes stayed fixed on him. The pale skin of her face made them stand out. The way her skin was stretched tightly across her hollow cheeks, emphasised the bones in her oval face. She looked hungry. The wavy hair, loosened from beneath her hood, was almost black. The lamplight shone on it, picking out red strands, making them shine like fine copper wires. Finn was surprised. He'd never before thought of electrical wires as anything but carriers of electricity. She moved her head slightly and the copper rippled across her head.

"I made some soup."

He offered her the bowl and spoon.

She didn't move.

"It's alright. It's not poisoned or anything. Look." He dipped the other spoon in the saucepan and sucked up the liquid. He held the bowl closer to her.

Still looking at Finn, she slowly reached forward,

took the bowl and after nodding her thanks, began eating.

Finn ate from the saucepan. When they had finished, he took the utensils outside to clean them.

He returned with two bundles. One was his sleeping bag, which he dropped in front of her.

"It's for you," said Finn.

She shook her head.

"Why not?" asked Finn.

She pointed at the sleeping bag and then at him, her head on one side, questioning.

"What?" Finn's question came automatically.

She pointed to her mouth and shook her head.

"Oh, you can't speak." His face reddened. "Sorry. I didn't... I mean... It's alright. You can have the sleeping bag. I'll going to sleep in the sledge cover with the blanket." He pointed to the other bundle beneath his arm and smiled.

The girl nodded. He turned to put the cover down.

Thank you, Finn.

Finn turned quickly.

"You can speak." He accused.

No. Her lips did not move.

A look of puzzled surprise crossed Finn's face.

"How…?" Finn was stunned. "How did…?"

She held her hands to her head, one each side of her temples.

Sorry. I didn't think you would hear me. People don't. They all think I can't talk. I can. The word echoed loudly in Finn's head. Only they can't hear me. I didn't know you could. There was another boy who could, but he died. There hasn't been anyone else since. I'm sorry.

"Don't be sorry," Finn smiled. "I've never even heard of it happening before. It's wonderful. You're unique."

Unique?

"Only one. No one else exactly like you."

Oh.

Finn smiled again. This time the girl returned it, a slow movement from the corners of her mouth. It was the cautious smile of someone who didn't smile often.

"What's your name?"

Moot.

"Moot?"

Yes

Another wave of understanding passed through his mind.

"Because you're mute."

Yes.

"I understand."

Questions crowded his mind.

"Where are you from? Where were you going? What happened when the snow pirates attacked you?

We were travelling from Our Place. I was being taken to the man who'd bought me.

"Bought you?"

Moot nodded. *Yes. I was to be his woman.*

"His woman?" Moot didn't look old enough to be someone's woman.

"Why did the snow pirates leave you?"

Moot hesitated and then shrugged.

If I make myself small and shadowy, people don't see me so well. They forget I'm there.

"I saw you."

And you can hear me. She shrugged. *Maybe that's why you could see me too.*

"Linda couldn't see you until I showed her where you were. You were glowing. A pink light was shining round you. Linda couldn't see that either."

Shining? Oh, I didn't know. Who is Linda?

"Linda is the woman taking me to London. I have

to go there to get things."

What if the snow pirates come back?

"Linda knows how to steer clear of the snow pirates. You're safe now. Linda will be going on alone after London. You can come with me into London or go somewhere else on your own."

I've never been on my own before.

"Come with me then and after London I'll take you back to Nisha in Eden."

Who is Nisha? What is Eden?

"Nisha is the woman I live with, in the place called Eden."

Nisha is your woman?

Finn went bright red, "No. I don't have a woman. Nisha is my friend. She is... old," he added.

The girl's smile was broader. *Sorry. I didn't mean to pry.*

Finn changed the subject.

"I'll tell you more tomorrow. If you want to stay."

I'll come to London with you.

"Okay. Now we must sleep. Linda will want to leave early tomorrow."

Only he didn't sleep. Too many thoughts crowded his brain, swirling through his mind.

Chapter 5

Their travelling became a routine again. They followed a trail only when Linda said they must. Mostly they journeyed across unmarked snow and ice. Linda chose their campsites: secret places that only she knew. She fed the dogs, who then settled down between their tents. Finn explained to Moot that the dogs would alert Linda of any danger. After sharing food, Finn and Moot prepared for sleep, safe, knowing that the dogs were protecting them.

Before they slept, Finn would tell Moot a little of his story; life in the pit, banishment, his journey to Eden and Nisha. Moot sat, enthralled. Finn told his story well and Moot always asked questions, especially about Nisha. Moot relaxed as the days passed. Almost as if she was in Nisha's presence. As if Nisha could give her the wise female companionship and guidance she had missed in her childhood.

Then, prompted by Finn's questions, Moot told of

her life in 'Our Place'. She shared a little of her memories of growing up in the nursery. She began to trust Finn. Unlike the children in the nursery, who had neglected and excluded her because of her 'difference'.

She explained her boring work in the kitchen. How she met Ben there. How they discovered they could hear each other and their friendship. How 'Our Place' became a happy place, until the day fever swept through 'Our Place' and Ben died. Moot's voice turned sad and lonely. Finn could feel Moot's loneliness. His eyes moistened with tears for her

Her voice changed again; she was somehow not present when she told of the trader who bought her.

Then she told of the snow pirates' attack when they were travelling to the trader's settlement. How the pirates sneaked into their camp in the darkness before dawn. How she was woken by screams and the sound of fighting. How she walked away from the camp, laid down on the snow, made herself very small and still and closed down her consciousness.

She told it all with matter-of-fact clarity, explaining that she knew the pirates would not be able to find her. She told of waking in Finn's tent, of feeling confused and of thinking he was a snow pirate. Of gradually realising he was not and being surprised that Finn could hear her. They laughed in disbelief at the strangeness of their meeting. Then, Moot's voice becoming almost shy inside his head, she thanked Finn for rescuing her. Finally, her voice changing to a whisper. *Thank you for listening and for being a friend.*

They both slept safe, sound and secure that night.

***

"What is your real name, Moot?" Finn asked one evening after they'd eaten.

My real name? What do you mean? I am Moot. That is my name. Everyone calls me Moot.

"Yes, but that's not your real name. That's just what they called you. You must have had a real name."

I don't remember.

"What did your parents call you?"

I don't know. My mother died giving birth to me. My father was never there. No one ever gave me a name. I've always been Moot.

Finn waited expectantly. Moot's small oval face screwed up in concentration.

The people in the nursery, who looked after me, always told everyone that I was mute. The other children heard and called me Moot. I became Moot.

"Don't you want to have a proper name? Like my parents called me Finn?

Moot smiled.

I think it's too late. I don't know if I could remember to answer to anything except Moot.

***

Time slipped away, as the dogs pulled them through the short days. Sometimes they moved fast on frozen snow that covered hard, smooth, ice, which allowed the dogs' feet to grip easily. They made good time.

Sometimes there was soft snow, the dog's feet sinking and progress was slow. Travelling over rough, uneven snow and ice were the worst days. Their passage became jerky, difficult and frustrating.

Yet, still they trusted Linda to guide them and tell them when and where they should camp. As the days passed, Finn and Moot ate sparingly, rationing the food so it would last until London.

The terrain changed. Tree tops gave way to rooftops poking through the snow.

Once, thought Finn, many people must have lived here.

Then came the morning they'd been waiting for.

Linda had been leading them along a road that went uphill. At the crest, she stopped. Finn drew alongside. She pointed down the steep hill, to where, across the white landscape, a sickly, yellow grey cloud shrouded the murky outline of tall buildings.

"London," said Linda.

They looked at the dirty smudge of cloud in the distance.

"That's London?"

"Yes."

"Is it always covered in cloud?"

"Sometimes."

Although he usually accepted that Linda was uncommunicative, sometimes Finn wished that she would say more. This was one of those times.

"Can you take us closer?"

Linda shook her head, "Camp now."

She left them the next morning. As Finn and Moot packed their things, Linda tied Finn's sledge on top of hers. As she rearranged her dogs, Finn tried to say thank you.

"Not thanks. Deal." She stopped and looked at him. A momentary look of concern crossed her face. "Careful. London dangerous."

She turned away, mounted her sledge and was gone.

Finn and Moot slung their heavy rucksacks across their shoulders and began their descent into a cloud covered London. Consulting the map Nisha had given him, Finn pointed to what must be the curling, frozen, River Thames.

As they went further down the hill, the morning light faded and London looked like some bizarre monster. Yellowed, grey cloud hair swirled slowly above the tops of tall structures sticking out of the snow like massive teeth. Glinting glass turned the tallest buildings into many faceted eyes.

Finn and Moot looked at them in amazement. Truly the ancients had possessed wonderful powers. They had seen nothing like this on their journeys through the white wastes.

They crossed the wide, frozen Thames. And as they penetrated further into the mass of buildings, more huge structures reared up on either side of them. The massive constructions hemmed them in, blocking out what light the clouds let in between their bulk.

Stillness enveloped them. Only the slight sounds of their movements broke it, echoing quietly around them. Was there any life in this place? Linda had said it was dangerous. What danger did she mean? Although he couldn't see anything, unsettling thoughts surfaced from the back of his brain. Occasional gaps of side streets between the buildings, allowed more light to reach them as they walked on through the shadowy concrete ravines.

Finn...

"Yes, Moot. I feel it too. It's... It's... I don't like it. We must be very careful. Come on. We'd better keep going or we won't find shelter before sunset and that wouldn't be good. We can work out where we are tomorrow."

Their disquiet persisted. These streets were nothing like the map Nisha had given to Finn. Its flatness had not prepared them for these huge buildings and the dark narrow gaps of roads between them. He had no idea where they were in the vastness of London. He glanced behind them. Was that a movement or a reflection from the cracked glass covering the building they'd passed?

Were they being watched?

"Moot," his whispered word was a slow echo along the road.

I know, Finn. I can feel them. There are people behind us. They mean us harm. He could feel her panic rising. *What do we do?*

He smiled to try and reassure her.

"It's okay. Pretend you haven't seen them. There's a side street over there." He gestured. "We'll hide inside one of the buildings when we're round the corner. Go that way, slowly." His murmured words went rolling along the road, distorting as they went.

They approached the side street. Closer...closer... Finn glanced back. Several figures had broken cover and were openly following them.

"RUN," Finn's shout cut through the quiet.

Skidding across the slippery surface, they raced for the safety of the corner.

There was a sudden laugh, as three more figures appeared from around the corner. Finn and Moot came to a skidding halt. The figures stood there, amused and smiling, as their trap closed on the two travellers.

Finn turned. The figures behind them were advancing quickly.

Finn, what do we do?

Finn looked around desperately.

His gloved fingers felt for Nisha's protection crystal

inside his pocket. He grasped it urgently as the figures came towards them. Would it help? He could feel its smooth shape even inside his coat pocket.

Now is the time, he thought.

Crystal. We need your help, NOW.

"HERE! Over here."

Finn turned.

A bearded man leant out of a window in the building to their left. He beckoned urgently. The figures from both ends of the street, broke into a run.

"QUICKLY."

Was this right? Should they obey this bearded man?

There were shouts as the figures slithered towards them.

As they closed in, Finn grabbed Moot's hand and sliding across the hard frozen snow crust, they raced to the open window.

"Quick or they'll get you."

Arms helped Moot though the window. Finn clambered into the shadows after her. The bearded man slammed the window shut and barricaded it with a wooden board.

"Come on. It won't take them long to get through this."

He led the way across a dark room. His right hand cranked a handle on something he held in his left. A dim light shone from it, illuminating their path.

They stumbled down a corridor. The sound of smashing glass and splintering wood told them their pursuers had reached the window.

They hurried along corridors and down stairs. Their rescuer led the way, telling Finn to shut the doors behind them. Together they pushed heavy furniture against some of the doors. Eventually they stopped. A pale light diffused through a snow-covered window.

"We're safe here for the moment," said their rescuer.

He sank down on the floor. The heat of the moment had passed and they could now see that their rescuer was not a young man. His sparse beard was grey and straggling. To judge by his wheezing breath, he was also not a well man.

Moot looked at Finn.

He is ill.

"I'm well enough. Give me a minute and we can go on."

You heard me!

"Of course I heard you."

But I don't speak.

"Neither did my wife and I could hear her perfectly. You're not the only one who speaks with their mind. You're few and far between, but I've known some," his voice became sombre. "All gone now."

There was a moment's pause.

Finn broke it. "My name is Finn. This is Moot. I want to thank you. Who were they?"

"I'm Dent. They're part of a slaver gang. They catch anyone they can. They need slaves to work in the caverns and tunnels underground." Dent heaved himself off the floor. "We need to get to my hidey hole now, before night falls proper. I'll tell you everything then."

Dent led them through a further labyrinth of long corridors, dark rooms and even more stairs, finally to arrive at his hidey hole. He stood before a blank panelled wall. Bending down he put his hand into a recess in a panel nearest the floor and pulled. With a click a whole section, about a metre square, opened inwards and upwards. He motioned Finn and Moot to enter. Following them, he pushed the door shut. In one corner, up against the ceiling, there was a tiny window covered by a metal grill. It allowed a shadowy light into the room. Dent went over to a table and lit a lamp. Its light showed the mess and clutter in the room. Despite the cold outside, the room felt warm.

Dent pointed to the table with its old plastic chairs, before slumping into a dilapidated armchair in one corner. The lamplight showed his face as a pale age-lined oval against the dark of his hood and scarf. His meagre beard scarcely covered his lower face beneath his scrawny, hollow cheeks. He sighed and closed his dark brown eyes. They disappeared into deeply recessed sockets. His shallow, unhealthy wheezing, was loud in the silence.

Moot and Finn looked around the room. Three of the walls were a dull grey. The other wall was covered in big pages of yellowing paper. They were stuck on randomly: upside down, sideways, some partly covering the pages beneath. It made it hard to decipher the words and pictures printed on them. The layers were very thick in places, less so in others, perhaps for insulation or maybe to keep the light from showing.

Books and papers were stacked haphazardly on the floor. Boxes of food, broken machinery, wires and tools were scattered around. Saucepans and unwashed crockery were piled on a steel sink in the corner opposite the bed. Finn recognised an electric stove beside it. Dent had electricity!

In the middle of the room was a metal fireplace. A chimney, cleverly fashioned from empty metal food tins, was suspended above it to take away the fumes. In a box beside it, there was paper, wood and shiny black coal. More food boxes were stored under the table they were sitting at. Finn nodded approvingly. Dent had all he needed in his hideaway.

Dent opened his eyes and looked directly at them. "What are you doing in London?" his voice was a wheezing rasp. "Don't you know how dangerous it is here?"

"We had to come," Finn paused, uncertain how to explain their quest for crystals and seeds. He told the story in a few words, keeping it simple. He ended the tale by getting out the London map and asking where The Natural History Museum and Kew were.

Dent took a cursory look at the map. "I can lead you to The Natural History Museum tomorrow. It's quite a way. Over the other side of London. In the west. I'll get you there, don't worry. We'll go at night."

"Because of the slave gang?"

Dent nodded, "They're easier to avoid at night.

They don't come out so much. They keep a watch during the day and take anyone who comes here. Snow pirates bring captives to trade. Under London are tunnels and huge caverns built long ago. After the survivors had eaten up all the food there was stored in London, they found a way of growing more down there. Enough to stay alive.

We are their children's, children's, children. Maybe. Who knows when this happened? There's water from underground springs. They get earth mining the old sewers and all the waste they can find. They brew ethanol. They use methane from their fermented waste and they get some electricity from the water mill I helped build when I was young."

You were in the slaver gang?

"They weren't slavers then. That was later when The Leader had taken control. He enslaved the survivors with the help of his initiates."

"The Leader?" Finn shivered. Memories of the presence he had felt at Eden sprang into his mind. Did that have something to do with The Leader?

Dent nodded. "He had a way of getting people to do what he wanted. He had some sort of power over them. He used a purple crystal." Finn's heart jumped. A purple crystal! Was The Leader somehow responsible for what happened to him at the church?

"It didn't work on me or my woman. Me and Jamila were immune. Might have been to do with her telepathy."

What's telepathy? asked Moot quickly, as if she already knew the answer and just wanted confirmation.

"That's the name for how you talk, Moot. I could hear but not speak. Jamila was really good at it. Me and Jamila escaped with the God man and some others. We had to get out. After we left, his followers hunted us. He couldn't have us as a separate group. He didn't want any rivals. They ambushed and trapped our people. One by one, all of our group disappeared, except for me, Jamila and the God man. We came here and hid. He couldn't catch us. He tried, but he couldn't do it."

Dent heaved himself out of the chair and walked unsteadily to the sink. He moved some crockery, turned the tap and a stream of pale green water gushed into the cup he held ready. He gulped it down, as if the talking had given him a great thirst.

Perhaps he hasn't talked to anyone for a while,

thought Finn.

"After a while The Leader disappeared with some of his followers. The God man left later. He wanted to find the Leader and stop what he was doing. He had a lot of faith in his God, did the God man. Why, when his God let this happen to his world, I don't know? He couldn't explain it to me, either. So that's it. I could tell you more, but that's the main story. It was all a long time ago. I need to sleep now."

He went back to his chair and soon his regular, wheezy breathing told them he was asleep.

"We'll take turns sleeping, Moot. You first."

She snuggled down in the sleeping bag and soon exhaustion claimed her.

Finn's thoughts raced. Dent's story explained the purple crystal and everything else in the church. The Leader and his followers must have been there. Where was The Leader now though? What had happened to Dent's wife, and where was this God man? Questions with no answers.

He looked around Dent's hiding place. Getting up from his chair quietly, so as not to wake the sleepers, he went over to the wall of printed yellow paper. Some of it looked as if it was cut out deliberately, mostly headlines in big letters with lots of typing underneath.

With a sudden sharp intake of breath, he recognised a phrase amongst the typing: 'The Amon Ra Project'.

He read avidly, his eyes going quickly from page to page, searching for more information.

"Ah, so that's it."

After he'd read it all, he sat down, a satisfied smile on his face. Now he knew the story of The Amon Ra Project. Well, some of it. And Nisha was right. It was important: very important. He must tell Moot when she woke, so she could read it too.

***

The next moment he was surprised to find Moot shaking him awake. He'd fallen asleep at the table. Moot was calling him.

Finn! Wake up. Dent is ill. He feels cold. Finn!

Finn jumped to his feet, almost knocking over his chair.

They went to Dent. His skin was freezing. His whole body was trembling. He kept shaking his head and mumbling.

What could they do?

Nisha would know, but Nisha wasn't here. If only he'd remembered to bring the emergency herb pack

Nisha had given him, but he'd left it on his sledge and Linda must have taken it by mistake.

Finn moistened a rag and wiped Dent's face.

I'll light a fire. We must keep him warm.

They took turns to sit with him.

Finn listened to his ramblings. They didn't make much sense. Suddenly, Dent grabbed Finn's arm and stared at him, "Follow my lead if you want to get out of here."

Dent laughed a crackling laugh and collapsed back into the chair.

"Follow my lead? What does that mean?" His brow furrowed. "Moot?"

I don't know, Finn.

Moot looked around the room.

Finn, there's something dangling from the ceiling.

She went over to the furthest corner. A thin line hung enticingly out of reach.

It's an opening.

Ah! He could see a black outline of a large rectangle on the ceiling. On one side there were hinges. A trapdoor!

Finn. A stick.

Moot grabbed a long thin pole propped against the

wall. She pushed one end against a dirty mark on the rectangle. There was a click and the trapdoor flapped down, exposing a folded metal ladder.

Using a metal hook screwed into the other end of the stick, Moot pulled the ladder. Finn grabbed hold and together they tilted it down into the room, opening its sections until the ladder's base rested in a clear space on the floor.

Finn looked at Moot. She smiled.

You explore it, Finn. I'll stay with Dent.

Finn nodded.

After fetching Dents torch, he climbed into the dark space. Winding the handle, he could see an electric cable coming out of a wall and leading off into the shadowy space.

Follow my lead? He grinned to himself at Dent's joke, as he followed it. It led to further ladders that led him on through a maze of shadowy spaces, until, eventually, opening a final door, he emerged onto the building's roof. He blinked in the pale morning sunlight.

Follow my lead! Ha! It would have been hard to remember all the right twists and turns and ladders to take, without it.

What now? Ah, in front of him, facing towards the sun, was a solar panel like the ones at Eden, only bigger. It faced directly south to get the best of the sun's rays. The cable went into a junction box. Dent must be using the electricity. What else? Another cable led from the junction box. It snaked off to another door in the roof. Dent had told him to follow the lead to get out of here. He must follow it.

The wire went under the door. He entered, being careful to close it after him. He followed it down more ladders, corridors and stairs until, after opening a final door, Finn found himself in a large storage room. A translucent skylight window focused its light on a shiny red machine mounted on short skis. Motorised transport! It had the word 'Snowmobile' painted on one side. There were two seats and in the lockers under them, Finn found containers of dried food.

The lead was attached to a battery in the engine. A trickle charger! The battery would start this machine. Finn looked around. Facing the machine was a large door with a ramp leading down to it. A complicated rope mechanism was attached to the door, which was set up to move back as the machine slid down the ramp.

This was what Dent had meant by, "Follow the lead."

This was Dent's emergency exit.

Where had he got this machine from? Finn dismissed the thought. It didn't matter where it came from. It was here and they could use it.

Dent was trusting Finn and Moot with this.

Oh thank you, Dent.

Yet, there were three of them. So, was Dent not coming with them?

Finn left the 'Snowmobile' and returning to Dent's hideout, told Moot about what he'd found. "How's Dent?" he finished.

Her hesitation told him all was not well.

Moot had propped him up in his chair, but his breathing was worse.

"Did you find it," he asked, his voice was a rasping croak.

"The Snowmobile?"

"Yes. What d'you think I meant?" he gasped for breath. "After you've finished… wandering around London… looking for those crystals of yours… you're going to need a way of escaping… the slavers and getting back to Eden… Don't even think… about me…

I'm old and ill... I'm not going to live long," he paused. "Use it... I've stockpiled ethanol... adjusted the engine... to run on it... If you find more on your journey... don't forget it's ethanol... or petrol...but you'd be lucky... to find that... Not diesel... not even winter diesel." He stopped: his breathing wheezy and uneven.

Moot held a cup of the greenish water to his lips. Finn took some dried fruit from his pack and pressed a morsel to Dent's lips. He seemed to gain strength from it. Finn gave him more. His breathing recovered.

Dent whispered, "Please God, forgive me. All food is flesh. All life is flesh."

What do you mean?

"What do I mean? How many years can you eat the flesh and not be guilty. The God man said to think of it as Christ's body."

"Christ's body?" asked Finn quietly, "What is that?"

Dent ignored him.

"Human flesh. There was nothing else left to eat. We didn't know. We all ate it. We thought it was the goats. The ancients had got them from the zoo when it happened. We didn't know. The Leader. He fed the bodies to us. His followers mined and cooked the frozen dead. And when they had to go further and further to find bodies, his gang of initiates preyed on the weak and helpless and took them too. But they don't get me. I'm too clever for them."

He laughed, stiffened with some pain deep within him and closed his eyes. Finn and Moot stared at him, both shocked and repelled by the thought of eating human flesh. Linda was right. The snow pirates and the London survivors ate the dead and the living. He shivered, despite the warmth of the room.

"We didn't want any part of what they were doing," Dent's voice dropped to a whisper. Finn and Moot listened in horrified silence. "There were millions of dead out there. All frozen. Whatever happened to our world, whenever it was, it was quick.

We were all free to begin with. Working for the common good. When people found out, there was fighting." Dent paused. "The Leader disappeared with some of his followers. Mary took over. She was ruthless. She and her gang made all the other workers slaves. The God man, Jamila and me and some of the others, we escaped when we found out and hid." Again he stopped. "I waited, Jamila, I waited till they came, like you told me."

Still with his eyes closed, Dent spoke again, "They take them as slaves. They grow their food now with slave labour in the tunnels and caverns. They're born slaves and they die slaves."

It's what I knew, Finn. They made us all work. I belonged to Smith. He owned me. I was sold when I was fifteen.

"Jamila told me... you... would... come," Dent's words came with more gasps for air. "But... she died," There was huge sorrow behind the words.

"Your woman died? How did she know we'd come?" said Finn, thinking back to when Nisha had said she knew he'd arrive.

Dent tried to shrug his shoulders and winced, "Jamila said you would. I didn't kill her, she died."

"Why would you kill her?"

"I didn't... I didn't," there was a desperate misery in his whisperings. A single tear coursed down his left cheek. "She fell down with a pain in her chest, when we ran from them... Ambush. She told me... go. She said... run. Save myself. She said I must be here to help them... I left her. I ran. No choice. I had to. But you took so long getting here... She didn't know when. And she was… gone… slipped away to the life beyond. I ran because I had to be here… for you." His voice gurgled in his throat.

"You did it, Dent. You did it," but Dent wasn't listening.

"I ate the dead. We all ate the dead, but it said in the book. The God man showed me. It said that God sent a man, Jesus, his son. His friends ate his body. It says so in the book. The God book. I got it somewhere. Somewhere?"

He flailed his hand helplessly towards the papers on the floor next to his bed. "Somewhere," he murmured again. "The book said it was alright. Not to kill, though. Not to kill. I didn't kill them. I only ate their bodies. There wasn't enough food. We'd eaten it all. Eaten it. That's why they did it. We didn't know. It said in the book. I kept it. Kept it somewhere. They didn't need their bodies any more. They were gone. Gone."

Tears oozed from his tired eyes.

"Gone. She was gone."

He lapsed into unconsciousness again. Finn could feel his eyes moistening in sympathy for this old man who had stayed alive for them. He could see Moot's eyes shining too, even in the dim light.

They sat for a long time, until the light faded. Then they sat in the dark. Dent's breathing grew shallower. There were longer pauses between his breaths. They fell asleep. When Finn woke, he realised he couldn't hear Dent breathing.

"I think he's dead, Moot."

He felt rather than saw Moot's nod.

He waited for us to arrive before he would allow himself to die. His Jamila would have liked that.

It was Finn's turn to nod.

"He was a brave man."

What do we do, Finn?

"We must do what I came here to do. We must get the crystals and seeds and take them back to Eden. To Nisha. We owe that to Dent."

Chapter 6

Finn looked out across London from the safety of the roof. He glanced down at the map Nisha had given him, trying to match the pictures of the buildings with what he could see of the cityscape spread before him. Where were they? Nothing seemed to fit. It didn't matter which way he turned it; the map made no sense. It was useless. Without Dent he couldn't tell where anything was? These names on the map of buildings and roads, how could he find them? It was impossible. He had no way of knowing where the Natural History Museum was or Kew. There was just a mass of buildings, their tops sticking out of the ice and snow.

Finn returned to Dent's hideout, miserable and frustrated.

"The map's no good, Moot. I can't make sense of it. It's from the before time. It's different now. I can't see any road names and I don't know where any of the landmarks are." Finn flung the map towards the fire and slumped onto a chair.

Dent's covered body on the chair felt like a rebuke.

Finn sat there, unable to think what to do.

Unsure how to help, Moot watched as the map flapped in the heat from the fire.

Without warning, she jumped up and grabbed the map.

Finn! Look. There are marks on the back. The heat's made them show. What are they?

She thrust the map at Finn.

He looked at it. There were brown marks all over the reverse of the map He held the map closer to the fire and looked at it more intently. It was another map, drawn in brown ink. A map of the city now. Someone had drawn a secret map of the city that showed in the snow and the heat of the fire had made it visible.

London was written at the top in bold brown letters. The main roads were drawn and there were pictures of landmarks in lots of places including Kew and The Natural History Museum. Better than that, there were several landmarks he recognised from looking at London from the roof.

"This is brilliant, Moot. I wonder who drew it. Look.

There's St. Paul's Cathedral. That is docklands. That's Victoria Railway station. That's Big Ben. I could see some of their shapes from the roof. We're in what was known as The City. Now I know which way to go, it won't be so difficult to get where we want," Finn smiled gleefully. He found a pen amongst Dent's things and traced over the top of the map so that he could still see it away from the heat of the fire.

They had a couple of hours before it would be dark enough for them to venture out.

"Moot, come and look at this wall," Finn pointed at the wall with its covering of yellow papers. "When I was in Eden, there was something on one of the computers. It was called The Amon Ra Project. I didn't know what it was about. I couldn't open it up. I felt it was important. So did Nisha. It's on this wall. Look."

Finn pointed.

"See."

Moot shook her head.

What does it say, Finn?

"There," said Finn impatiently.

I can't read, Finn. You have to tell me what it says.

"You can't read?"

No.

"But you read the map."

NO. YOU read the map. I only saw the marks. You were important in the pit, so you were taught to read. No one bothered to teach me to read. I was not important.

Finn looked at Moot in dismay.

"You were not important?" Finn parroted her words.

No, Finn.

"I'm sorry, Moot. I... I... didn't think." He went bright red.

Moot laughed.

It's alright, Finn. You couldn't have known. I didn't think to tell you. Why would I?

"When we get back to Eden, Moot, I'll get Nisha to teach you. She will be a good teacher."

Can't you teach me?

"I've never taught anyone anything, Moot. I wouldn't know what to do." Finn felt strangely shy of telling Moot. He'd always known what to do, except when he couldn't find what was wrong with Eden. Somehow that felt a bit like this.

Tell me about this Project, Finn?

Finn nodded.

"Project Amon Ra was a last effort by experts from some of the countries of the Earth, to stop the world from overheating and billions of people dying. A billion is a million, million, Moot."

A million? I don't know what that means, Finn.

"It means a lot of people. It's hard to think of how many."

Thank you for trying, Finn. Moot smiled at him.

Finn smiled back and began again.

"They had been burning fuel that made the Earth warm up. All the ice on the Earth had melted. Huge amounts of frozen methane gas were released from beneath the frozen seas. This made the Earth warm very quickly. The oceans warmed too. All the creatures in it were dying or had been fished out to eat. There were too many people. There was not enough land to grow food and not enough animals to feed people.

Some countries were fighting over water. They'd tried all sorts of things to cool the Earth. Nothing had worked. Some scientists had a plan to move the Earth a bit further from the sun, so the world would be cooler. They called it The Amon Ra Project and started work.

This is a map of where they were building it. It's

where three big pieces of the Earth fitted together. Plates they called them, tectonic plates. They joined together in some big water called the Atlantic Ocean. That is what it's about, Moot. It doesn't say what happened."

What do you think happened, Finn?

"I think they succeeded and then something went wrong and the world got too cold. That's why the world is like it is"

And the people died and are under the snow and ice. Is that it?

Finn nodded. "I think so."

I wonder when this happened.

Finn shrugged. "I don't know. A long time ago. Hundreds and hundreds of years ago, according to what Dent said."

Finn couldn't stop himself from looking at Dent's body lying under the blanket on his chair.

"I think we should go, Moot. It's dark enough.

They crept out of the building, rucksacks on their backs, their warm breath steaming in the freezing night air. As Dent had said, it would take them all night to get to Kensington where The Natural History Museum was. Finn already knew that the crystals were in the part called The Geological Museum. He used the pen to mark their route on the map so they could find the window after they returned.

When they left Dent's hideout, Finn tied one end of a ball of string to a nearby door. Then they walked the corridors until they found a window to the outside. Finn tied the string to the outside of the window. It would return them to Dent's hideout, so they could find the Snowmobile and escape from London.

They sneaked through the silent streets. The cloud had lifted and the snow reflected light from the stars and a sliver of a crescent moon. The frozen buildings were beautiful, but it was a cold, frosted beauty, harsh and mean.

Almost half the night had gone when Finn came close to Moot and whispered, "I think someone is following us."

How do you know?

Finn shrugged his shoulders. "I'm not sure. It just feels like it. We're safe for now. It's one person. They won't try anything until there's more of them."

Moot nodded.

They walked on.

As they rounded a corner, they saw a long, low

building of pale blue and yellow, mottled stone. It had central twin towers with smaller towers at either end. Their spires glittered with an icy covering. Rows of windows stretched all along the front of the building, rounded at the top, with thin columns on either side. Modelled into the window sills were creatures and plants that Finn had never seen before. There were more creatures and plants decorating the eaves. The building was at once beautiful and forbidding.

They hurried across the street and stood in the recessed shadows of a massive doorway that was now almost filled with thick drifted snow. Thin columns supported graceful half-moon arches above them.

They moved on quickly, looking for a way in. Reaching the east end of the main building, the architecture changed and there was a broken window. They climbed through.

Are we still being followed?

"Maybe. I'm not sure. We may have lost them."

Them?

"I think there's more than one now."

They walked along dark corridors and through shadowy rooms. Some full of furniture, others empty. How could they find their way to the crystals?

Going through a door labelled, 'No Entry', they found themselves on a wide balcony lined with stuffed animals in glass cases. To one side it was open to a great hall filled with the bones of a long dead creature. Even in the darkness, its size was impressive.

They walked down a wide staircase which joined another from the far side and continued on one grand set of steps to the floor of the hall. A statue of a long dead person watched them go with unseeing eyes.

Finn's skin tingled strangely.

This is a very odd place, Finn. Why is it full of dead things? I don't like it.

Finn shrugged and beckoned her to follow him. He led the way to the front of the hall, their feet setting up echoes that reverberated around the vast space. Just as he had thought, here was a map of the whole place.

Finn studied it.

"This way," he whispered.

He led them to the other end of the hall, around and under the huge staircase and along corridors lined with more dead animals.

They took a right turn.

Finn, stop. This display feels important. Part of it looks like the map that was on Dent's wall. Do you recognise it?

"Yes," he turned to her excitedly. "It's a map of all the big pieces of the Earth: the tectonic plates. See where they join together here in the Atlantic Ocean. This is where they built The Amon Ra Project. The map on the wall in Dent's hideout was just a small part of it. See? The Atlantic Ocean isn't so very far from Eden. We must go there."

Go there? What about the crystals, Finn?

Finn smiled. "I don't mean now, Moot. I meant after we've collected the crystals and the seeds at Kew and returned to Eden. Let's go find the crystals."

They walked through a wide corridor with circular glass cases built into the walls. Despite the shadows, they could see crystals behind some of the windows. They sparkled in the diffused light.

Is this them?

"Some of them. There are more, further on. I can feel it."

He led the way again and they came out into a large high-ceilinged room. A staircase, starting from the furthest end, towered above their heads. It cut across the whole room. Statues of people in strange clothes stood on either side. At the top of the staircase Finn recognised an enormous representation of the earth. They walked up the staircase and went through the earth into another room.

Display cases were everywhere. Each one contained different varieties of crystals. There were so many, how could he choose? What had Nisha said?

"You will know."

"How?" he had asked.

"I'm not sure how it will be for you," Nisha replied. "You will know. Choose wisely. Eden depends on your choice."

There was row upon row of beautiful shining stones. Laid out in their display cases, they waited for him. Walking to the nearest case, his practical mind began working out how best to open it. He took tools from his pack.

The easiest way, of course, would be to smash the glass. The easiest and most deadly. The noise would tell whoever was following them, exactly where they were. There was a better way.

He selected a case to work on. Removing his outer gloves, he used his tools to unlock the case. He levered at the lid. A heave and the lid opened, exposing the crystals. He stared at them. The fate of Eden depended on him choosing the right ones. He flinched at the responsibility. He had not asked for this. Why did it have to be his responsibility? The words stuck in his mind. His responsibility.

Reaching out, he made a grab at the nearest crystal. He hesitated and his hand hovered above a crystal. What was that? For a moment he had felt something. What? What was there to feel? Moving his fingers slowly from side to side, he felt a tingling sensation of heat in his palm. The feeling changed as his hand went over each crystal. It disappeared completely over one or two and became stronger with others. One particular purple crystal, about fifteen centimetres long and maybe ten centimetres around with five, no six, flat, glinting sides, felt stronger than the rest. He grasped it, closing his fingers around its smooth faces, feeling it through the thin inner lining of his glove. He felt the sharpness of its point and the blunt slightly ragged end where it had been wrenched from the rocks that had formed it.

Was this what Nisha had meant by choosing wisely, this feeling in his hand. Was that it? Were these the ones to choose? Holding the purple crystal in his right hand, he moved his left across other crystals and again felt the tingling as his hand reacted to them. He smiled at himself. He knew which the right ones were. Why had he doubted? Trust, Nisha had said. He had to learn to trust. Trust his feelings, be aware of the energies around him and he would make the right choices. Nothing Nisha could have done would have prepared him for this. He'd had to experience this himself.

The purple stone seemed to want to stay in his right hand. It stuck. He held on, choosing more crystals with his left. When he found one that felt good, he gave it to Moot, who wrapped it and placed it in the bags with the others.

He worked fast. It was important to choose what they needed and be gone. He moved on to the next display. This case held bigger crystals. Running his left hand across the glass cover, he was surprised to feel nothing. No tingling, no heat, nothing. The crystals lay there, inert.

He moved on. Ah! These felt good. He levered the case open and chose the crystals that he knew were right, before moving quickly to the next case.

The bags were becoming heavy. How many crystals could they take? The temperate biome was huge. They only had one more bag. He looked at the next case.

Would these be enough? It held large, transparent, clear quartz crystals. Nisha had explained that these were the crystals that focused energy.

This display felt different. These crystals sparkled with bright white energy. He could almost see the power. Inexplicably, he felt the crystals were asking to be taken. They wanted to be chosen. How could that be? The crystals weren't alive. He had felt their energy though. Was there a sentience to them? Were they alive? He took the first one. He placed the crystal in Moot's hand and reached for another. There was a gentle crackling sound.

Finn.

"What?"

He turned quickly with the next crystal in his hand and gasped. Moot was enveloped in a bright white light that shimmered and danced around her head and shoulders.

It shone all around her, like an outline.

"Moot. You're shining. There's a white light all around you."

She held up her hand holding the crystal and Finn could see the light shining from between her fingers. Moot took an age to reply. Yet it could only have been seconds.

Shining? Am I? Moot's voice seemed far away. Her voice inside his head felt different, brighter, as if it too had absorbed the sparkling energy.

"What happened?"

I don't know. I feel a little strange. Something's happening to me, Finn. I can feel more than I ever could before. A light is shining into some darkness in my mind. I can see things. I can see them.

"Them?"

People. Tracking us. They're in the museum. I can see them.

"You can do that?"

Yes, I don't know how. Yes, I do. It's the crystal. She opened her hand. The crystal was glowing with its own light. Pulsing from within. *It's helping me to do it. It's making me, making me...* Moot struggled for words. *It's making me bigger. No, I don't mean bigger. It's increasing my, my...abilities. You said about the crystals in Eden intensifying the energy. It's doing it to* me. *It's changing me, Finn. Like you said the purple crystal did to you in the church.*

She turned, looking into the darkness of the museum.

They're coming for us Finn. I can see them. They're coming. Lots of them. Five... Six... Seven. They mean us harm. We must go now... quickly.

She slipped the crystal into her pocket.

Hurriedly, they packed the rest of the crystals in the last of the bags.

Swinging his bags carefully across his shoulders, Finn began to go back the way they had come.

No, Finn. This way. We can't go back the way we came. That's where they're coming from. I see where we must go. Follow me.

Finn followed. Moot led without hesitation.

They went down stairs, across display areas and through doors, some marked private, until they could see starlight shining through a set of windows set high up on the side of an office.

Moot pointed.

Out. Through the windows. They haven't got here yet.

Fin dragged a high desk across to the window. Placing his crystal bags on top, he vaulted up and held a hand out to Moot. She slid her crystals bags over to join his and he pulled her up beside him.

He examined the window catch. It opened with a

soft click. A cold draft of air rushed in, carrying a cloud of soft snowflakes with it.

Finn wriggled through the narrow window and dropped down on the ice a metre below him. Once outside he reached back in and Moot passed him the crystal bags one by one. She clambered up and he pulled her through the window. He pushed it closed behind them and they hurried off into the thickening snowstorm.

A smooth blanket of snow covered everything. The snow must have been falling steadily while they were inside the museum.

Moot led the way again. The heavy crystal bags made them slow.

Finn, they're catching up.

There was acute anxiety in Moot's voice.

This way.

She dived down a side street that Finn could only half see. The snow changed, blowing sharp bursts of harsh crystals straight into their faces.

FINN!

The loudness inside his head, almost made him cry out in pain. He stopped, nearly dropping the crystal bags.

"What is it," his voice almost lost in the howling wind.

It's a trap! They're in front of us. They've got someone who can see like me and his powers are as good as mine, even with the extra crystal energy. He hid himself with some others. I didn't know they were there. They're coming. They want us for our powers Finn.

Her voice was strangely calm.

"Get behind me Moot. I'll stop them."

Finn reached for his knife.

No. Don't. It's alright. I know what to do.

"What?"

Let me cover you. He can't do that. I can.

She pushed him into a doorway and pressed herself against him.

Something came out of her consciousness. He felt it slide over him.

Moot covered Finn and Finn wasn't there. Whatever made him Finn, she covered it. He felt calm and at peace. Finn had disappeared. Hidden within himself! They wouldn't see Moot either. She had hidden them.

He went deep down within his mind, moving slowly along a grey road, his face close to the surface. White emptiness on either side of the road's grey surface. He travelled slowly, deliberately, floating across the greyness.

His brain felt stroked, smoothed, blissed? He did not feel the sensation. It happened within him. He was mesmerised, hypnotised, compelled, absorbed. Unable and unwilling to do anything except travel the road's surface, close to his eyes.

He travelled endlessly. He travelled for so long he didn't realise it had ended and what he could see was the grey light of dawn shining between the buildings. He could see the buildings. He was back in London. He was Finn again.

"Moot."

She lay crumpled at his feet.

At her name, her eyelids flickered.

A feeling of immense relief passed over him.

It's alright Finn, I am still alive. I fooled him, Finn. He was not so clever after all. I made him think we had escaped. The rest followed him to another part of London. They will not bother us again. We can get back to the Snowmobile and leave this place.

"You did all that Moot?"

Yes.

"Have you always been able to do it?"

I could do some of it. I hid from the snow pirates when they attacked us. I had no control then. It just happened when I wanted to get away from something. Now I can control it. The crystals gave me the power to see what I did and how to do it. I didn't have that before.

Finn smiled.

"I thought I would have to fight them and I wasn't sure I could win. Thank you Moot. When we are away from here, you must tell me where you sent me. It was a very strange place."

I'm not sure I know, Finn. Now we must get back to Dent's hideout.

***

Their journey took most of the day. Moot guiding them, they slipped from shadow to shadow, grateful that the sun was unable to shine straight down on them. They avoided open places and saw no others.

It was almost dark by the time they reached Dent's building. Finn located the string in the window. They followed it down the dark corridors to Dent's hideout. Finn winding it back into a ball as they went. Despite Dent's body on his chair, they were grateful for the shelter. They slept together in the opposite corner. Dent was dead, yet they both felt he still welcomed them there. It would have pleased him to know they had escaped the slavers.

In the morning they gathered all they needed from Dent's supplies, followed the lead up to the roof and down to the Snowmobile. They loaded everything the best way they could: including Dent's spare fuel in a large plastic container. Finn tied it all on with the string.

"All we have to do now is collect the seeds and return to Eden," he said, as Moot hunched down behind him.

The noise of the Snowmobile's engine filled the space. Finn pulled on the rope above him, the door grated opened and they slid down the ramp and out into the street.

They roared into the morning.

Chapter 7

The sound of the Snowmobile's engine broke the quiet of the silent streets. Finn made for the frozen River Thames. He wore all his spare clothes beneath his anorak to keep out the intense cold. His balaclava helmet and goggles kept the wind from his face.

He steered upriver, towards Kew, driving through the dark shadows cast by the half-frozen buildings and bright sunlit patches from the rising sun. Moot, sheltered by Finn, held the map, keeping track of where they were.

Travelling on the rivers smooth unbroken snow, they sped along. They left the City's huge buildings that pushed their bulk through the snow crust, moving into the larger expanse of London. There were fewer landmarks here, yet all those that were near the river, were marked on the map.

Later, Finn steered into Kew Gardens and stopped the engine.

A sudden quiet, enveloped them.

Kew had been easy to find. Whoever had drawn the map must have been to London and seen the landmarks. Finn wondered how the map had made its way to Eden. It must have been before Nisha was born or soon after. What strange coincidence had made her give him that very one? Although Nisha wouldn't have said it was coincidence, thought Finn, smiling, despite himself.

They looked around. Nearby they could see the tops of orange brick buildings. Each roof of red tiles obscured by their covering of snow. Not far away, in the opposite direction, something shiny glinted in the sun.

"No tracks, Moot."

That's good.

"We have to search these buildings for the seeds. The Snowmobile could attract people. We need to hide it somewhere and then return afterwards."

Moot pointed to a squat tower in the far distance.

There. Go there. That's far enough away to hide.

The Snowmobile broke the silence again as Finn steered it past the tops of what would have been very tall trees.

The tower was unlike anything they'd seen in London. Each of its stories decreased in size as it went higher. Each story was an octagon with windows at intervals. One set of windows was gone, leaving an open space. It was exactly level with the snow and Finn steered straight in. There was more than enough room.

"Are you coming with me Moot or do you want to stay with the Snowmobile?"

I need to stay here Finn. Two sets of tracks would be too many. You do this.

Finn nodded, picked up his pack and slinging it across his shoulders went off in the direction of the red roofs.

Moot watched as he became smaller and smaller, until he vanished.

Finn?

There was no reply. Was he out of range of her thoughts?

She waited.

Eventually, Finn emerged from a building and lurched back across the snow towards Moot.

There was something about his walk that disturbed her.

What is it, Finn? His mind was a muddle she could not read. *Is this the seedbank?*

Finn said nothing.

There was a look of frustration on his usually positive face. Like when he couldn't read the map.

He flung himself down against the Snowmobile.

What's wrong, Finn? Tell me.

Finn looked up; disappointment covered his face. His voice was a whisper, "We're in the wrong place, Moot. The seed bank's miles away. Somewhere called Wakehurst. I found a poster advertising it, but it didn't say where Wakehurst is. How will we ever find it? I've failed Nisha."

Moot was stunned. This was not the resourceful Finn that she had come to know.

It's getting late, Finn. We must stay here for the night. We have Dent's lamp and we can use this paper to make a door to cover the entrance so no light escapes. We'll think what to do tomorrow.

Finn nodded, too tired to protest. He stayed slumped on the floor, while Moot began covering the door with big sheets of paper from a pile in the room.

She fetched small sticks from nearby tree branches and used them to hold the paper together, carefully overlapping it and making small holes to push the sticks through. She chose longer sticks and poked them through the top. She leant the whole thing against the opening, completely filling it. She lit the lamp, laid out their sleeping bags and prepared food, ignoring Finn, who still lay against the Snowmobile.

Finally, she went and stood above him.

Finn! We still have the crystals. Nisha will be pleased you got them. Do not lose heart. I have prepared food. You must eat.

Finn nodded and slid over to where the food lay in the flickering light of the lamp.

He picked at the meal. Chewing slowly, saying nothing, his spirit crushed within him, his mind seeing only his failure, not their success.

The light from the lamp glinted on the Snowmobile and the shiny surface of the paper Moot had used to block the door. It threw fuzzy shadows across the octagonal walls.

Finn glanced idly around their den. His detached mind taking in, but not seeing the dark tiled walls, the wooden floor and the posters that Moot had used to cover the entrance.

WAKEHURST!

There were posters advertising Wakehurst. Moot had used them to make her door. He grabbed the lamp, stood up and lifted it high above him, illuminating the posters.

Finn! What is it?

"It's the posters Moot! These are posters of Wakehurst. Look, there's the address," he pointed. "And there's a map showing where it is and how to get there. It's got London on it and it has the compass rose at the top. Wakehurst is south west of London. It shows the roads too. There's enough information on it for me to find our way to Wakehurst. There's even a separate poster about the seed bank." He shook his head. "It's incredible. Moot, we can find the seeds. You are wonderful," He flung his arms around her. She didn't move. "If you hadn't used the posters for a door, I wouldn't have seen it. Thank you, thank you, thank you." Finn released her and they stood back awkwardly.

He shook his head and laughed. His dark mood was forgotten. He felt energised and optimistic again. They could find the seed bank now.

He smiled at Moot in the light of the lamp.

He was sure of it.

Chapter 8

They looked at the snow on this freezing morning. Nothing moved in the stillness, the silence. It had closed in after Finn turned off the Snowmobile engine. They stayed still for long moments, feeling the quiet serenity, knowing they had reached their destination.

This was Wakehurst. Even though they could see nothing of the buried buildings, Finn knew this was Wakehurst. It had taken three days and many false directions to find it. He had used the stars, the compass and any landmark that stood up above the snow drifts.

Then Finn removed his outer gloves and brought out the plan of Wakehurst. He had found whole piles of posters, maps and other papers at the back of the tower. It was strange to have found them all piled there. He laughed. Nisha would say they were looked after and it was not strange at all.

He aligned the map to north and tried to make

sense of it. The snow had hidden everything. This must be the right place. It felt like the right place. The buildings must be beneath their feet. The only thing that stood above the crust of ice was a treetop.

It's the tree in the picture Finn. The one that was so tall it stood out above all the others. The one you said was a Giant Redwood. If we find it, we can get the map the right way round and dig in the snow to find the buildings.

Finn nodded and when they stood beside the top of the dead Redwood, Finn looked again at the map and pointed.

"That way."

This time Moot nodded.

They turned and walked towards the setting sun, down a short slope and there were the tops of the buildings. They had been impossible to see from the tree. Hidden by the slope, the snow had looked unbroken. The wind had carved out the snowdrifts and there was the side and part of the roof of an ancient stone house.

"The map shows the seed bank further down the slope and to the right. North west."

Moot smiled, *Follow me.*

She slid down the side of the house and walked confidently across the snow crust. Finn followed. Ever since the sparkling crystals had awakened her latent talents, Moot could feel her way when she needed to.

Finn trusted her.

She walked maybe fifty metres and stopped. Then she paced out a few metres more to the west and stopped.

"Here?" asked Finn.

Here.

He started digging into the snow crust with the short-handled metal spade from his rucksack. Moot using a trowel she had brought from Dent's hidey hole, to help with the softer stuff beneath.

It took a while before they reached anything. His thoughts flashed back to when he had cut down to the trapdoor in the church tower.

A clunk, as his spade hit something solid, drew him back to the present. What was that? He poked hard with his spade and there was a splintering crack. For a moment nothing happened and then came a series of cracks. Almost in slow motion, the snow around him collapsed and he sank with it. His world turned ice blue. Moot was left sitting on the edge of a rectangular hole.

Finn! Are you alright? shouted Moot.

"I'm okay." his voice echoed up from the bottom of the hole.

He looked about him. Beyond the piles of snow that had fallen with him through the shattered glass of the half barrel roof, a smooth tiled floor ran away left and right into a dark blue twilight. The half-light allowed him to see posters on the walls and exhibits of seeds with printed information. Glass partitions showed spaces for workers. This had to be the right place.

Finn. How do I get down?

"Wait. I'll find a way."

He got up and began to explore.

Through a glass partition he saw a step ladder. He tried a nearby door and amazingly it opened. Moments later the step ladder was in place and Moot clambered down.

They looked about them.

You said the seeds were locked away?

Finn nodded. "The leaflet said they were in a special chamber, to keep them cold and dry so they didn't start growing."

Then how will we get to them?

Finn shrugged.

"I don't know Moot. Do you?"

Wait.

She closed her eyes, opened her arms, turned her hands palm up and stood for a moment.

This way.

Finn followed as Moot walked to the western end of the building the sound of their boots on the concrete floor disturbing the sepulchral silence. The light was like the church, thought Finn, with a rueful smile. He half expected to see a purple crystal hanging from the roof somewhere. He caught himself looking for it, even though he knew it couldn't be there. The Leader hadn't been here. He would have felt it.

At the far end of the building there was a glass screen and then a five-metre drop. Going through an open glass door at the right-hand end of the glass screen, they made their way down an iron staircase that spiralled to the floor below. On the left was the seed vault and there she was.

Her body lay against the open door, preventing it from closing, a strange half smile on the lips of her perfectly frozen, alabaster face.

They stood looking at her for a long time.

I wonder why she did it.

Finn took a long time to reply and when he did, it was with a technical answer.

"Perhaps she opened the doors to let the cold into the seed bank. She had to keep the door open. With no electricity to drive the cooling machines and keep the air circulating, it might have become stagnant and damp inside. The seeds might have gone mouldy. Without the outside cold, the seeds could have been lost forever."

He is still a tec, thought Moot.

I don't think so. She paused. *I know why. If she hadn't, no one would ever be able to get in. This lock is too complex to break. She did it because she hoped someone would come for the seeds. Like us. This door locks itself. She had to stay there to keep the door open.*

Finn looked at Moot in admiration. She was shining again.

What she did saved the seeds for us to take to Eden. What she did, she did out of hope for the future. She sacrificed her life for Earth's future.

They stood there for a few minutes, looking at the woman in silent respect.

Then Finn led the way, carefully stepping over the frozen sentinel and entering the seed bank.

What do we want?

Finn opened his coat and delved into a deep pocket. "Here. It's Nisha's list."

They explored the rows of shelves, with their neat alphabetically labelled signs telling them what plants the seeds were from. Using Nisha's lists they worked diligently, searching the shelves for what they needed.

They piled their selections in small heaps at the ends of the aisles. It took hours to find everything. Eventually they collected the piles of seeds together, packing them into the cloth seed bags Nisha had given Finn.

They climbed back up the spiral staircase, leaving the woman to her frozen vigil. Finn looked about them. The light blue twilight had turned a darker hue. They had spent a long time in the seed bank.

"Should we camp down here tonight?" asked Finn. Yet even before Moot's reply came into his mind, he knew the answer was no.

Not here, it doesn't feel right. Not with the woman at the entrance. It's almost like she's still guarding it. We're only welcome to take what we need and then we must move on. It's what she would want.

They took their precious load and carefully climbed up the ladder and out through the broken roof. They made their way back to the ancient house.

After hiding the Snowmobile beneath Finn's white tent, they dug around until they found a window to climb through. Beyond, there was a series of empty rooms. They made themselves comfortable for the night.

The following morning, they searched through the house to see what they could find. There was a kitchen without food and an empty office.

Moot searched through the other rooms and came back to the office to find Finn looking at a plan of the whole of Wakehurst.

"Moot, we need fuel for the Snowmobile. We haven't got enough to get us to Eden. I have to fill the fuel tank from our containers and that'll leave them half empty. We need more fuel or we'll have to walk to Eden and that'll take a long time."

What do we do Finn?

"It said in the booklets they did a lot of work here with machines. Something called a tractor and there were mowers and diggers too. They would have needed a large tank for all the fuel. I think it's here, where it says workshop. Look." Finn pointed to a large rectangular shape on the map. "The fuel might have evaporated or there might still be some left. We have to dig and find out."

Taking measurements from the map they paced out where they thought the workshop would be. Digging down they were soon rewarded with broken tiles and wooden slats. The weight of the snow above it had caused part of the roof to collapse. They dug further until they found the huge fuel tank in the corner. The tank didn't sound empty. After more digging they found a tap. Finn eventually managed to turn it and the fuel ran, filling their containers. Finn used some cloth to filter it.

"We must take all we can Moot. I'll do the filling. See if there's anything else about that we can use to put the fuel in."

Rummaging around beneath the sagging roof, Moot found a pile of plastic bottles with a funnel. They were saved again.

They packed everything, tying the new containers of fuel across the Snowmobile with rope from the workshop. They roared off, heading back to Eden at last.

For three days they travelled until, a short way from Eden, the fuel ran out and they abandoned the Snowmobile and everything they didn't need. They walked the last few miles, carrying the crystals and seeds.

Moot gasped when she saw the domes of Eden. They stood on the edge of the old quarry and watched the plastic and aluminium sparkling in the afternoon sun.

Finn remembered his feeling of awe when he'd first seen the rainforest and Mediterranean biomes? He wondered what Moot would say when she saw what was inside them. Despite all the challenges he'd had to face, he'd returned to Eden with the crystals and the seeds. And just as Nisha had said he would, he'd had help. He couldn't imagine Moot not being with him now. He couldn't have completed his task without her.

Smiling, Finn led the way down the path.

Part four-Return to Eden

RETURN TO EDEN

Chapter 1

They are sleeping now, exhausted from their journey and our celebrations. It has been a day for celebrating. Finn has returned, bringing Moot, his companion, with him. She is delightful. They complement each other so well and see each other as equals. How I have longed for this. It is so good to have him back. He has grown into a man on his journey, yet he does not see how much he has changed

I asked spirit to help you Finn and you have been kept safe. I feel I can let out the breath I was holding for so long. Thank you.

Nisha replaced her pen, closed her journal and sat crossed legged on her mat. She closed her eyes and deepened her breathing. Her face relaxed and a faint outline of golden light appeared around her.

***

Lying comfortably in his bed, Finn smiled as he thought of all that had happened the day before when he and Moot had arrived in Eden.

Nisha had been weeding the vegetable garden. Glancing up, she'd seen them. With a shriek of, "Finn!" she'd run to him, wrapping him in her muddy arms just like a mother would welcome her child. Moot had stood in amazement at Nisha's display of love for him. She was even more amazed when Nisha hugged her too.

Now I know why Nisha's not your woman, laughed Moot. *She's your mother!*

Moot's piercing shriek burst into Finn's mind and he blushed bright red.

He went red again as he thought of it.

Nisha laughed, too. "No Moot, I am not Finn's woman or his mother. I am his friend."

Moot's hand went to her mouth, as if she had spoken aloud.

"You hear her!" the words had jumped from Finn's lips, despite his embarrassment.

"Of course I can hear her Finn," a mischievous look came into Nisha's eyes. "Why would you think I couldn't? Are you going to be his woman, Moot?"

Then it had been Moot's turn to blush.

"You two are like beetroots," said Nisha, laughing.

Beetroots?

"A round red vegetable," said Nisha. She had sighed, "I'm sorry Moot. I am only playing. I have been a little lonely since Finn left. You must find your own way. May I ask where you get such an unusual name?"

As Moot had explained, Finn's thoughts had run along a different path. Would Moot be his woman? Would they have children to help repopulate the earth? He'd pushed the thoughts from his mind. He did so again. Not now. They had work to do.

He had seen Nisha's joy as they placed the crystal and seed bags before her. She had touched them reverently. Her eyes had shone as she thanked them. She'd stumbled over her words as she'd tried to express her joy and gratitude. She'd listened intently as he'd described his journey with Linda, how he had found Moot, what had happened with Dent and the slavers in London and their escape to Kew on the snowmobile.

He had noticed Nisha's brow furrow when he told her about The Leader and how it must have been him who placed the purple crystal in the church. He didn't mention what he'd found about The Amon Ra Project.

He hadn't been ready to talk about that.

"Finn! Breakfast."

Nisha's shout shook him from his daydream. When he arrived at the table, Moot and Nisha were dressed and Nisha had already shown her some of Eden.

"I knew you wouldn't mind, Finn? You were so tired and Moot had woken early."

There was a bird, Finn. It came and ate from my hand and a butterfly landed on me. It was wonderful. We had nothing like this in Our Place.

And he hadn't minded. He was not jealous, as he might once have been. They talked contentedly as they ate.

He showed Moot his room, where Nisha had treated him when he'd fallen into Eden.

His room. He was surprised at its comforting familiarity.

This was his room.

This was his home.

He was home.

His thoughts startled him. He hadn't realised how 'home' had crept up on him.

Eden was home. Nisha was home.

He grabbed Moot's hands and laughed and

shouting, they danced joyfully around the room together. Swinging round and round until they were dizzy, collapsing into a heap of happiness and contentment.

Later Nisha examined the crystals.

"You chose well Finn. These crystals are wonderful," she smiled. "Moot, tell me, how did the crystals open your mind?"

I don't know what happened, Nisha. When Finn placed the first shining crystal in my hand, I suddenly found I could see things clearly. Finn saw what happened.

Finn described the white light he had seen around Moot and Moot explained how she had been able to sense the slavers and outwit their leader despite him also having the gift.

Finn showed Nisha the crystals that had woken Moot's abilities.

Nisha examined them, one by one, holding them, feeling their energy.

"They are wonderful Moot. There is more to be learned. We must work together, you and I."

Again, Finn was not jealous. They shared each other's time and company.

***

A few days later, Nisha chose new crystals for Finn to insert into the generating machines and then he reset the fuel cells, so that power could flow into the temperate biome.

He watched Nisha and Moot work together to place new crystals in the cleansed temperate biome. He saw the energy flow and the crystal patterns shining brightly in the twilight, powering the biome and protecting its structure.

It took time for the heat to spread, even though the soil was now sterilised. It needed time to warm enough for seeds to grow. "Like it would in spring, in the before times," explained Nisha.

She sorted the seeds and made plans for sowing them. Finn and Moot found themselves caught up with Nisha's excitement. She set them to work and they learnt quickly.

Each day, after working with Nisha in the garden, they all wandered in Eden.

As they followed Nisha beneath the trees, something startling happened to Finn. The pale sun, now at its highest, shone down through the latticework of leaves above Nisha, making shadow patterns on her pale clothes.

Finn stared. Light dark, light dark and he was in the pit again: a growing gallery. The high stalks of sweet corn towered above his young body. The glaring lights shone through the featherlike leaves and there was the pattern of light dark, light dark on his arm as he reached up to pick the enormous cob of corn. He flinched as he remembered the pain of the corn spider's bite. The poison spread quickly through his little body. He'd seen others, grown men, die from such a bite. How had he survived such agony? A slow smile spread across his features as he answered his own question. To be here of course!

Was he starting to accept Nisha's incredible explanations? He laughed in triumphant disbelief. Nisha had stopped and turned at his laughter. She and Moot stared at him quizzically. He grinned back at them and then suddenly dashed off along the path, offering them no explanation.

Moot found him later, after Nisha had gone to pick vegetables for their evening meal. He was sitting on a bench listening to Eden's life, its noisy chatter.

Finn was relaxed. Contentment oozed from him. Moot looked at him intently.

This is your home Finn, isn't it?

"Yes Moot," Finn smiled. "This is my home and it's yours too."

Moot looked at him in surprise for a moment.

Yes, I think it is.

Moot smiled. She had a home.

***

They dug the earth, and bringing barrow loads of compost from the heaps in the other domes, they began sowing seeds in the temperate biome. Nisha directed them and they worked hard at completing the jobs. They settled into comforting work routines. Days passed. Together they celebrated when, after a few weeks, the first green shoots pushed their way up through the dark earth.

***

A week after arriving, Moot and Finn returned to the abandoned snowmobile to collect the things they'd discarded. He didn't want to leave it any longer in case of a heavy snowfall. After collecting and putting everything they wanted into their packs, they stood looking at the snowmobile.

"It's a beautifully made machine, Moot, but without fuel; it's of no use to us."

Is there anywhere we might find more fuel, like we did at Wakehurst?

"Perhaps. We'll need to take a lot of equipment with us when we go to the Amon Ra islands. Even if we did find fuel, I don't think the snowmobile is powerful enough to pull everything we need."

Why haven't you told Nisha about the islands yet? She thinks we're here to stay?

"I don't want to spoil her happiness. She is so pleased." He smiled. "She loves you Moot."

I know Finn. Nisha is my friend. I wouldn't want to upset her either, but you have to tell her sometime.

"I will Moot. Just not yet. I can prepare things without saying. We need to be ready first and I'm still thinking of how we're going to get there anyway. If I hadn't traded my sledge to Linda, we could've pulled it easily between us."

If we had two sledges it would be easier still. If I pulled one too, we could take a lot more with us.

"Are you strong enough to pull a sledge Moot?"

He could easily pull a sledge. Moot hadn't had his training. The tasks she had worked on at Our Place wouldn't have made her fit enough to pull a sledge.

I'm sure I could do it Finn. I know I'm not as strong

as you, but if I trained, I would get stronger. You could teach me how to ride the bicycles, couldn't you?

Finn nodded. "Yes. We'll start as soon as we get back," He smiled. "It'll be fun."

Looking at the snowmobile, his mind went elsewhere. Their journey would take a long time and there was a limit to what they could pull, even with two of them. Could he make two sledges? Were there enough resources in the supply store? Maybe there was timber and metal he could use from around Eden?

They couldn't take enough food for a return journey. He wasn't even sure they could take enough food to get there either. They were leaping into the unknown. Yet they had to go. Nisha said they were always kept safe and after all that had happened, he believed it.

The snowmobile pushed back into his mind. It had runners to slide over the snow and ice. Moot helped him remove the runners using the tools in the snowmobile tool kit Dent had provided for emergencies. He would fit them on a new sledge.

***

"Moot, today I will teach you how to ride a bicycle."

Moot smile was broad as they made their way to the

storeroom. She was impressed with the big, fat tyres on the bicycle she chose, the shiny paint and chrome. She watched Finn cycle. She admired his easy balance.

I don't think I can do that.

"Yes, you can," insisted Finn. But she couldn't. He had forgotten how long it had taken him to learn. He had spent hours of practice on the exercise bike in the pit and he was determined not to be defeated when he learnt to ride his own bicycle in Eden. That now seemed so long ago, yet was just a few short months.

Moot wasn't used to it. Her legs ached and despite Finn's help; she kept falling over and hurting herself.

She pushed the bicycle away and stood looking at it with folded arms. She was almost in tears.

I can't do it.

It was Nisha who helped.

It was Nisha and her patience that gave Moot her confidence.

It was Nisha's kindness, her praise for every small step, which kept Moot going.

It was Nisha who ran behind her and pushed.

It was Nisha who massaged Moot's limbs with sweet smelling oil to take away their aches.

It was Nisha who cleaned Moot's grazes, applying

soothing ointment and dressings to help them heal.

And finally it was Nisha who cheered first when Moot eventually managed to stay upright and not fall off when she put the brakes on.

Together, Finn and Moot cycled along the paths in Eden. Moot gained confidence and most importantly, strength and fitness for their journey ahead. Finn practised most, showing his determination to be ready for their journey.

Moot glowed with health. Good food, exercise, the light of the sun and above all, good companions. She thrived amongst those who loved her. Nisha was so content and happy. She called Finn and Moot her Earth Children and caught herself singing a song her father had taught her. Something she had not done for a long time. Her heart felt full to bursting, she was so happy.

Only, something in the back of her mind said, enjoy it whilst you can Nisha, it will not last. Yet she ignored the signs and lived only in the moment.

Chapter 2

I can feel it, Finn. You are preparing to leave. You are making your plans and Moot will go with you. Something calls and your purpose waits for you.

I did not think I would have to say goodbye so soon. It has been such a short time since you returned. I had thought you would stay longer. I had thought we would plant more seeds and watch them grow and nurture them together. I had thought I'd teach you about the crystals and I would have taught Moot to read too. All this must wait for your return.

I know you will return.

Only... only... without you and Moot, Eden will feel so empty, as it did not before your arrival, when I was truly alone? Perhaps my heart did not know what it had been missing since my father died.

I understand why you do not wish to tell me yet.

I too will say nothing... until I must.

Nisha put her pen down and sat still, only her lips

moved as she repeated words that Finn would not have recognised. A vague shadow emerged from a mist in her mind. An ancient animal sat upon a human head. It spoke to her, yet she could not grasp its meaning. An arm extended and a bird's wing cut the air. A shinning green light appeared. She followed the light and her face and body relaxed. A brightness came across her features as if a light shone upon them. Now she understood. They were to be helped. Something was to be fulfilled. She sat for a long time.

***

Finn looked at the computer screen, studying The Amon Ra Project page. Despite everything he'd tried, there was nothing more than the one page and its message remained the same.

There was no choice. They must journey out across the frozen Atlantic Ocean and find the islands where The Amon Ra Project had been built. It was a vast distance, much further than travelling to London and back. Yet what else were they to do? The papers on the wall in Dent's hideaway had shown him where they must go.

How would they get there? He had solved challenges easily when he was in the pit? He always knew what to do with machinery. This was different. He wrestled with it, unable to tell Nisha and unwilling to burden Moot. He lay sleepless at night, staring at the dark ceiling. When he did sleep, he would wake suddenly in the middle of dreams, knowing the answer was within his reach, only for it to fade before he could remember it.

***

He walked the paths in the rainforest biome: tramping round and round on his own. Something began to surface in his mind. Was that a voice he could hear in the distance? What was it trying to tell him?

Later, trying to sleep, Finn caught himself thinking of the puzzle his father had made for him in the pit. He watched his father helping him fit the pieces together.

Why did he remember that now? He put the thoughts out of his mind, trying to let the pieces of the puzzle join and connect themselves without his conscious interference. A warm glow spread though him as he remembered his father helping him. He sensed his mother's gaze and then the memory was gone, leaving an indefinable feeling of happiness entwined with a sense of loss. Momentarily his mind became a torrent of emotion and then sleep ambushed him unexpectedly with confused dreams of his childhood in the pit.

***

When the sun started creeping across Eden's vast domes, Finn crept from his bed. As he washed, he looked in the mirror at the dark circles beneath his eyes. His restless nights were taking its tool. Nisha said nothing, but she knew what was in his mind, he was sure.

Yet he felt an answer had inserted itself somewhere in his mind and he must follow it. He took food from the kitchen and finding his way out of Eden from behind the restaurant, he went searching. For what, he wasn't quite sure.

He hadn't explored this side of Eden, so he climbed the snow-covered road that wound up to the quarry edge, until, behind the stark limbs of dead trees pointing to the sky, he came to an area of storage sheds and outbuildings.

He stood in front of a wide galvanised metal door set in a single-story building with a red tiled roof. His palms tingled as they had when he felt the crystal energy in the Geology Museum. Was this telling him he'd found what he was looking for?

He grabbed the handle mounted near the bottom of the door and pulled. It didn't move. It was frozen shut. He kicked away the snow and ice along its bottom edge and grabbing the handle again, he wrenched it upwards. The frozen metal screeched and moved. He pulled once more and with a squeal of grinding metal and ice it lurched up overhead and slid back to reveal a huge dark space.

Massive irregular shapes, covered with grey dust sheets, filled the interior. What did they cover? He pulled at the nearest sheet; it slithered from the shape and slipped to the ground.

Finn gazed in awe at the machine before him.

A TRACTOR!

He'd seen pictures of tractors in books in the pit library. They were farm equipment. With their enormous wheels, tractors could move effortlessly over rough, muddy ground. They would travel over snow and ice with ease. Excitedly he walked around the vehicle that just might take them to The Amon Ra Project.

This was what he'd been led to. This was what they needed. More and more he was accepting what Nisha said about trusting. Every time he'd needed something, it somehow turned up.

The tractor's blue and white bodywork shone. Its massive black tyres, on their white rims, looked flat. He must inflate them? A transparent cab with a blue roof covered the driver's seat and controls. A tall black exhaust was attached vertically to the right of the cab.

He laughed and smiled to himself as he examined the engine. He climbed up and sat in the cab. He could put another seat in here for Moot. The ignition key had been left in place. He could start it.

He climbed down and walked around it. What a marvellous piece of machinery. Whatever their faults, the ancients had known how to make things that moved.

Would it use the same fuel as the snowmobile? A label beside the fuel tank filler pipe said 'Diesel'. Where had he heard diesel before?

It was Dent. What was it he'd said?

"Don't put diesel in the snowmobile. Even winter diesel. It'll damage the engine. You want petrol."

How had Dent known that? He hadn't asked him. Dent hadn't looked strong enough for questions. Finn had heard of diesel though. It was a better fuel than petrol for big vehicles, only the ancients had gradually stopped using it because it gave off a lot of pollution. Winter diesel made sense. Diesel must freeze in the cold and they added something to stop it. It was certainly cold now. Would there be any winter diesel stored here? Would it still work the tractor engine? If he could find some, it would help them travel at least some of the long distance they needed to reach the Amon Ra Project.

He removed the other covers one by one. There were other tractors and a black, electrically powered vehicle. Its range would be limited and he couldn't recharge it on their journey anyway. He'd stick with the tractor. It offered them their best chance if he could find some diesel.

The final cover slid off to reveal a wagon with passenger seats. It must have been used to take visitors on tours round Eden. If he removed the seats there'd be plenty of room for all their gear.

Now, where did they store their diesel? It didn't take him long to find the pump. It was outside, next to the road. Behind it, almost hidden by a snow drift was a huge cylinder fixed to the ground. He scraped away the snow and ice and eventually found a gauge. It was over half full. Finn jumped up and down in delight.

Was it winter diesel though?

The lid on top unscrewed easily and he climbed up and shone the torch inside. A blast of fumes hit him. He coughed and looked away. It was a liquid! He could see a liquid.

It must be winter diesel!

It was still only mid-morning. He had enough time to service the tractor and fix anything that needed it. Then if he could transfer some diesel from the storage tank to the tractor, he could try starting it.

At the rear of the building, there was a workstation with tools, a work manual for the tractor and everything else he needed. He worked fast, enjoying the challenge. His knowledge and intuition of how machines worked helped him understand the manual. He lost himself in his work and forgot about eating the lunch he'd brought.

Much later, in the afternoon, he stood before the tractor. He'd serviced and checked everything, using parts from the other vehicles when necessary.

It was ready. There were just the tyres to inflate. He could do that after he'd started the engine, using the tractor's power to work the pump he'd found.

Geordie would have been proud of him. Geordie… It had been so long since Finn had thought of Geordie. It was not that he'd forgotten him, how could he ever forget. It was more that he was now in Finn's memory and not in the front of his mind. He thanked Geordie for being there when he needed him.

Now for the fuel.

There was a drainage tap beneath the tank, just where he thought it would be. He levered the tap open slightly and used a plastic bucket to catch the fuel as it dribbled out.

Using a funnel he poured it into the tractor's fuel tank and primed the fuel line and pump.

It was ready. Would it work?

"Nisha, I wish your god to please help this tractor start," he whispered.

This was as close to praying as he could get.

He sat in the cab, breathed out and turned the key.

With a stammering throb and a shuddering roar, the engine stated. A burst of foul-smelling smoke belched from the exhaust as Finn hit the throttle and the engine thundered. An ear-splitting boom.

Finn grinned. he'd done it. He'd made it work.

He shouted, "Thank you!" to Nisha's god, put the

machine in gear and drove it out of the garage.

He smiled. They had everything they needed.

All he had to do now was tell Nisha they were going.

He could delay it no longer.

He drove the tractor from the garage and carefully began the slow descent on the access road. He swung it around the southern end of Eden and drove to the entrance.

From inside, Nisha looked on in amazement as the tractor roared up to the doors and stopped. Finn put the hand brake on and turned off the engine. He climbed down from the cab, went through the doors and there was Nisha. Moot was close by, but she hung back a little, waiting.

"Is this what you will use on your next journey?" Nisha's voice was soft.

Finn was reluctant to say the words. Yet he must.

"You know I have to go, Nisha."

"Yes, Finn. I know." There was a sad inevitability in her voice. "I have known ever since you returned with Moot, and Moot shall go with you." Nisha sighed. "I just didn't think it would be so soon. You have been home for such a short time."

There was that word 'home' again, thought Finn.

"It has been seven weeks, Nisha," he replied.

"Only seven weeks!"

"Yes, but it feels like a lifetime," he smiled. "A good lifetime."

Nisha smiled too.

"What is this machine, Finn?"

"It's a tractor. I found it in a building up near Eden's rim. It will take Moot and me to The Amon Ra Project. We found more, so much more, about the Amon Ra Project than I have said. I know what it is and what needs to be done,"

"Where is it, Finn?"

"It is a long way out in the frozen Atlantic Ocean."

"Tell me why you must go there."

"The ancients' world began to heat up, unbearably. There were many, many problems. You said they were warned. You were right. They caused it. They weren't as clever as they thought they were. Their lack of action made it worse.

In a last desperate measure, their scientists decided to move the earth further from the sun, so it would be cooler. Something went wrong. The Earth moved too far. It cooled too much, too quickly, and the earth became a ball of snow and ice. Civilisation collapsed.

We are the survivors."

"How do you know this, Finn?"

"It was written on paper stuck on a wall in Dent's hiding place."

"Waiting for you to read it," Nisha smiled.

Finn grinned.

"Dent told me some, too, and I worked the rest out. In the Atlantic there is a crack under the sea. The ancients constructed two islands there and used the power of the molten core to move the Earth. That's when something went wrong. We must go there and I must fix it."

"It will put you and Moot in great danger, Finn."

"Yes," he shrugged. "We have to go. There isn't a choice."

"The Leader will be waiting for you."

"Yes."

"Could you not go alone?"

"No. Moot can do things I cannot. I need her help, just as I need your help, Nisha. You've known all along I couldn't stay. Haven't you?"

Nisha nodded.

"I ignored it." She laughed. "You are not the only one who hides things Finn. I do it too." She looked into his eyes. "Yes, you must go. The Earth demands it. You know what needs to be done. I understand this. I... I... I cannot be..." Nisha struggled to say the word. "Selfish. Since you have returned, I have wanted everything to stay the same. Before you first arrived, I was," Nisha had tears in her eyes. "I was so used to being alone; I had closed off my heart without realising it. You opened it. I didn't want you to go to London. I sent you because I had no choice. I don't want you to go now Finn, but I know you have no choice."

Her tears turned to sobs and she crushed him to her as if she would never let him go.

"I love you so much, Finn. I know you have to go, but part of me pleads with you, please don't, please don't." The love in her voice pierced his heart. As if she had grasped it in her hands, touching that which made him Finn.

"Go then, Finn," whispered Nisha. "Take Moot and heal the world. And then come home and heal my loneliness."

She dropped her arms, wiped her eyes and stood back from him.

"How can I help you prepare for your journey?"

Finn smiled. She was back to the Nisha she was and always had been.

He spent long hours with Moot in the workshop, making the sledges for when the tractor's fuel ran out. He taught Moot how to use the tools as they worked. She learnt quickly and became skillful in a very short time. She helped him with the designs and everything else they had to do; it took almost a month to complete the sledges and be ready.

He serviced the wagon they would take for their supplies. They transferred the diesel fuel from the storage tank into containers to fit in the wagon.

He worked out how far they could travel with the fuel they had. It wouldn't take them all the way. They'd have to walk with the sledges over the last part.

He calculated the weight of the tractor and checked the thickness of frozen sea ice in the Survival Handbook. The sea ice was usually two or three metres thick in this sort of cold, which was more than enough to support the tractor, although they would have to look out for pressure ridges, from sea currents moving below the ice.

The preparations took over their lives, yet soon they would be ready.

Chapter 3

Early one morning, clad in her warmest clothes, Nisha stood outside the dome's main entrance. The last few weeks had gone by so quickly.

They had cooked a mountain of food, placing it outside to freeze. Finn had helped Nisha refine the oil they would need for cooking and the lamps. Nisha had taught Moot how to dry the fruit they picked.

They had harvested fish from the pond: freeze drying them outside on the racks Finn constructed. Everything had been packed on top of the fuel containers in the wagon. The new sledges were lashed to the roof. All was ready. The tractor waited.

They said their final goodbyes. Nisha gave them each a shining protection crystal. She hugged them both in turn and then they embraced together for a very long time. Finally, silently, she let them go and they climbed into the tractor's cab.

Finn started the engine and Nisha watched as they

climbed the slope to leave Eden. She returned their last farewell wave when they reached Eden's rim. She kept watching long after they disappeared from sight, listening to the sound of the tractor's engine until it faded to nothing. It was only then that she whispered, almost as if they could hear her, "May the Source of all things be with you on your journey, Finn and Moot. Return home, safely."

***

Finn drove the tractor into the white, Moot at his side. His thoughts whirled as they travelled across the harsh land. Could they have stayed a little longer with Nisha? She had so loved him and Moot being there. They were her Earth Children.

Yet, he was the child that had to leave home, to make his own choices. And it was only because of Nisha that he was able to do this. Nisha had helped him become the strong young man that he now was. She had saved him from being stuck in his childhood. And now he had to leave, taking Moot with him. There had been no other choice. The world could not be allowed to remain in winter.

They exchanged the peace of Eden and Nisha's love, for the perils of the white waste. Moot and Nisha's friendship, begun with Nisha's warm welcome, and blossoming as they all worked together, was left incomplete.

Since the awakening of Moot's abilities, Moot had shown how gifted she was. Being mute did not matter. She worked with the crystal energy, talked to the deva spirits and used the crystals to help the plants grow. He still sometimes saw their emerald green figures from a distance. Moot saw them easily, at any distance.

They had planned their route together, drawing it on the map they found in Eden. They would travel along the Cornish coast for as long as they could. Then after crossing the frozen channel there was Brittany and the Bay of Biscay until they reached Spain's northern coast. Finally they would go due west over the frozen Atlantic Ocean to the Amon Ra islands.

The Amon Ra Project was out there waiting for them. Together they must find it.

Inside the cab, they were sheltered from the white waste. The heat from the engine kept them warm. This was travelling in luxury compared to pulling the sledges or even riding the snowmobile. That had been fast, but intensely cold with the wind whistling past them.

It had been difficult for Moot, too. Reading the map and using the compass had been a challenge. Being inside the cab was much easier. She became expert at map reading. The only time they had to stop was so she could get out and away from the tractor's vibration and magnetic influence to check the compass to make sure they were going the right way.

Even so, the ever-present rumbling growl of the engine was tiring. The ear defenders they wore kept out the noise, but it could not stop the vibrations. Only when Finn turned the engine off, did silence return, giving a wonderful sense of peace.

The tractor's huge tyres made it easy to travel over the ice and snow that covered the Cornish countryside. The trailer bumped along behind them. Even deep drifts were not a problem, although eventually the rising cliffs meant they had to go down onto the sea ice to cross the Channel and head south to France.

Finn drove the tractor across a flat beach onto the ice-covered sea. Travelling on the frozen sea was very different from the even terrain of the land. The pressure from the currents moving beneath the ice had pushed it into great ridges. Where it had cracked, huge, irregular blocks of ice had been thrust up, to tumble down on either side.

To make it worse, a sudden mist formed around them. Even with the compass, it was hard to keep the right direction.

The tractor lumbered along in low gear. Its tyres, gripping well on snow, sometimes slid on smooth, wind-swept ice. They avoided the huge chunks of ice sticking up around the pressure ridges. Carefully, they threaded their way through the twisted landscape.

"Do you know exactly where we are Moot?" he shouted above the noise of the engine.

Moot grinned.

I can hear you Finn, no need to shout. I'm not sure where we are precisely. The map's no good on the sea ice. We will find the French coast so long as we keep going south. She smiled. I don't think we'll miss it. I'll use the compass to correct our direction as we go and then I'll be able to feel where we are when we get closer.

Finn smiled and nodded.

They drove on.

***

The sun moved closer to the horizon. Finn gauged the

amount of daylight left. He felt Moot's gaze.

"What do you think?"

We won't reach land tonight.

"Do we need to stop and camp?"

Moot shrugged.

Finn gave her an anxious look. They drove on.

We have to stop soon, Finn.

"I know," he replied. "Even with the headlights, I can't see properly anymore." He looked around. "I was hoping we wouldn't have to camp on the sea ice. The thought of all that water beneath us..." He stopped and Moot caught a glimpse of his mental shudder.

What about over there?

Moot pointed to some strangely shaped, smooth ice, caught in the beam from the headlights.

Finn smiled as he steered the tractor towards it.

"Is this a feeling or do you just want to stop?"

Moot laughed. *Both, I think.*

Finn turned off the engine. They got down from the cab, adjusting their clothes for the cold.

The ice curved up and away from them. It had a darker tinge than the rest. Finn stared at it and rubbed his glove across the surface.

"Look!" he exclaimed, "It's wood, frozen under the

ice. Just like at the church. Remember I told you?"

What is it then? It can't be a church in the sea.

"I think it's a ship. A wooden one. I saw pictures of them in books in the pit library and there was a small boat on the pond, remember, in the Rainforest Biome. Ships float on water and the ancients travelled over the sea in them. This one must've got frozen and couldn't escape. We might be able to shelter in it."

How do we get in?

"There must be a door somewhere."

Finn walked along beside the curved ice, stopping to rub at the surface occasionally as he went. Moot walked the other way.

Finn.

"What?"

Bring the torch. I've found something.

Her side of the ice-covered ship was smooth and flat. Almost hidden behind a large mass of ice, was a small dark opening.

I'll go in. It feels okay.

After winding Dent's torch, she squeezed herself through the opening. Finn followed.

Moot held the torch high in the space below the deck of the ship. It was cold but dry. The ice had pushed the ship over and where bunks had been at the side of the ship, they were now on the floor. Someone had made the space into a comfortable living area. Bedding and clothes were strewn about.

"This hasn't been used for a long time. We can stay here tonight," said Finn. "It'll be better than the tent. We can see where we are tomorrow."

There are cliffs marked on the map. If we can find a place where you can drive up, I'll be able to work out where we are on the French map and point us in the right direction.

"I'll fetch what we need."

There was no food in the ship, just a bin full of empty packets. Finn pushed a makeshift door shut from the inside, being careful to leave an air gap.

After eating, they settled down for the night, climbed into their sleeping bags and huddled together for comfort and warmth.

* * *

Finn opened his eyes. He floated high above the ice. Below him the land and sea were spread out like a map. He blinked. The last thing he remembered was lying next to Moot and thinking about tomorrow.

Was this a dream? Something within his mind said

no. This was like him floating out of his body when he fell into Eden and injured himself. That was because he'd hit his head and the fever caused by the bad meat. Whatever had triggered this, he could see the ship, far below him, where they lay sleeping. It stood out, illuminated by a pale blue light. He was flying high above their sleeping forms.

A sudden force, like the wind, but not, blew at him, twisting him around. A shape flashed past him and as he looked, there was Moot coming back towards him. It was a Moot he hadn't seen before. She was flying, too and she was silver. She was silver starlight; she was glistening moonlight and she was smiling and laughing at him. He grinned back as she hovered in front of him and she spoke. Her words poured into his head like a rushing mountain stream.

Finn, this is wonderful. How did we do it?

He spoke and heard his thoughts go straight into Moot's mind.

I don't know. I think we're asleep. Maybe it's the crystals that Nisha gave us for the journey.

Moot nodded. *It doesn't matter Finn. Look, that's what we need to see.*

He turned his gaze to where she pointed.

To the south, there was the coast with the cliffs they were heading for. The land dipped in and then jutted out again. From above, the peninsular looked like the ragged outline of a massive bird, with wings to the north and south. Its tail was joined to the land in the east. In front of its head, like some strange sharp beak, disconnected knife-like shards of land stood up from the ice. On the point where its eye would be, was a bright silver, violet light. It pulsed like a beacon.

That's why we're up here Finn. We needed to see this. It's somewhere we have to go.

Yes, Finn nodded. That was it. They must go there. Why, he didn't know. Moot obviously didn't either. Yet they must go there. Something was guiding them.

Then he saw it. Something back on the cliffs, not too far from where they slept on the ship, something long that glowed with a paler violet light.

Look Moot. Over there. We must go there first.

Moot nodded.

Yes. You're right Finn. It's important.

Abruptly, the land was gone. All was black and he could hear Moot's gentle breathe beside him.

***

There'd been no chance of getting onto the land that morning when they reached the coast. Huge cliffs reared up out of a thick mist that held them in its cocoon of white, muting the noise of the tractor's engine. Moot struggled to locate where they were. What was so clear, when they'd floated over the land last night, was much harder to find at ground level.

After spending hours slowly following the shrouded coastline, a gusting wind tore the mist to shreds and the ascending sun showed them the cliffs. Much later, with the sun raised high above the land; they found the estuary leading to the site of the pale violet light.

The tractor pulled its loaded trailer across the wide frozen bay. They could see where they needed to go. An ice-covered headland pushed out into the bay, its highest point dominating the whole area. Travelling around its western side, they could see a rounded shape sitting on the summit, widening as it flowed down the hill.

The north western side looked as if something huge had taken a giant bite out of it. A series of wide, flat, interlinked pathways and platforms, like massive steps, were built into the outer edge of the monument.

There were more steps on the southern side, above a series of dark openings that were spaced along the whole of that side.

The wind had cleared the snow from the smooth area surrounding it, leaving a mottled white layer with dark clumps of dead grass poking through. The shape itself sparkled. Was this the source of the pale violet light they had seen pulsing in last night's darkness?

They found a way onto the riverbank and drove up the hill from inland. Finn brought them to a halt a short distance away from the shape and they dismounted, walking the final part. It felt the right thing to do. The wind had died and without the tractor's engine, a cold silence closed in. Only the snow crunching beneath their boots disturbed it.

As they drew closer, they could see why the surface glistened so strangely. The huge monument was built from thousands of different sized flat rocks. The gaps between them were crammed with frozen snow and ice, which must have been partly melted and frozen many times over. The sun shone on these cracks, making the massive grey structure look as if it was covered by a huge, irregular, sparkling white, net.

From this high point they could see across the

whole of the ice-covered bay and out across the frozen sea. Slowly, they walked around the stone structure.

What was this place for? There, as in their travels last night, was the part that looked as if something had taken a giant bite out of it. As well as the dark openings, there were several tunnels going right through it.

Unlike the huge buildings in London, it hugged the ground, growing organically out from the land like some strange gigantic fungi.

Cairn. The word came to Finn's mind.

They walked to the eastern end and stood beside it, wondering. Why had they been directed here? Was this a special place?

Finn's palms began to tingle. What was happening?

A mist arose, quickly rolling in across the snow and ice, isolating them.

Then as suddenly as it had appeared, the mist rolled back before them, restoring their view of the bay. They gaped in surprise, for the snow and ice in the bay had vanished. In its place the estuary and the sea beyond had changed and was now a vast plain of golden green grass that the wind blew into swirling patterns. Herds of browsing animals roamed amongst the occasional clusters of trees and bushes.

Is this what the before times were like?

No Moot. I think this is the very old times. Long, long ago.

Finn's mouth had not opened. He grasped Moot's arm.

Moot, did you hear me?

He felt her nod.

They turned and looked at each other. Finn had sent words from his mind, straight to Moot, as he had last night in their floating experience.

Had he become like Moot? Would he always be able to hear others now?

Only if you want to, Finn.

Moot's thought startled him. If he wanted to? Did he? Perhaps.

As they watched, the sun set, evening approached and the scene grew darker. A bright moon rose in a star strewn sky, turning everything to silver and black.

Out of the shadows, walked a column of people dressed in furs and vividly patterned, woven clothes. Some carried heavy loads, others held weapons and were obviously hunters and perhaps, warriors. They climbed the steep path that wound to the top of the hill.

Leading the column was a man wearing an animal headdress. To Finn it looked almost like one of Linda's husky dogs, yet not. Then he remembered! A picture from a book in the pit came to him and he knew. It was a wolf's head! The wolf man carried a bird's wing in his right hand and a leather bag hung from a belt at his waist. Behind him walked a group of men and women with skin covered wooden drums. A single drumbeat kept the walkers in rhythm.

They reached the south side where the openings were waiting like dark caves. They gathered in a half circle, Wolf Man standing before them. A low crying sound, almost like singing, started from one end of the watching people. It travelled back and forth from one end of the line to the other. All the while the single drum was pulsing, like a slow beating heart.

More drums joined, adding a rich texture to the rhythms. A fire was started in a big clay pot in front of the crowd, smoke pouring from it. They smelt acrid smoke and then the sweet sharp smell of herbs. It engulfed the people and some of them entered the smoke, moving like shadows in and out of the swirling fog of smoke and herbs.

The drums and singing stopped abruptly and a slosh of water doused the fire. The smoke dissipated and Finn and Moot watched a group of men and women carry a heavy fabric covered shape towards one of the dark openings. It was unmistakable. They were witnessing a burial.

The group ducked their heads and carried the shape into one of the dark entrances to what must be burial chambers. They returned empty handed a few moments later and stood outside the chamber. One by one people from the crowd carried things, a stone axe, leather bags, animal skins and woven containers, to the burial group, who took them into the burial chamber.

The singing and drumming started again. The people began to move in rhythm and then started a slow, shuffling dance. It felt as though they were saying goodbye. There was a sad happiness to the music.

The drumming stopped and Wolf Man took something from his bag and held it aloft. Finn's heart jumped. Wolf Man was holding a purple crystal. The people sank to their knees. The warriors watched, standing as a ragged group.

Wolf Man said something and a warrior lit a flaming torch. He brought it forward and stood before the people. Wolf Man held the purple crystal in front of the flaming torch and a flickering, violet light shone out across everyone watching. Finn and Moot stared too, mesmerised, unable to look away.

The light penetrated deep into their minds. Relaxing and reassuring, it drove all fear away. To Finn it felt like a return of the light in the church. This time, though, it was different. It was benign, unthreatening, loving. He felt a gasp from Moot. Their minds touched for a moment and he saw something settle, protective, waiting, in Moot's mind. Waiting for what?

Who is he?

A reply came, almost as if Moot had asked the question out loud.

"I am shaman, healer, mage, priest and wise man. I am linked to spirit. I am The Leader."

The shaman's words were not in any language they had ever heard, yet they understood him and the pictures that accompanied the words.

He knows we're here, Finn.

The shaman pointed at a young man of around Finn's age, who sat on the ground. A slim, muscled figure, head bowed, brown shoulder length hair obscuring his features.

"It is time," the shaman's voice was soft, yet piercing.

Two men helped the young man to his feet. Another took a leather bag and put its straps across the young man's shoulders. A spear was placed in his hand and a belt holding a stone axe and knife was tied around his waist.

He stood before the shaman; head bowed; dejected, listless.

The shaman reached out a hand and, not unkindly, lifted the young man's head.

FINN! Moot's voice was a shriek. *It's YOU.*

Finn felt icy finger's moving up and down his spine. The hair on his neck prickled. His face paled.

He stared, astonished by the young man's uncanny resemblance. What did this mean?

Using the bird wing, the shaman brushed its feathers over and around the young man's shoulders and across his face. As the feathers touched his forehead, the young man's body jolted.

Finn's body jerked, too.

The young man's muscles tightened; his expression changed. Like someone waking from a deep sleep, he looked around him and tried to break free from the warriors.

They held him tight. The shaman chanted and used the feather again. The young man stood still.

The shaman pointed the feather at the young man and then aimed it exactly at Finn.

"This is your path. Go!"

Finn gasped. He was being sent away! Banished. Had this happened to him in this, another life? How was that possible?

The shaman pointed beyond them with the bird wing.

The mists retreated further and then they saw it: a silver green, shining ribbon of light that sprang from the centre of the cairn. It twisted and turned, shining, glistening, moving, as if it was alive, sliding down the hill and over the land, yet also a part of the landscape.

"See your path. Follow your path. Be the path. It is yours. Go!"

The young man looked about him. His gaze crossed Finn's. For a moment Finn felt almost a glint of recognition and then the young man strode away, walking alongside the shining ribbon of pulsating light.

The mist returned and the young man disappeared within its tendrils. Behind them, the single regular drumbeat restarted. The mist closed about them.

The scene began to fade, all except for the insistent drumbeat and the shaman. Finn stood there long after everything else was gone. His intense blue eyes looked straight at Finn.

"Go! Follow the path."

Was he waiting for a reply?

"Thank you," said Finn.

The drum faded. The shaman nodded and was gone.

***

It was still dark when he woke. They had talked about their shared vision at the cairn until late into the night. Moot came back again and again to the young man and his amazing likeness to Finn.

The purple crystal had brought Finn back to his memories and experiences in the church. None of it made sense. Finn felt Nisha might have explained it, but its meaning was beyond them. The only thing that was clear, the shining path must somehow lead them to the Amon Ra islands.

He shrugged off those thoughts and concentrated on the day ahead. Rubbing the sleep from his eyes, he wound the torch. The frost on the inside of the tent glittered in its beam. There was a little of Moot's pale face peeping from under the hood of her sleeping bag. He could just hear her light breath. He nudged her. They must leave early today.

***

Finn stood within the incomplete circle of stones. It had taken them two days to get here. The route had not been straightforward. They had followed the shining path. Sometimes it would disappear and Moot had to rely on the map and her feel for the land.

Now they were here. Standing on the eye of the bird they had seen on their first floating together. It stood on a flat piece of land not far from the cliffs towering above the sea. A series of huge stones ran east west in a long line. Coming off them, going north were lines of stones curving in towards each other like a broken circle with the missing stones along the northern edge. They stood together in the centre of the circle.

Energy suddenly poured into him.

Moot!

They touched hands and the energy flowed between and around them. It coursed and pulsed and for a few fleeting moments that seemed like hours, they became one, the primal energy of their spirits joined.

Separated, they were suddenly soaring through the sky as they had before. They floated high above the frozen sea. There was the incomplete stone circle, the tractor and their camp. What else? Ah, there was the bird image and running from its eye was the green ribbon of light. Their eyes followed as it zigzagged across the white waste of ice. Every time it changed direction; it left a small circle of light before it struck off again in a different direction. Where was this trail leading?

Then they saw it, their destination, far to the west. Two peaks: tall cones, one higher than the other. The tallest towered far above a ring of green at its feet and the circle of ice-free ocean surrounding it. Though that was not what held their attention.

It was the angry red light which held their gaze. Splintered with yellow and orange flashes, it pulsed above and around the peaks. This was where the danger to Eden had come from. This was the source of that which stopped the earth being what it could. This was the home of the computer terminal that needed Finn's attention. The Leader would try to stop Finn from fixing it and Moot had as big a part to play in this as Finn. He didn't know what she must do, but they had to do this together.

Chapter 4

They travelled west for several weeks following the shining path, hoping they were going in the right direction. And then one afternoon, as the wind began to rise and powdered snow was flung in their faces, they came across a ship in the frozen sea.

If a pressure ridge hadn't pushed its bow up out of the ice, they might not have seen it. Nearby, there were snow covered humps and bumps where supplies looked as if they had been unloaded by sailors trying to escape the frozen ship. They looked at the rope ladder hanging down from the deck. Should they go in?

"Look Moot, there's a boat missing." Finn pointed at the ropes dangling from the empty davits. "Maybe they used it as a sledge to carry their provisions. I wonder if they left anything we could use."

Could we shelter inside d'you think?

"It might be better than spending the night in the

tent."

He held the ladder tight whilst Moot climbed and then scrambled up after her. They explored the ship, finding food and fuel they could use.

It was when they reached the crew's quarters that they found the frozen bodies, huddled in their bunks.

Finn looked at the opened bottles of pills and alcohol. His mind went back to his journey from the pit. He remembered the castle and the frozen couple.

"They made their choices Moot."

I wonder if those who left ever reached land.

Moot's voice was sad, regretful. He glimpsed pictures in her mind, of the desperate survivors, struggling to drag the boat across the ice in a raging snowstorm. He understood her compassion.

"We'll never know, Moot." There was a note of kindness, of comfort, in his voice.

They left the bodies and spent an uneasy night in another cabin.

The following morning they woke early and stood in the dark beside the ship's rail, where the rope ladder hung.

Oh! Moot turned to Finn. *This is why we saw the shining green ribbon. Do you remember how it zigzagged between small circles of light?*

She pointed and they could see the ribbon of light in the darkness, leading away from the ship.

Ships, Finn, abandoned ships. The light's showing us a route we can follow from ship to ship. We'll have shelter and supplies to get us there.

Finn laughed at the simplicity of it. They were being shown. He thought of Nisha and smiled.

So they travelled, going from frozen shipwreck to frozen shipwreck, following the shining path whenever they could see it.

***

The storm struck fast. The wind blew wildly, uncontrollably. It grabbed snow and ice crystals and hurled them into the air. Tossed and pitched by the wind, they were driven horizontally, straight at them. It tore at the cab windows like the white wraiths scratching to get in that the pit dwellers talked of.

The memory arrived instantly in his mind. How he had listened with the other children as they talked of the snow spirits, the souls of the banished. They said the guards on the pit rim would be lured from their posts, to freeze to death as revenge for banishment. Where had that forgotten memory come from?

Stronger blasts of air snatched at them. The trailer was almost lifted from the ice, held down only by the weight of the tractor. Finn felt his very core shudder at the battering. He stopped the engine.

"I can't see," Finn shouted to Moot above the howl of the wind. The wind shrieked louder and the ice crystals cascaded against the window.

"We'll stay inside until it eases." He was shouting still. The noise of the gale deafening them.

Moot nodded.

Don't let it get inside your head, Finn. Focus on calm. Moot's voice was a small haven of quiet to sooth his battered senses.

They made themselves as comfortable as they could and Finn slipped into dreams.

He was walking, the last in a procession of the banished. Wrapped in mushrobes, they struggled through the snow, one footstep at a time. All around, snow spirits laughed at them, pulled at them, holding them back. And one by one, the banished fell over to sleep and die in the snow, except the figure in front of him. It stopped and turned to Finn. Its hood was pulled close about its face. It put out an arm and pointed forcefully with its mushglove. It raised the arm and brought it down, pointing, again and again. Finn looked on sleepily. He stood, unmoved. He was so sleepy, oh so sleepy. He looked at the figure helplessly. The wind caught at it and the hood went flying back to reveal the face of his mother.

Dream Finn accepted her presence. She shouted. He could see her lips move. What was she saying? He didn't understand. She pointed again and Finn turned his head and looked. There was the tractor. The ice in front of it was moving. A pressure ridge was pushing it up. It grew quickly, towering over them. He looked on powerlessly as blocks of ice began to topple. They crashed down onto the trailer, crushing it. More fell beside the tractor. Finn looked on, transfixed, as the ice rose up beneath the tractor. The vehicle turned over and his arm was jerked painfully as he was almost thrown from his seat. He cried out with the pain. He could hear his mother's voice shouting again. Tears sprang from his eyes.

Moot was shaking him, pulling at his arm.

FINN, FINN. Wake up, Finn. What's the matter? Why are you crying?

His mother's last shout finally made sense.

He started the tractor's engine and heedless of

direction, pushed the accelerator. The tractor jumped just as the ice began to crack and move beneath them, grinding and groaning like an awakening, predatory animal. Finn jammed his foot to the floor and the tractor leapt forward.

They'd stopped on a pressure ridge. If they'd stayed any longer, they'd have been crushed. How had his mother come to him? Was she still a banished spirit, doomed to walk the ice forever?

It was then he felt the presence once more. A shadow appearing from nowhere. A head nodded as if he'd passed a test and he felt, rather than saw, a mocking smile on its hidden lips.

***

The tractor's engine stopped. Finn grimaced. This was as far as they could drive.

"That's it Moot. We're out of fuel. It's all gone."

She looked at the map.

There's still a long way to go, Finn. How many days will it will take us?

Finn laughed, "I don't know Moot, but I think we're going to find out." He looked at the sky. "It'll be dark soon. Come on, let's get the sledges sorted. It'd be good to have a full day's walking tomorrow."

They packed the sledges as full as they could, yet still be able to pull them. The rest of the supplies they'd have to leave on the trailer. Finn marked it as accurately as he could on the map. Maybe they could find it on the way back.

The way back? Yes, there would be a way back, he was certain of that. How it would happen, he didn't know. They just had to keep going and everything would be fine.

***

The first day of walking was exhausting. Fit as he was, Finn hadn't pulled a fully laden sledge since arriving in Eden. Moot had never done so. Their progress was slow. They stopped frequently, to rest and adjust their harnesses.

Moot used the map and compass and sometimes they glimpsed the green ribbon of light, confirming they were going in the right direction.

The wind blew in their faces all day. The next day was slightly easier, with a little less to pull and a little less far to go

They became accustomed to pulling the sledges across the long smooth surfaces between the pressure ridges, then climbing the next ridge and finding their way between the huge slabs of ice. A succession of similar days passed.

Until the day came when Finn stopped and pointed to where, in the far distance, a cloud, darker than most, hung above the ice.

The word **'destiny'** formed in his mind.

Destiny? That sounds like Nisha, laughed Moot. *If that cloud is our destination, we're almost there, Finn.*

Finn looked back at the ice where they had walked for the last few weeks.

"It must be. There's nothing else here, Moot. That cloud must mean something."

They walked on, heading towards the dark cloud.

Days passed, the sun rose and set, they camped and travelled and camped again. The rhythm of their travelling became another settled routine.

The cloud enlarged: bigger, but the same. The terrain didn't change. Enormous blocks of ice tilted at angles by pressure ridges. Then flat ice and snow until they reached the next ridge.

As they consumed their supplies, their sledges lightened and moved more easily.

A wind arose and for two whole days they rocketed along with their parachute kites billowing out before them. The cloud enlarged more quickly in those two days than in all the weeks previously.

The first night of the blowing wind, they lay sleepless, side by side, the parachutes pulled in and the wind buffeting their tent. They rose early after the second day to find a thin layer of snow covering a still world.

They trudged on. Finn thinking about their supplies. The last ship had been completely empty, stripped of everything useful. Did the islanders come out this far?

If that were so, there would be no more provisions to find.

Moot caught his thought.

Would they arrive before their food and fuel ran out?

They continued, knowing that what they had on their sledges was all there was.

As they got closer to the islands, something began to well up inside Finn. A part of him felt as if he was going home, felt almost as if he belonged.

The feeling grew stronger as they gradually drew closer to the cloud.

Did The Leader know they were coming? Was he

being welcomed?

As they approached, they could see the two peaks more easily. The larger of the two belched dark clouds.

At last, after climbing over the tumbled ice blocks of a ridge, they saw, just a few miles away, the end of the ice. Beyond the ice, the shifting green sea glinted in the pale afternoon sun.

They stopped. Never had they seen open water like this before.

Finn.

He turned.

Moot held out her open hand.

A pale purple crystal, rounded and smooth, lay on the palm of her glove.

An image flashed into his mind, of Dent reaching into a pocket, holding out this crystal to her.

It was a gift from Dent when you were looking for the snowmobile. It will help us to keep in contact more easily.

Finn took a deep breath. It was a similar colour to the crystal in the church.

It's alright Finn. This crystal is like the shaman's crystal at the cairn. Here, take it. She slid it onto Finn's gloved palm. *Feel its protective energy.*

He took it from her gratefully.

Keep it safe Finn. Our lives may depend on it. She turned to her sledge. *We'd better get going. Night is not far away.*

They camped a short distance from the open water.

It didn't take long to reach the sea, next morning. There was a shout and several circular boats changed course and made for them. They waited, looking at the small group of people dressed in grey, that approached.

Before they arrived, Moot walked a small distance away and knelt down. Finn could see the pink glow around her that he'd seen when he and Linda found her. It became harder to focus on her physical body. She was invisible to the men from the twin peaks.

Saying nothing, the grey people landed their circular boats and made straight for Finn. Saying nothing, they took him by his arms and marched him to the edge of the ice where the water lapped. He did not resist.

One of the circular boats waited for him. He had seen lots of boats in pictures, yet none had been circular. It was tiny, compared to the ships they had sheltered in on their journey.

Finn was curious as to how it would move over the water. It was made of a mass of sticks, woven of something like the split mushstalks that they made things from in the pit. A silvery skin covered the outside that rested on the water. It shone and glistened as if it had oil or grease rubbed into it. A young woman sat on a wooden plank seat that went across the boat.

The boat bobbed up and down on the moving water. The grey clothed men held the boat still whilst Finn clambered in.

The woman propelled the circular boat with a short wooden, spoon like, tool he had no name for, which she pushed into the sea. This circular boat bounced over the water, giving him a strange disquieting sensation in his stomach. He was glad when the boat landed on the black sandy shore of the smoking peak.

There were more people dressed in grey to meet him. They led him along the black sand beach towards a large squat building built on the black rock that started several metres back from the beach. Constructed from stone and timber it had a rusted metal roof. The entrance was the bows of a huge upended wooden boat, its sharp prow pointing to the sky.

It took just a few minutes for them to reach it. They opened the wooden doors set in the bottom of the boat and entered the building. As his eyes got used to the shadowy interior, Finn could see that the floor had been dug out and was almost a metre below ground level.

With a guard on either side, he went down several deep steps and walked towards a man sitting at the far end of the huge spacious building. A short, stocky man, with long, coal black hair, sat on a carved wooden chair. His clothes were made of smooth grey animal skin, embroidered with swirling red patterns.

He stared intently at Finn. Grey eyes in a paler face looked him over. Finn felt evaluated. His strengths and weaknesses noted for future use. He could feel the power of this man's gaze.

Finn's eyes were drawn to the heavy silver necklace hung across his chest. No other white metal shone in quite the same way. Large flat turquoise stones were threaded around and entwined with flat engraved pieces of silver.

Finn's eyes followed the swirling pattern of lines that coiled around the central boss of turquoise, which was inlaid with more lines that curled into a central silver point. It felt as if he was being pulled down into a silvery turquoise whirlpool of rushing water. He dragged his gaze away.

The Leader, for who else could it be, attempted to smile. Yet he was unable to stop his lips curling back from his even white teeth into a mocking sneer.

The Leader.

That was what his initiates called him. Finn could hear it in their minds.

Suspended above the carved chair, a large, six-sided, dark purple crystal hung, suspended within a wire metal holder. It moved slightly, glinting in the light of lamps hung at intervals along the sides of the hall. The lamps burnt with clear yellow flames, filling the room with a strong smell of fish.

Take care, Finn, this man is dangerous. He is clever and calculating. Beware his tricks and deceptions. Do not look at his purple crystal. It is full of darkness. Focus on the crystal I gave you. It will help me protect you. My protection will be different from London. This time you will be aware of all that is happening.

Finn could feel Moot's fear and anxiety mixed with her warning.

He felt Moot cover him. A silver/violet, translucent gauze curtain grew from Moot's protection crystal. It came between him and The Leader's world.

Welcome Finn. I am glad you have come to join me. I can feel that you have many talents. That is why I have drawn you to me. Let me help you develop your abilities. Then we can rule this world together.

The leader's lips did not move.

Finn gasped.

Moot, he's telepathic too.

Yes, but he can't hear you talk to me, Finn. So he's not that good.

If he could hear The Leader's thoughts, what other abilities did Finn have that he didn't know about?

He remembered Moots words

Only if you want to, Finn.

Did he want to?

Did he have a choice? No, he must do what he had come here to do.

Finn smiled.

The Leader looked at him curiously.

Why are you smiling?

He doesn't know, thought Finn. He can't hear me. Moot is protecting me. He doesn't have all the power he thinks he has.

Finn's smile became broader.

You smile, yet you are here and I have the power.

The Leader paused for a moment, examining Finn's bearded face for any sign of weakness.

Observe. See the power that I will share with you.

He gestured with one hand.

A ring of shining crystals floated from a low table and hovered in the air before him.

It is not magic Finn. They, he gestured at his followers, **think it is magic, but it is not.**

"I can't do that," blurted Finn.

The Leader looked at him, considering.

Not yet, but you have the ability or you wouldn't be here. You must realise you can do nothing to oppose me. Join me. He paused. You went to my church, didn't you.

Finn nodded. There seemed little point in denying it.

The Leader smiled. His voice became measured, slow and hypnotic. **You have already experienced the purple crystal, Finn. Everything is simple. Look into the crystal above us. Let me direct your mind. Let the crystal do its work and the power I have, will be** yours, too. I will share it with you and teach you how to use it. Together we will rule this world. What you experienced in the church was only the beginning. There is more, so much more.

Don't trust him, Finn. I can hear the deceit in his voice. Remember what we came here to do. Focus on my crystal.

Finn, you understand the workings of the ancients' computers. Make them work for me.

So, he didn't know about the Amon Ra project. He just wants my abilities.

I will teach you how to control others. We will have power over all the earth. I will show you how we can live forever. I will teach you how to use your power. We can exert control over my frozen empire. Us, Finn. Together.

"No. The people of the Earth must have their free will. Nisha has told me of this. They are supposed to make their own choices. The earth must not be manipulated just for your benefit."

Look at what the ancients did with their free will. I can control everyone and everything. Our empire on earth will be what we want it to be. You have the ability to help me do this, Finn. Join me.

The Leaders voice had become wheedling, almost pleading in his eagerness to have Finn on his side.

The purple crystal above them shifted slightly. In Finn's mind, he could see it move towards him. A sudden shaft of light, from the window behind it, shone through the crystal, just as it had in the church. Its beam turned a deep purple and it shot straight into Finn's eyes. It felt totally delightful, soft and caressing, unlike the church ray, which had felt cold, hard and somehow harsh. He began to give way to its delicious appeal. It had a fascination to it.

The Leader's voice became blurred and indistinct. Its smooth flowing tones soothed and stroked Finn's mind. He began to see pictures. The Leader was showing him visions of what could be if they ruled together. Pictures of what could be if he let The Leader take over his mind. Even though they were blurred and indistinct when seen through Moot's curtain, Finn let his mind go there. He could feel the power of the crystal surge into him. He could use that power. All he had to do was let The Leader completely into his mind. All would be well. It was all for everyone's good. It was for all the good of the world.

He could see The Leader's smile. He could feel more

and more of The Leader's power flooding into him.

He must let The Leader help him help the world. The Leader's way was for the benefit of all.

Finn knew this. It had to be.

He surrendered to the purple crystal light. The Leader's mind was like a delicate purple hand. Its violet, tendril-like fingers coiled and twisted as they came through the purple crystal. Carefully, so as not to break the spell, the finger-vines began to dig their way into Finn's brain. Curling around to grasp his very essence and enslave him.

But the fingers closed on nothing.

Finn was gone.

Finn felt the safety of Moot's crystal protecting him, covering him, shielding his mind and spirit.

He laughed.

The hand groped in the space Finn had left. Instantly it was withdrawn.

The Leader jumped up and yelled.

For the first time Finn heard The Leader's voice. Finn was surprised at the thin, high-pitched screech. It was so incongruous. It didn't fit with The Leader's powerful, body. Ah, that was it. He's changed his body to keep it young and that had changed his vocal cords.

The Leaders face turned red and angry.

He looked wildly about him, as if unsure of where Finn actually stood.

Finn laughed again. Somehow the noise echoed around the room when it had not before.

"Where are you? What have you done? Let me back in."

The Leader's shrill tones revealed his anger.

He stared around the room, searching for his prey, but Moot had hidden Finn from him.

His voice cut across Finn's laugh.

"Where is he? Hold him." The voice was a shriek, wrathful and confused. The guards came forward hesitantly, confused by The Leader's strange actions. Finn could hear their puzzled thoughts. They grasped Finn's arms.

"You will regret this, Finn," The Leader's thin voice grew icy. Vengeance lay beneath its ugly thwarted tones.

"Take him to the ice prison. Put him with the other one."

Chapter 5

Finn was flung into the ice room. He sprawled headlong, sliding across the slippery floor. He heard the key grind in the lock of the metal door fixed onto the ice wall.

"Good evening," said a deep voice.

Finn looked up from where he'd landed. The figure of a man sat with his back to the wall in the icy shadows

"Is it?" said Finn.

The man moved forward slightly before replying, a movement that obviously gave him a certain amount of pain. His face contorted with the effort.

"From my point of view, yes, it is. I have few visitors to talk to."

A smile grew between the straggling hairs of his unkempt grey beard. The brown skin of his face creased into a myriad of fine lines as the cracked lips parted, showing extraordinarily white teeth for someone of his obvious age. The warmth of his smile was genuine.

Finn returned the smile. "I am Finn. Who are you?"

"Pleased to meet you, Finn. I've had quite a few names in my time." He considered for a moment. "Perhaps Godfrey would be good. It is the one I started with."

Leaning against the wall for support, Godfrey rose to his feet, slowly, gently.

"Here," he held out a hand. "Let me help you up."

Without thinking Finn grasped the hand, noting the roughness of the skin and the strength in Godfrey's arm. Nonetheless, Godfrey gasped as Finn pulled himself upright.

"What's the matter? Are you hurt?"

"A little bruising from an earlier encounter with our host's followers," Godfrey smiled ruefully. "My muscles have tightened. Nothing to worry about."

He moved himself into an easier position.

"It's so good to meet you, Finn. Even if the circumstances could be better. I don't have to ask you why you are here. You have obviously met our host. Otherwise," Godfrey chuckled. "You would not be incarcerated here with me."

Finn grinned. He liked Godfrey's good humour, despite their situation.

"That's right. He didn't like what I had to say. What do we do about him?" asked Finn.

"I don't know. I'd rather hoped you would."

"Me?"

"Yes," Godfrey looked at Finn with his head held to one side, quizzically. "It's not me. I'm not the one. It's you. You are the one to do it."

"That's what Nisha said."

"I don't know the lady, but she is right."

Godfrey wobbled slightly and sat down. Finn joined him, leaning back against the icy wall.

"Tell me about yourself, Finn. Where do you come from? Who is Nisha, the wise lady? Why are you here?"

"I was banished from the pit, a mine I was born in and journeyed to an amazing place where they have forests and plants and creatures that live in them. Nisha lives there too and it's covered with domes and it's full of crystals. It's called Eden."

Godfrey laughed. "I wonder if they knew when they called it Eden. Eden is paradise. It said in the Bible, the Good Book, that we came from a paradise called Eden. Will you return to Eden after this adventure? I would dearly love to go with you and meet this wise Nisha."

"Godfrey!" In a sudden flash of insight, Finn knew. "You're the God man. Dent's God man."

"Dent!" Godfrey's expression was one of extreme amazement. "You know Dent? You've been to London?"

"Moot and I met Dent in London."

"Moot?"

"Moot is my friend. We met after I left Eden to get seeds and crystals from London. Dent saved me and Moot from the slavers when we arrived there."

"When was this? Dent must be very old now."

"I'm sorry, Godfrey, Dent died the day after he saved us. He was very ill. He told us he was waiting for us. Jamila had told him we were coming."

"He wasn't in good health when I knew him." A flicker of sadness crossed Godfrey's face. "He was a good friend. They all were. Jamila was blessed with some unusual abilities. They all called me The God man; Dent and Jamila, Alana, Minip, David, Jermaine and Jasmine. Is Jamila still alive?"

"Dent said Jamila and the others were dead."

"Then I'm the last of us."

Godfrey suddenly looked very old and tired and

then in an instant his expression changed and he was full of light.

"Someone once told me none of us get out of here alive. We all go back to God in the end," he laughed. "I think I'm almost there, Finn," Godfrey's laughter made Finn smile. "I would know more of Eden. How did you come to be there?"

So Finn told him.

Godfrey listened in rapt attention. When his story was complete, Godfrey nodded gently and looked down in quiet contemplation.

Finn risked breaking the silence.

"Why is the earth covered in ice and snow Godfrey? Why did your God do this to the earth?"

The God man turned his head and looked Finn squarely in the eyes.

"Something like this happened before. Last time it was a flood. Massive amounts of water covering the earth. God took everyone back to him. We are given free will. We can choose what we do on Earth. He gave them freedom and they abused it. He gave the earth back to those that he trusted to look after it. You know this, don't you?"

And Finn could hear Nisha saying, "They were

warned they were destroying the planet."

Yes, he knew this, but he did not feel it.

"Why did you come here Finn?"

Why had he come here? He'd told Nisha he had to and Moot had come with him. Apart from knowing he had to fix The Amon Ra Project, there had been something else. Not a proper reason. He'd just known that's what he had to do.

He realised Godfrey was still waiting for an answer.

"The Amon Ra Project of course and," he shrugged. "I felt I had to. Something was unfinished. I had to come and end it. I don't know what. It's different for Moot. She wants to be with me." He stopped for a moment, realising that that was the real reason why Moot came with him. She wanted to be with him. "Something drew me. I was shown the way."

But who or what had shown him?

Godfrey laughed, "It was him, Finn. The Leader, he calls himself. He did it. He knew you were coming. He knew where you were. You've got something he wants. Be careful. He'll take control of you. You'll be his servant, his slave. He mis-uses his gifts and he'll mis-use yours too. He can manipulate matter at a molecular level. You think he wears that turquoise and silver necklace just to look good." Godfrey shook his head. "It keeps him young and healthy. He has lived long and he wants to live longer." Godfrey looked at him carefully. "People think it is magic. It is not magic."

He looked sideways at Finn. "You can do it too or you wouldn't be here."

"Me," said Finn.

Godfrey shifted again.

"Many, many years ago, before a man was considered a man, he had to be initiated: to leave the world of women and join the world of men. Grown men. Not the boys who never grow up and instead try to control the world and fill the hole within themselves with worldly things. The lost and lonely men.

Do you know of this Finn? Do you need initiating? Do you need a mentor to guide you through your initiation?

The Leader controls his followers with initiation. He uses crystals. Did you see the purple one hanging in his hall? You didn't let him get you near that one, did you?"

Finn was silent. What should he tell Godfrey?

Godfrey looked at Finn's face. "Oh Finn, you did,

didn't you? That's why he could find you easily. He wanted me too, but I wouldn't do it. I used the power of prayer. I resisted peacefully. I didn't look at the crystal."

"Godfrey," began Finn. "I..." he stopped. What should he tell Godfrey? Would The Leader read Godfrey's mind and find out their plans if he told Godfrey everything?

Godfrey smiled, "Don't worry Finn. He cannot read me. He knows this. I did not look at the crystal. He has no power over me. I march to a different drum. What do you wish to tell me?"

"I have seen the purple crystal before. I was in a place called a church and the crystal was hanging high up in the rafters. Its brightness flashed into my mind. It changed me. After, I found a storehouse of everything I needed. I felt I was directed there. Did The Leader do that?"

"Yes Finn, he did. I went there too when I followed him. The hole dug in the floor. The equipment stored at the church. He had his initiates do all this for him."

Finn looked at Godfrey.

"Why did he put the crystal there? I don't understand. The crystal helped me. It opened a crack in my mind. It enabled Nisha to unlock a door I had closed within me. It was a good thing."

Godfrey considered before replying.

"Maybe it helped you then. Do not be fooled into thinking it left you. It is still there, hiding somewhere in your consciousness. It may still have control over you. He uses it as a tool to control his followers. It was the rite they went through for their initiation. Oh, they undertook it willingly. He has the power and charisma to command. Yet his is a selfish end. He uses his gifts to further his own power here, on earth. He wants Eden to die. He knows you have looked into his purple crystal. He thinks he can complete what the crystal started. He wants to control you, so you will help him keep his earthly empire. He thinks no further than that."

Godfrey sighed.

"I've seen his initiates do his bidding, Godfrey. Yet he says nothing to them. He puts his thoughts into their minds. He makes them do what he wills. Can he look into my mind?"

"I don't know Finn. Can he?" there was uncertainty in Godfrey's voice.

Moot interrupted, *No Finn. He cannot. I would*

know if he did. He has not. You are safe. Do you understand how I hid you from him, Finn?

Yes, Moot. Finn nodded.

Then tell Godfrey. He needs to know The Leader's crystal did not make you his initiate. I saw inside your mind, Finn. I know. Tell him.

Finn looked straight at Godfrey.

"Moot says The Leader cannot. She knows. We shared each other's minds when we stood together in the broken circle of stones. All The Leader saw in my mind was a smiling image of Little Finn. The Leader could not see that I was hiding. That was what enraged him. You cannot hear Moot, Godfrey?"

Godfrey shook his head.

"I do not have that talent, Finn? So, Moot, she protects you from The Leader. What must we do, Finn?"

"I have to find the control room the ancients built for The Amon Ra Project. I must repair and complete what they started. That is what I know I must do. What I don't know is how to get out of this gaol."

Finn looked around at the thick icy walls and then the metal door. How could they escape from this place?

"Think Finn. You know what to do. It's still inside

you. You can release us from this prison as you released yourself from the prison of your past. DO IT NOW."

Godfrey's words were powerful. They stirred something in Finn, something in his memory, something that had escaped his recollection. What was it? What had he done?

"Moot. Help me? What do I need to do?"

Open your mind, Finn. What you seek is not hidden. It is within you. All we must do is find it. Let me help you.

"There was something I did. Something I had the power to do. Something unexpected. I need that knowledge now, but I don't know what it is. I CAN'T REMEMBER," Finn's voice grew loud with frustration.

Moot soothed his anger. She held his mental hand as they searched for the memory he needed. She guided his thoughts. They went together through his childhood and his journey from the pit. Searching, experiencing.

"What if I can't find it Moot?"

Do not worry Finn. We will find it.

"What if we don't?"

Beads of sweat formed on his brow. He was hot. He

undid his coat. Sweat collected faster than he could wipe it away. His face turned red. His palms felt so hot. What was happening to him?

Why are you so hot Finn?

Hot? Why was he hot? A picture formed. He was in the pit, taking his turn at stoking the furnaces.

"I'm in the pit Moot. It's so hot. I'm so hot," a sudden understanding hit him. "I sat on the ice and it melted beneath me when I thought of stoking the furnace." He laughed in triumph. "I can melt the ice around the door."

That's it, Finn. Do it! Melt the ice with the heat from the pit. I can see you doing it. Go to the pit, Finn. Feel the heat. Let the heat build in your hands. Melt the ice. DO IT FINN.

With his memory unleashed, Finn pressed himself against the door. Reaching out, he put his hand on either side of it and let the heat from the pit spill out from his palms. The walls dissolved in a rush of steam and water. The door fell away into the corridor outside.

They were free!

Finn's hands were shaking and his legs trembled. The sound of running feet stopped him from sinking to the floor. Three guards dressed in black with yellow bands around their arms and their chests, ran along the corridor. For a moment Finn stared as they ran towards him. Then he laughed. Wasps. They looked like wasps. He knew what to do with wasps. He laughed again and held out his hands. The men stopped, hitting the wall Finn held before them. They gasped and were held still. Finn pushed them along the corridor, towards an open door and in a moment, Finn had pushed them through the door, which Godfrey slammed shut behind them.

"Moot. Listen. Can you hide both of us?"

Yes, Finn.

"Then do it. The Leader thinks I've come here because of his purple crystal. He thinks he can use my psychic and technical abilities to rule this earth. He doesn't know about the Amon Ra Project. But we do and I can fix it. I can mend the earth. Not because Nisha wants me to. Not because Godfrey wants me to. Not because their God wants me to. I can fix this earth because this earth deserves another chance. We can make it work. Hide us Moot and we'll give this earth its other chance. Come on Godfrey. Let's go find the main computer. I need to access the Amon Ra Project."

Godfrey nodded and they went.

Chapter 6

Silver necklace man.

Who calls me that? I am The Leader.

I am Moot and you are not my leader.

The Leader sat up on his carved wooden chair.

Moot?

Yes. Moot. I'm here to talk to you.

You are here? Where? Show yourself.

Ah, you would like me to do that, wouldn't you?

The Leader chuckled.

You are clever, Moot. Are you a companion of Finn? Finn will be joining me soon. Won't you join me?

First tell me why, silver necklace man? I need to know more.

Moot used all her skills to distract him, letting her power show a little at a time, just to tantalise him.

He tempted her to join him: offering eternal life, the world and many other gifts.

Moot kept him busy, giving Finn the time he needed.

***

Finn and Godfrey stood before a metal door set into rock. They had left the ice behind them on their way along tunnels and down stairs. Finn pushed and the door opened with a whoosh of pressured air. No locks. No guards. Perhaps the ancients thought they were far enough away from civilisation that there was no need.

As Finn crossed the door's threshold, rows of recessed lights flicked on and screens crackled into life. Had they been waiting for him? Finn smiled. No, of course not. They were made to come on automatically whenever someone came in the room.

"Godfrey. Guard the door. Tell me if anyone comes."

How was this equipment powered?

The answer came to him. It was the power of the molten earth from deep within the fissures. The ancients had amazing technology. Yet they had not kept pace with it. They had remained children with dangerous toys.

The room's high white ceiling reflected the light, casting sharp angular shadows around the serried rows of equipment which stretched to his left.

A low whining hum started. It reminded him of the insect buzz in Eden, even though he knew it was coming from hidden air conditioning units that had begun cooling the computers and the other electrical equipment, now they were working.

Finn walked between the stacked computer servers, into the empty space in the middle of the room. His movements disturbed the very thin layer of fine dust that covered everything. It rose into the air in clouds, to be sucked out by the whirring fans hiding behind metal grills set into the walls and ceiling.

He surveyed the array of computer terminals and flat screens, arranged in a half circle on a shelf built against the curved wall in front of him. Above the array, the biggest monitor he'd ever seen, at least two metres long and a metre high, stretched across the whole of the wall. A flickering light indicated it was on standby, ready and waiting. For what?

For him. Waiting for him to mend the glitch in the program, so that something the ancients started could be completed. It was time.

Memories of the pit's control room edged into his mind. He'd always been able to repair the computers there with chips from other machines. Could he do the same here? He still knew how to fix things. He'd repaired Eden. He knew. Why then did his mind feel confused and baffled? Was he missing something, like how he'd blocked his memories and abilities when he first arrived at Eden? Yet after Nisha had helped him, he had repaired Eden. He must be able to do the same here.

He looked around. The small screens were all turned on: their screens bright with the Amon Ra Project logo. They all said, 'Welcome to The Amon Ra Project.'

Was he welcome?

One corner of his mind could hear Moot's dialogue with The Leader and at the same time he could feel her presence surround him and Godfrey, protecting them so he could concentrate on what he had to do.

He took out the shining crystals from his pack that the initiates had, strangely, let him keep. He placed them in a half circle before him and the giant screen. He slipped into the chair at the curved desk mounted beneath the screen. Getting comfortable, he prepared to enter the system.

He leant forward and touched the massive screen

before him. There was a slight crackling of static as the huge screen came to life. The familiar message of welcome appeared below the pyramid and disc logo.

Where was the mouse pad? He looked across the bank of computers. Ah. Each one had a headset. He picked one up and examined it. Where was the connecting wire?

How did it work, he wondered?

There was a band to fit on his head. The inside of the band felt slick, smooth and malleable, yet slightly sticky to the touch.

Cautiously he placed it on his head. The band gripped his temples, the inside moulding to his forehead.

Instantly, two handprints appeared on the desk in front of the computer screen, glowing pale green beneath their covering of fine dust. His hands slid onto them. A small keyboard appeared on the screen. Finn lifted his hands in surprise and the keyboard disappeared. He chuckled quietly in admiration. The ancient's scientists and engineers had been so clever. Suddenly Nisha's voice echoed in his head.

'They were too clever for their own good. They were told to listen to their heart and not just follow their head.'

What did he do now? He looked at the huge screen. This logo was slightly different. The edges of the pyramid... moved. Each of the blue lines thickened at the base and the bulges slowly moved up to the apex of the pyramid, where they joined together, disappeared and started again at the base. He followed the lines. They became brighter. When they reached the apex, their blue brightness stayed there. He followed the line in the centre of the pyramid up to the apex, returned to the base, up to the apex. As the light accumulated at the apex, it overflowed upwards into the disc, which brightened. His eyes were drawn to the shining disc. It shone intensely, filling his eyes with light. He closed them. The light still shone within him. Not just his mind, it filled his whole body. He was dimly aware that this was not an effect of the computer. This was him. This was his abilities guiding him, directing him to where his awareness needed to go.

He was subsumed into the program. Focused entirely upon what he must do.

A screen appeared inside his mind, covered with iridescent blue signs and symbols. Despite his closed eyes, he typed at great speed, filling the screen. The symbols joined together. A clear pathway of bright yellow light ran across them and as he looked, the picture became three dimensional. The yellow light pathway sank into the signs and symbols which now towered over him like thick blue hedges and he was standing on the yellow pathway within a maze of blue light.

He laughed. That was it. This was a maze. He was being shown the computer system as a maze. He must follow the path and see where it led.

He travelled along the yellow pathway of light. When he came to forks and turnings in the path, he knew exactly which way to take. He knew.

He travelled the pathway until it came to a junction of many ways. The golden light became thick, like syrup, and he was forced to stop. The light separated and went along each pathway in turn, only to return to the junction through one of the other paths. It was a feedback loop. The light endlessly spooled around upon itself; following its looped pattern round and round and round. Going nowhere.

Finn smiled. This was it. This was where the path of light was blocked. This was what prevented the program from running correctly. They must have set it running remotely and it should have worked automatically. Something had gone wrong. Why they didn't fix it he had no idea. He'd found it! He watched the pathway of light as it wound round and around in its elliptical feedback loop.

His hands jerked and he found himself typing furiously, his hands flying over the keys. Numbers and symbols appeared in a blue line at the bottom of the screen. They merged into the code that was needed to make the new pathway. The blue code shimmered and the signs and symbols of the maze changed. A new opening appeared and the shining pathway went through the opening. The energy of the feedback loop dissipated as the path went through the new doorway. It did not return.

He'd done it.

The light shone brightly and he opened his eyes wide to find himself looking at the Amon Ra Project welcome logo on the screen. There was a series of symbols beneath it and at the end of the line one word.

Run.

The cursor was hovering over the word. All he had to do was press the pad and the computer program would start. The ancient's original plan would run and his mission would be accomplished.

Yet he hesitated.

Why?

What was wrong?

Nothing. Nothing was wrong.

When he set the program running, something would happen, something known in the original plans.

He felt fear.

It was the unknown.

What if he'd got it wrong?

What if...

Yet he had no choice.

He pressed Run.

For a moment nothing happened.

Then a message appeared.

Inappropriate human presence detected.
Tsunami in one hour.
Evacuate human presence.
Simulation starts now.

Tsunami? What was that?

A timer began counting down from one hour in a

corner of the screen. Words appeared.

Expected size and duration of the tsunami after the EVENT.

A picture of the islands appeared.

The bigger peak belched gigantic clouds of computerised grey smoke. All around the islands, the sea shivered as something happened beneath the surface. The water drained away from the islands, forming a circle around them of about 100 metres.

Then the water at the circle's edge bunched up and a wave at least thirty metres high began to move towards the islands. It gathered speed and raced forward to crash against the islands. Gradually it dissipated and all returned to normal.

The time counter showed one hour and forty minutes.

Finn sat there in dismay. What had he done? The wave would run under the ice and it would race to the islands, sweeping all before it. He'd sentenced The Leader and all his people to death.

No, The Leader had travelled his path and this was the consequence. It was not Finn's fault. He could not have known what would happen.

That was not true either. He could have checked before pressing Run. He'd felt something. But what could he have done? He'd had no choice. He'd had to repair the program and set it going. If he tried to warn the initiates now, he, Moot and Godfrey would be held and would die with them. They had all made their choices. They had doomed themselves.

It was not his fault.

"Moot!"

Yes Finn.

The voice within his head gave no indication of the effort it was taking Moot to keep The Leader occupied and stop him knowing she was talking to Finn.

"It's done. I've set the program running. But there's going to be a tsunami, a flood. I didn't know. We're in great danger. We don't have much time to get away. I'm coming now." He scooped up the shining crystals

"Godfrey!"

Together they ran from the room.

There were several circular boats on the shore. Finn put his pack down and held one still while Godfrey climbed in. Finn turned to pick up his pack.

"Godfrey! What are you doing?"

The boat was already several metres from the shore and Godfrey was quickly padding it further away.

"Godfrey, that's the wrong direction. You'll get caught in the tsunami."

Godfrey continued paddling and shouted his reply. "I have to warn them. They are not all his mindless drones. I must try to save them."

"Don't Godfrey. You'll drown. Save yourself."

Godfrey's green eyes looked at Finn.

"We all die Finn. They are all God's children and I am a man of God. They must have a chance to choose. I will warn them, that some may choose to live. Go to your friend. Return to Eden and renew the earth. It is God's will. Say hello to Nisha. Goodbye Finn."

He turned and paddled vigorously towards the volcano.

"Goodbye," Finn shouted. "You're a brave man Godfrey. I'll miss you."

He watched the boat for a moment, before climbing into another and began paddling towards the edge of the ice where he knew Moot waited for him.

As he paddled, something, he had no idea what, exploded from the tip of the volcano and shot into the air. Something bright and metallic that climbed into the night sky. Finn knew it was something that would change everything, something that would give this world another chance.

Whatever the ancients had set up had now happened. They may have been too clever by half and they were warned where their technology might lead. Yet he had set their legacy in motion.

This world had been frozen for long enough.

***

As Finn and Moot pulled the sledges away from the ice edge, it bulged beneath them. Pieces came away from the edge with thunderous cracking sounds. Fractures appeared all over the ice. They held on to the sledges and waited for the tsunami to pass.

The ice subsided, with more pieces drifting away. They looked back to see a huge wave headed for the island. They could feel the surge even from where they were.

"Moot."

Yes.

"I must see what happens. I know you see it. Show me."

Moot shared her visions.

Together, they saw the wave rear up before the

beach, ready to crash down and destroy the followers. The Leader stood before it, resolute. Whatever else, he was courageous. He stretched out an arm towards it, willing it to part and go around him. And for a moment it did. He half smiled and then something else happened.

In Moots eyes, Finn saw the white crescendo of the wave tops turn from mere foamy water into something else. A silver green, shining ribbon of light topped with an iridescent chaos of flashing rainbows.

He saw The Leader's face change from absolute power and confidence to disbelief. The wave descended and broke upon the base of the volcano. It took everything with it, scouring the rock clean of all traces of the village and the people who had lived there.

Chapter 7

Godfrey had been right after all. A few, a very few, of the islanders survived. They had been sent to a recently discovered ship as a scavenging party. So they had lived and now were free from the influence of The Leader. From far away they saw Finn and Moot walking across the ice and came to join them.

They had tents, crude wooden sledges, some food and they brought a surprise.

"I didn't get there in time," Godfrey smiled ruefully. "I floated over the tsunami wave. They found me, still in the boat. I was flung up on the ice as the wave returned. I don't think God wants me back yet after all."

They stood in a smiling group around Godfrey. He pointed at them one by one and named them: Gemma and Nemma, the twins, Gurlain, Pedro and Pietro, Tommy, Astrid, Darain, Yatty and Plen. They would bring so much to Eden: love, laughter and most importantly, babies. They would have babies and humanity would prosper.

And then Gemma asked Moot, "Why does your head glow?"

Finn caught his breath. She sees it.

Finn shook his head and smiled.

Geordie, you were right. There were others. More than you'd ever have guessed and they have gifts. Dent was right, too, and Nisha. They all had gifts they could use for the future of people on the Earth.

How surprised Nisha would be to see them all. He could almost feel her welcome everyone. She could pass on her skills and knowledge.

Who knew how long it would take for the ice and snow to disappear? He didn't think it would be fast like when it first came. What he did know was that Eden had plants and seeds enough to green the Earth and truly the Earth itself would be an Eden once more.

Afterthought

Finn sat in the shadow of a tree directly above the story space in the Mediterranean biome. He listened to Nisha telling the children the tale of how he had repaired the Temperate Biome. They sat very still. Nisha was a wonderful teacher and a captivating storyteller.

He smiled wryly to himself as he heard how he had climbed the outside of the main dome right to the very top. Nisha was good at adding to the stories. It didn't really matter, although he couldn't help feeling that he'd like her to be more accurate.

He could tell the children exactly what had happened. Even though six years had elapsed since they'd returned from The Amon Ra Project, every detail was etched permanently onto his memory. But then, would he really want to sit like Nisha and be the centre of attention in that way?

Nisha brought the story to an end and the children

clapped. Their parents emerged from their waiting and listening places and the children ran to them, a multi-coloured wave of Eden tee shirts and shorts. They excitedly waved pictures they'd drawn earlier and told the smiling adults their favourite parts of the story.

In a few minutes everyone had said thank you and goodbye, leaving Nisha and Jasmin to collect the pots of crayons the children had used in their lessons. All was quiet for a few more minutes until Jasmin turned and shouted, **Mother.**

A smiling Moot joined them.

Not so loud Jasmin. Nisha is beside you and your father is somewhere nearby. You must remember your telepathic voice is very powerful.

She smoothed her six-year-old daughter's unruly black hair with its flashing red strands. Finn always said the only thing Jasmin had from him was her green eyes.

"Yes mother," said Jasmin, dutifully. "Where is Daddy? You said he was coming to collect me, too. I can't hear him."

You know how Finn shields himself. He likes to be private sometimes. You do too. We all do now and again. I expect he'll be here soon.

Finn smiled. Moot was right, he did like to turn off his abilities for a while. He liked to be private. It relaxed him. Now it was time to re-join his family. He walked down the path.

"Daddy!"

Jasmin raced to Finn, just as he reached the edge of the story space, and jumped into his arms. Holding her tight, Finn whirled her round and round, Jasmin shrieking with delight, until they were both dizzy and Finn collapsed to the ground, grinning, with Jasmin laughing in his arms.

Nisha and Moot laughed, too.

Finn was so good with Jasmin, thought Nisha.

"Not that you aren't, Moot. Only it's different for a mother. You and Jasmin will always have the female bond."

I know Nisha. It's okay.

Finn and Jasmin disentangled themselves. Moot and Nisha joined them and they began to make their way home to their quarters. Jasmin clasped hands with Moot and Finn. Nisha walked beside Finn. Their shadows moved before them as they walked between the crops.

The afternoon sun was bigger and stronger than any of the adults remembered. It reminded them that the Earth was changing as its orbit moved fractionally closer to the sun every day.

"Nisha told us the story of how Daddy climbed the big dome," said Jasmin as they walked.

You've all heard that one many times, haven't you?

"Yes Mother, but Nisha changes it every time she tells it. So it's always different. I like to see how it's going to turn out."

"Do I really change the story, Jasmin?"

"Oh yes, Nisha, but it's all right, we don't mind. I'd like to know the real story, though."

Only Finn can tell you that Jasmin. He's the only one that knows the whole story.

"I'm no storyteller, Moot."

You told me the story of the pit and your walk to Eden. After you and Linda found me and she took us to London.

"That was different, Moot. It was only for you."

"Why don't you write it, Daddy? You wouldn't have to tell it out loud. I could read it and practice my reading and everyone would know 'zactly what happened and Nisha wouldn't need to make bits up."

They stopped.

You could Finn.

"Yes, you really could," added Nisha.

"Would you do it please, Daddy?"

Finn thought. Could he? Should he?

"Okay, I'll try, but I'll need lots of help with the parts you were both in."

Nisha and Moot nodded.

"Will you come home with us now Nisha and help Daddy write it tonight?" asked Jasmin with a winning smile.

"It's my turn to cook for Godfrey tonight," said Nisha. "You know we always take it in turns."

"He's invited, too," said Finn. "We'll cook together. I'll need his help with the writing. He knows what happened in London with Dent and the others and at the Amon Ra Project."

Nisha nodded.

Jasmin chattered away as they walked on, sometimes out loud and sometimes with her thoughts.

"How are you going to end the story, Daddy?"

"What do you mean, Jasmin?"

"Well... Can all the children be in it when we play?" she asked, smiling sweetly at Finn.

They all laughed at Jasmin's obvious plan.

"Okay Jasmin. You and the children can be in the story," said Finn.

"And you have to put in how the ice is melting a little bit and about the icicles hanging off Eden's roof. The story can't end without that or it wouldn't be finished, would it."

Finn stopped and looked at their daughter. What a clever little thing she was.

"Yes Jasmin, I'll put all that in and I'll keep a diary like Nisha. Then when I've finished the main story of Eden up to where you and the children play, maybe we'll add more bits and the story won't end, because the story of Eden and all this Earth hasn't ended. Perhaps it never really will."

Jasmin's eyes shone, "I'll keep a diary, too and when I'm grown up and you don't want to write it any more, I'll write the next chapters of Eden."

"Thank you, Jasmin," said Finn. "That would be very good and now that's settled, can we all go home and have something to eat. I've been working on Eden's electrics all day and I'm getting very hungry. I'm sure everyone else is, too."

As they walked to their quarters, Jasmin talked

excitedly about what she'd write and draw in her diary.

On the way, they collected Godfrey from the rooms he shared with Nisha and as the noisy group walked on, Finn followed behind them, reflecting on all that had happened and what he might write.

Despite the dangers he had faced after leaving the pit, with Nisha's help he had found his past, mended Eden, found Moot and set the Earth on course to gradually warm. Jasmin was a lovely daughter and their community worked well together. Perhaps Nisha and Godfrey were right about their God helping them when they needed it, although they still had long discussions about that.

How fortunate they all were to live in Eden and how wonderful it was that they and their children would help rebuild the Earth. He looked forward to when the ice had retreated far enough for them to live outside. In time, Jasmin could write that story. For now, she was right, it was important to tell the story of what had happened and how they had all come to the sanctuary that was Eden.

Whatever the future might bring, today he was content.

RETURN TO EDEN

Acknowledgements

Thanks to Susanne, my wife, for reading Eden. Also thanks to Celia, Audrey and Kelli who also read it and made suggestions.

Many thanks to Christine for reading Eden, her encouragement and suggestions for improvement.

Lastly, thanks to Paul of publishingbuddy.co.uk for an eye catching, imaginative cover.

A Word from the author

I've taken a few liberties with the Eden Project. When I started writing the story, The Eden Project had entered a competition for a grant to build a desert biome and it fitted my story. Eden didn't win and the desert biome wasn't built, but I didn't want to leave it out.

Also the big carved seed project wasn't built. I did leave that out.

Although Eden were kind enough to send me a plan of Eden, I added rooms and buildings to it and they use solar and ground source heat pumps for power.

Hydrogen can now be split from water using electrolysis and solar panels can obviously produce electricity. Many people would say that enhancing anything with crystals is pure fantasy. This is a fantasy story and who knows what can done with crystals. Crystal healing is a thing.

Petrol goes off. I've taken liberties with the stuff

Finn and Moot find in Kew at Wakehurst. Diesel can last for a longer time at lower temperatures so long as it has a stabiliser. It would need to be filtered to stop the engine gumming up. I did look all this up, but I needed fuel for the purposes of the story and stretched points.

I looked up how far people can travel pulling a sledge. It varies, apparently, but it suited me to allow it to happen how I wrote it.

That's it. Hope you found the story interesting. Go to Amazon and leave a comment, any comment. Feedback is great.

For more of my stories:

www.colintaylortales.com

Printed in Great Britain
by Amazon